Making Love Work

PAT SIMMONS

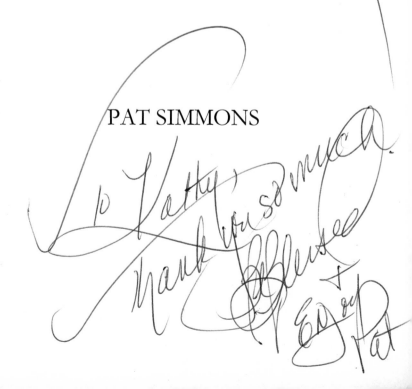

To Kathy, Thank you so much. Blessed & Enjoy Pat

Making Love Work is dedicated to all the romantics in the world that believe it's never too late for love and know love can blossom in unexpected places.

Delight thyself also in the LORD; and he shall give thee the desires of thy heart—Psalm 37:4

This is a work of fiction. References to real events, organizations, and places are used in a fictional context. Any resemblances to actual people, living or dead are entirely coincidental.

To read more books by this author, please visit www.patsimmons.net.

Printed in the United States of America

ISBN-13: 978-1482794908

ISBN-10: 148279490X

ENDORSEMENT

Making Love Work
(Three novellas)

A Mother's Love

Words of Love

Love at Work

MAKING LOVE WORK

CHAPTER 1

"He's here." Jillian Carter said, startled as the doorbell's chime echoed throughout her two-story St. Louis suburban condo.

She swept the comb through her thick, jet-black mane one more time. A year shy of forty and she could still boast not one gray strand.

Leaning closer into the mirror, Jillian scrutinized her eye makeup. She grinned, practicing a genuine smile before stepping back and scanning her attire. "Not bad." She shrugged at her toned figure before flipping off the bathroom lights and hurrying to the stairs. Her heart pounded with excitement and trepidation.

For her daughter's sake, Jillian wanted to make a good first impression on Shana's soon-to-be in-law whom she was meeting for the first time. Since she technically had never had any in-laws to claim herself, Jillian was excited for her daughter.

At the stairwell landing, Jillian peeped through the

white shutters and recognized the familiar SUV that was parked in the driveway.

With her smile in place, she opened the door, expecting to see Trent, her future son-in-law, and meet his father, who was a widower. Instead, she came face-to-face with a very handsome man with an engaging smile of his own. A well-defined salt-and-pepper beard showcased his perfect white teeth. He was tall—six foot-something—with skin that reminded her of dark pecan.

Remembering to breathe, Jillian stared as she appreciated the formula God used to create this man. She had only seen a handful of good-looking men she would label as drop-dead fine. He was definitely a King Solomon in her book.

If money had a scent, then Jillian was intoxicated from the fumes. Nothing on the man appeared second-hand like some of the outfits she had worn for decades. And by the custom fit of his suit, Jillian felt under dressed in her two-piece sweater dress and jacket—and it was new.

Money meets middle-class. She would not be intimidated in her own modest home. Jillian swallowed and regained control of her senses, but her lips wouldn't move.

His eyes twinkled as he chuckled. "I'm Dexter Harris, Trent's father. I apologize for being early. At the last minute, he and Shana wanted to make a stop, and since I not too long ago got off a plane, they suggested that getting to know you would be more relaxing than going with them. Trent programmed your address in his GPS. I hope that was okay."

"Absolutely, Dr. Harris." Jillian stepped back and

Dexter walked into her house. Towering over her five-foot-five frame, he filled her foyer with his presence.

"There is no reason for the formality. Please call me Dex."

"Sure, and I'm plain old Jillian." She took his trench coat as he removed it.

"Trust me. In that dress, there is nothing plain about you," he complimented her.

Jillian couldn't contain the blush as she closed the door. Whirling around, she didn't make eye contact as she thanked him. *Wow,* she thought.

"Follow me." She led him past her dining room on one side of the marble foyer and her small living room on the other. Her foyer dead ended into a large kitchen that overlooked a great room.

"Please make yourself at home while I bring out the snacks. I prepared sandwiches and salads. I just need to pop in the dessert and whip up the spinach dip. It will just take a few minutes."

"If I am to make myself at home then I must offer to help," Dexter said, following her into the kitchen.

Charming. So that's where her future son-in-law got that trait. And that's what won Shana over and Jillian, too. She shooed Dexter away to no avail. "All I have to do is mix the spinach dip and warm the pastries." She set the temperature on the oven and grabbed the tray out the refrigerator and slid them inside in no time.

"I can do either."

"Not in a suit, you can't. Plus, this is your first visit, so you're a guest. After that, you'll have to help yourself in my kitchen," she joked and looked away to keep herself from drooling or fainting at the tease of his cologne. Trent definitely had good genes in his family. Her son-in-law and Shana should have beautiful brown babies with jet-black hair and expressive eyes like Trent and his father.

Dexter's deep rumbling laughter was mesmerizing. "I'll remember that." Stuffing his hands in his pants pockets, Dexter pivoted on a heel and appraised her family room/great room from the kitchen. He whistled. "This is nice. Did you decorate, or Shana?"

"Both of us. We enjoy doing projects together. We've come a long way from the bungalow we used to have years ago where Shana excelled as an interior designer. I'm proud of her."

"We're proud of her," he corrected, catching her off guard with his statement.

She was flattered by his swift inclusiveness. "Yes, well, I started with dollar store craft kits, which was all I could afford at the time. Soon Shana began to create artwork from anything she could find, literally—socks, utensils and even worn shoes. She had an eye for color coordination and contrast and an imagination to feed her obsession."

Even with her back to Dexter, Jillian knew when he returned his attention to her. It was as if she could feel his eyes on her. Without turning around, she heard the leg of a barstool rub against her floor. Dexter had taken a seat.

"Do you add red peppers to your dip?" he asked as she set the ingredients on the counter, which also served as the breakfast table.

Jillian was about to pour sour cream into a bowl, but stopped with a spoon in her hand. "No...why, are you allergic to peppers?"

"Oh no, I'm not allergic to food of any kind. The first time I ever tasted spinach dip was at a restaurant. The red peppers and chopped pecans made me want to eat the entire appetizer with no regard for my colleagues at the table. All I can say is umph. Now, when I prepare it, I add red peppers along with the standard ingredients."

"Really?" Jillian smirked, entertained with his animated expression, subtle cologne, and tempting smile. "So you're a doctor and a cook?"

"I like to eat." Dexter patted his stomach.

Jillian tried not to peep, but she did. The doctor definitely didn't have a beer belly. *Did Dexter even drink?* she wondered. Trent had gotten saved shortly after he met Shana, and he exemplified a superb example of a practicing Christian, but he never mentioned his father's relationship with God.

She stepped to her refrigerator and began to rummage through her vegetable tray to see if she had any red pepper left over from the salad she had prepared. Twirling around, Jillian held up the plastic wrapped vegetable. "Ta da."

"Excellent." Dexter chuckled as he reached across her granite countertop. He took the liberty of opening the package of dip mix and sprinkled it into a bowl.

His simple gesture made Jillian chastise herself as he began to stir. Dexter was down to earth, not high-minded as she had judged him by the suit he had on. Shame on her. *Forgive me, Lord.*

Besides being a doctor and living in Atlanta, all she knew was he was a widower with an honorable son. How the women in Georgia had failed to snag him was a mystery to her, but his social life was his business.

Dexter had his privacy and she had hers.

It's not like she had time for any meaningful relationships, anyway, while she reared Shana. Jillian's focus was on her daughter and that left only so much time for dating. Now that Shana was a grown woman and moving on with her life, what would be her excuses for not getting out?

Chopping up bits of the pepper, Jillian cleared her throat. "Trent is an amazing young man. You should be a proud papa."

Sitting straighter, Dexter seemed to puff out his chest as he grinned. "I did my best. My in-laws made sure of that," he griped, then retrieved his smile. "And you have a sweet and beautiful daughter. You two could pass as sisters."

Jillian blushed, accepting the compliment as she avoided eye contact. Dexter had no way of knowing that she had been fifteen years old when she got pregnant and sixteen when she delivered Shana.

However, it was because of her youth that she and Shana did have a strong relationship, more as sisters, especially since both had to answer to Lavera, Jillian's mother. Too bad she had died when Shana turned ten. Lavera would be proud of her only grandchild.

As the silence grew between them, Dexter must have sensed he struck a nerve. For a moment, neither said anything. At least she had programmed her satellite radio earlier, so the music floated in the background.

Jillian sighed. She was the hostess, so it was up to her to make her guest feel comfortable. "It's been Shana and me for twenty-three years. She has been my baby, best friend, and confidant...and at times like a sister, but I'm still Momma." Jillian didn't play when it came to being a disciplinarian, especially if she didn't want Shana to fall under the same fate as she had at fifteen.

"Anyway, three schools were vying for her to enroll. I convinced Shana to attend The Illinois Institute of Art in Chi-town. I missed my baby, but we both agreed I had been right. When she graduated, we had a similar discussion about which job offer to accept. She wanted to set up her own business. I suggested she work for a firm one or two years to build relationships. She agreed." Jillian sighed. "You can imagine how proud I am of the woman she has become."

She paused and sprinkled the pepper bits into the dip. "Now, the Lord is blessing her with a good man, but nothing will change about our relationship. We'll still be close and I'll treat Trent as my own son."

Realizing she had been rambling, Jillian glanced up and caught a glimpse of the oddest expression on Dexter's face—almost menacing. *Why?* she wondered as a brilliant grin swept away the frown when he caught her staring.

CHAPTER 2

Being a good listener had paid off, Dexter thought as he allowed Jillian to babble on without interrupting. He refused to let her beauty distract him, and that was hard. Dexter's main concern for being there, besides finalizing the details of his son's wedding, was to keep a watchful eye out for an overbearing mother-in-law as he endured.

Exactly how much influence did Jillian have over her daughter? he pondered. From the few times he had spoken with Shana, she seemed to be a woman in charge of her own destiny. And this evening, when he met her for the first time, she appeared confident and in love with his son. Up until a few minutes ago, that was the only thing important to Dexter.

Now, he wondered would his son be marrying Shana, or Shana and her mother. Dexter refused to allow his son to go through what he did as a young husband. If his wife, Marsha, had lived instead of succumbing to breast cancer, his in-laws would have ruined their marriage with their constant interference beginning the day after they returned from their honeymoon.

Footsteps and voices jolted Dexter back to the present.

"Hi, Mom," Trent said with a peck on Jillian's cheek as he walked into the kitchen. Glowing from his attention, she rewarded him with a tight hug and pat on the back.

"Hey, son."

The scene softened his heart to hear the foreign endearment coming from Trent's lips.

"Hey, Dad," Shana said as she made a beeline to him as he stood and welcomed her hug. The moment was surreal. He always wanted a daughter, and to hear those words humbled him. He heartily welcomed her embrace.

"So Mom—" Shana sniffed and then hurried to the oven. Peeping inside, she turned off the stove. Slipping into gloved potholders, she pulled out the baking tray lined with pastries and placed it on the stove top. "See what a great father-in-law I'm going to have." Shana beamed. Dexter winked at her, wondering if Trent would be able to say the same about Jillian.

"God has truly blessed you," Jillian agreed and joined the couple in carrying plates and platters into another room. Dexter relieved Jillian of her load and trailed them into the dining room where books and magazines were neatly stacked to the side.

The first thing he noticed was the décor. It was striking. The seat upholstery on the chairs and the drapes complemented each other, as well as the artwork. The room was an impressive showpiece. Had it been the handiwork of his future daughter-in-law or mother and daughter? Before he could inquire, Jillian's voice invaded his thoughts.

"Dex, do you mind blessing our snacks?"

Aloud? Dexter wasn't a fan of outward piety. His son knew that.

"I got this, Pop." Trent bowed his head and the ladies followed. "Father, in the name of Jesus, I thank You for allowing us to fellowship this evening. Please bless and sanctify this food and blend our families as one."

After the chorus of Amen's, Trent pulled out his seat for Shana, and Dexter followed suit for Jillian who gave him a dazzling smile. *Enchanting.*

They reached for the luncheon plates to fill them with miniature sandwiches, pasta salad, the dip and chips. Dexter watched the couple drift into their private world of communication. It was reassuring that they really loved each other three months after they first met. He wasn't the only one observing them.

Jillian seemed to have a whimsical expression. The slight smile made her entire face glow. Although Shana didn't have as dark a complexion as her mother, it was undeniable that the two were related. Judging from Jillian's physical attributes, the woman took care of herself. As a doctor specializing in internal medicine, Dexter appreciated a person's attention to good health.

However, it was going to be a struggle for him to be a role model with that spinach dip in front of him. Already he had devoured two servings. The red peppers made the difference.

"Mom," Shana said as she nibbled on her finger sandwiches, "Trent and I have made some slight changes to the wedding."

Wiping her mouth, she gave her daughter her full attention. "Such as what, sweetie?"

Trent jumped in, "First…Shana and I decided to move the wedding up one month to April." He squeezed Shana's hand.

"That's not even three months to plan a proper celebration. This is the end of January," Jillian reminded them.

Dexter frowned. He had a sinking feeling in his stomach. "Why, son? Please tell me it's not because she's…" He didn't want to think it, much less voice it.

Shana gasped. Jillian swatted at his hand. Trent's nostrils flared and shot daggers at him.

"What's the rush?" Dexter cringed. "I'm not judging one way or the other. I love you both. It's a valid question."

"But not with my daughter and your son!" Jillian slapped her hand on the table.

"Pop, the Lord saved me not long after Shana and I started dating. That meant we would walk with Christ together without violating each other." Trent paused and stared into his fiancée's eyes. "And it's been hard for both of us, but the scripture says it's better to marry than burn. My first responsibility to her is to protect her soul. I'm determined to do that."

"You have really taken your salvation seriously," Dexter said with a bit of awe.

"The longer we wait, the more temptation is at our door," Shana said.

"God will bless you two for honoring Him." Jillian lifted her chin and cut her eyes at Dexter.

Chastened, he felt like the bad person. "I'm sorry,

son, to imply differently. Shana, please forgive me. Either way, I will love you as my own daughter," he repeated himself.

"Forgiven, Dad."

"What about the butterflies? Shana, we always talked about the butterfly release. It will be too chilly, even if we happen to have an unseasonably warm day. We always dreamed about the butterflies."

Did the woman pout? Dexter stared at Jillian's lips. Man, she was such a distraction.

Shana picked with her napkin. "I know, Mom, but Trent and I had to compromise. That's why we're moving the wedding to a smaller chapel and going for an intimate candlelight ceremony."

Jillian nodded, but Dexter could clearly see she was disappointed. Dexter admired her for not pressing the issue as she scribbled down the change.

"Okay, next?" Jillian hesitantly prompted.

"We decided to further reduce the guest list," Trent said.

The flashing lights seemed to dim in Jillian's beautiful brown eyes. For a brief second, her long lashes fascinated him. Snapping out of the hypnotic trance, Dexter concentrated on the conversation.

Jillian gnawed at the remaining lipstick on her lips. "Okay, how many are we talking about?"

"From two hundred to eighty," Shana explained.

Dropping her pen, Jillian reached for a napkin and began to fan herself. "Well, that's going to be tight with my coworkers who have watched you grow up, our many church members, your friends and clients...."

Clearly flustered, Jillian took several deep breaths, then cleared her throat. "Okay, well at least we have a small family. You still want a princess wedding dress, don't you?" Jillian subtly crossed her fingers.

Nothing Jillian did escaped Dexter. She was really taking the changes hard. Had he rushed to judgment based on his own experience?

"We also decided against those three-tiered cakes and opted for cupcakes. That way we'll have more variety," Trent added.

"No traditional wedding cake? But…" Jillian's eyes glazed over. "Cupcakes are expensive even with a reduced guest list. Most people would probably want two or three and—"

Uh-oh. Was this a sign that she was about to force her point? Dexter stepped in and usurped his authority. "If that's what the kids want, we will abide by their wishes. I'll cover the cost of the cupcakes, daughter."

***

Jillian started to tell Dexter it wasn't all about the money. She had been saving up for her daughter's big day since her first day on the job at a fast food joint. She and Shana had planned her wedding ever since they played with paper dolls together.

Since Jillian had never married, she was looking forward to the Monarch butterflies taking flight and the three-tiered cake intrinsically decorated with the bride and groom topper. Still, it was Shana and Trent's nuptials, and she would give them the moon if she could. Those were small things, considering the couple insisted on footing the bill for everything else. As long as there were no major surprises, Jillian was fine.

"Thank you so much, Dad. There is one more thing, Mom. I took a chance and reached out to Alex and his side of the family."

"Sweetheart, that was very considerate of you to include your father, but I don't want you to get your hopes up too high, because he might not respond," Jillian said. Alex Nixon didn't acknowledge Shana and hadn't tried to get to know her in her entire twenty-three years. She was ashamed to discuss this in front of Dexter. He had already made an insensitive remark inferring Shana might be pregnant.

She could only imagine what he thought about her having a baby out of wedlock and never marrying. *Lord, please don't let him be a terrible in-law.*

"Mom, he offered to walk me down the aisle."

Mixed emotions battled for Jillian's attention: anger, confusion, joy and fear. She stood abruptly. "Excuse me." She hurried to her bathroom off the kitchen. By the time she locked the door, the first tear fell. She gave in to the anguish. Alex had some nerve to parade Shana down the aisle like he had made her feel like Daddy's little girl. He had given her away in his heart the moment she was conceived. "God, if I ever need you to show up so I don't show out, it's at the wedding."

CHAPTER 3

What was that all about? Dexter didn't know the details of Jillian's relationship with Shana's father, but evidently Alex walking Shana down the aisle didn't sit well with her.

"Why don't you go see about her?" Dexter urged Shana as tears pooled in her eyes and she turned to Trent for comfort.

"Okay." Her voice cracked as Trent released her.

Once she was safely out of hearing range, Dexter questioned his son, who looked just as concerned. "What's going on? You never mentioned anything about discord between Shana's parents, but judging from Jillian's response, it doesn't look good."

Trent rubbed his chin. "There is no relationship. After I proposed, Shana confided that she always wanted her dad to walk her down the aisle. I don't want to say too much. I'm sure Shana will open up about her childhood without her father to you soon enough. Until then, know that when she calls you Dad, she means it."

Dexter's heart ached for her. He was proud that his son was protective of Shana. That was a good thing. Dexter wished he had been more protective of his marriage and safeguarded things said between him and Marsha. "Maybe we better head out."

"No. Not until I make sure Shana's okay, Pop." Trent stood, but Dexter put his hand out and prevented his exit.

"Let's give them a few more minutes."

Reluctantly, Trent fell back into the chair. "You're right." He drummed his fingers on the table and darted his eyes to the doorway.

Dexter smirked. Neither he nor his son had an ounce of patience. He did his best to draw him into a mindless conversation while they waited for the ladies to return. "I'm still considering closing my practice and moving up here."

With his chin firmly in the ball of his fist, Trent mumbled. "Umm-hmm."

His son wasn't listening. Trent had been hounding him to either retire or set up a practice in St. Louis. "Nothing's final."

"Okay," Trent murmured without taking his eyes off the entryway.

When mother and daughter reappeared, they both had mustered up identical smiles, but glassy eyes told a different story. Shana raced into Trent's open arms. He dragged her into the foyer for more privacy, leaving Dexter alone with Jillian, who didn't look his way as she began to tidy up the table and remove dishes.

Dexter sensed it would be better to pitch in than to ask if she needed help. Briefly, he wondered what his son was getting into. As he trailed her into the kitchen, she whispered her thanks.

"I'm here, Jillian, for Shana and you. I'm a good listener, too, if you want to talk about it."

Dexter heard her sniff as she rinsed off the plates and placed them in the dishwasher. For the next few minutes, they worked silently to restore her kitchen. Dexter was honestly at a loss for what to say. Clearly this was something beyond his control.

As if she could read his mind, Jillian glanced over her shoulder. "Thank you."

Before he could question her, Trent and Shana strolled into the kitchen with their fingers linked.

"Pop, are you ready to go?"

No was on the tip of Dexter's tongue, but Trent had turned his attention elsewhere.

"Mom, are you all right with Shana's decision?" Trent asked as all eyes were on Jillian.

"Yes," she answered weakly, then repeated stronger, "Yes."

Dexter wasn't convinced as Shana and Trent seemed to exhale in sync. Jillian dried her hands and trailed everyone to the front door. She suddenly paused in her steps. Behind her, Dexter peeped over Jillian's shoulder. The couple was having a private moment. Shana was in Trent's arms as he whispered to her, then pecked her lips with quick kisses.

Jillian sighed. "Nothing like the love of a good man," she mumbled more to herself, but Dexter heard her.

Now he was really curious about how much drama was going to tag along with their marriage. Maybe a move to St. Louis might be a good idea. When the couple realized they had an audience, they slightly separated and waited for Dexter.

At the door, he hugged and kissed Shana, then surprised himself when he turned around and brushed a kiss on Jillian's cheek and squeezed her arms.

"Goodnight." Dexter strolled out the door behind his son as if it was routine to kiss a woman he had just met hours earlier.

***

While Shana waited in the doorway to wave them off, Jillian headed upstairs to her bedroom. She needed to sleep off the tension Shana's news caused her. The evening had been full of surprises and not just with the major wedding changes.

It wasn't the first time they had reached out to the only known address she had for Alex Nixon. Jillian had just come to accept that Alex wasn't interested in Shana. Now, all of a sudden, he not only responded, but offered to give her away. Shana might be happy, but Jillian was mad.

Correction: Alex had responded after Shana was born to say that the baby wasn't his. The rejection had hurt, but it toughened her skin. As a courtesy, Jillian had sent an announcement when Shana graduated from high school at seventeen and college at twenty-one. No word from him.

Alex's interest now was a bit suspect. Jillian prayed as she removed her makeup and brushed her hair. Whatever his intentions, let them be for Shana's good. Jillian smiled as Shana's cell rang minutes later down the hall.

A popular love song was Trent's ringtone. The two couldn't get enough of each other. Yes, it was better that they moved up the date.

Closing her eyes, Jillian paused and praised God for the firsts in her daughter's life: college graduate, marriage, and getting married before having a baby. Despite all the wedding changes, Jillian was grateful the two didn't want to get married at city hall.

Jillian showered and slipped on pajamas. Opening the bathroom door into her bedroom, she saw Shana was in her room and stretched across her bed. Trent had restored the bright light in her daughter's eyes. Thank God for happiness.

"Mom, Trent and I were going to check out three places to hold our reception, but he thinks I need some pampering. Do you mind going for us? Trent's dad will even tag along."

"I'll go, but I don't need Dexter's help."

"I want him to go," Shana countered. "He's here to help us and you. Please, Mom. Alex agreed to walk me down the aisle. He didn't offer to pick up the slack as far as any other planning."

Jillian hissed at the mention of his name. "I won't bad-mouth your dad."

Shana hugged her mother when she sat on the bed. "You never have, and I know it's because God gave you peace, but I need you to understand this: He's my father, but Dr. Harris will be my daddy from here on out, so you might as well get to know each other."

CHAPTER 4

Saturday morning, Dexter accompanied Trent to Jillian's condo to tag along with her for the day. He didn't know what kind of mood to expect after the previous night's announcement about Shana's biological father.

Dexter wouldn't consider himself a praying man—until now. He prayed there wouldn't be any drama.

When they parked in the driveway, Shana was waiting for them at the door—rather waiting for Trent. She greeted him first with a hug and then went to her fiancé. As their greeting lingered, Dexter strolled inside as the smell of bacon and coffee permeated the air, beckoning him.

Jillian came out of the kitchen at the same time, meeting him halfway. Some women had it and some didn't, but Jillian Carter could work whatever she wore to her advantage. Dexter couldn't believe she was a knockout in casual clothes.

"Is it a good morning?" Dexter asked.

"As a matter of fact, it is. The Bible says joy comes

in the morning, so I prayed last night and joy woke me this morning."

He wasn't expecting that cheerful response. "Okay." Dexter stroked his beard. He hadn't grown accustom to Trent's attribution to God on the simplest of things after his salvation experience, but coming from Jillian, it seemed refreshing.

"Are you hungry?" Her eyes twinkled.

"I don't miss a balanced meal, and breakfast is the most important."

"Then come on back."

Following her to the kitchen, he admired the airiness of her walk. She had a slight bounce to her step as if she was a dancer. He washed his hands in the sink. "Have you eaten?"

"Not yet." Jillian busied herself with pulling the tray with turkey sausage patties out of the oven.

"Here, I'll get this. Why don't you let me take it from here? You've cooked, so I'll serve."

The shock on her face was entertaining. She genuinely looked perplexed. Dexter liked that. It was heartwarming.

"I believe my visitation pass expired last evening." Dexter winked as he opened her overhead cabinets and located her plates and glasses. She already had the utensils drawer cracked. With her elbows anchored on the counter bar table, she rested her chin in her fists and quietly watched him. Dexter whistled as he quickly scooped brown rice, eggs, biscuits, and sausage on their plates.

He was in his element. Although he was a successful internist, his passion in life had been to be a good husband and father. One thing he enjoyed was cooking breakfast and serving his wife in bed. That dream was short lived after she was diagnosed with cancer. Eating any meal after that was a challenge for his wife.

Dexter blinked. Those memories seemed like another lifetime ago. He had a live flesh-and-blood woman to share a meal with, so he refocused. Once he was seated across from her, Jillian seemed to wait on him, but when he didn't bow his head for grace, she took the lead.

"Lord Jesus, thank You for the cross and the blessings seen and unseen. Please sanctify this food and provide for those who have nothing, in Jesus' name. Amen."

The cross? What did that have to do with saying grace? At least it wasn't long and drawn out.

"You're a great cook and wonderful host," Dexter complimented after taking a few bites. Her scrambled eggs were stuffed with ingredients as if she had planned to make omelets and then changed her mind.

"Thank you, and you're a good server. Do you cook all the time at home?"

"Actually, no. Since there's no one at home besides me and I don't like eating alone, I eat out most of the time." Of course his housekeeper would prepare something if he asked her.

Dexter realized that was too much information about his boring life. He had to regroup. His concern was whether Jillian might interfere in their children's marriage. "So what was the verdict last night after we left? Did you talk Shana out of letting her father walk her down the aisle?"

"Why would I do that?" she asked with the oddest

expression.

"Well, you didn't look too happy, and I just assumed you would have talked her ou—"

Jillian lifted a brow. She didn't blink or speak. Tilting her head, she continued to stare as if she was daring him to say what was about to come out of his mouth. One thing he would have to learn was to hold his tongue around her.

"How many halls do we have to preview?"

"Three." Jillian sipped her decaf coffee as if he had not said anything to upset her seconds earlier.

He nodded and they finished their meal in silence, but that didn't stop the questions from forming in his mind. Maybe Jillian shouldn't be his focus. Perhaps it was Shana's father who Dexter might need to be concerned with. The couple needed a chance to grow and learn from their own mistakes without anyone moving them like puppets. That was Dexter's gift to his son: not to interfere in the marriage or allow the other set of in-laws to cause a division between the couple.

As Dexter assisted Jillian in tidying up the kitchen, he couldn't resist asking, "About Alex, Shana's father..."

"Alex Nixon and I never married. We had a summer fling when I was fifteen, and I delivered Shana when I was sixteen. With the help of my mother until she died thirteen years ago and other family, I reared Shana into the woman she is today. Thank You God very much," she said with finality in her tone. Lifting her wrap off a wall hook, Jillian glanced over her shoulder. "I hope this answers all your questions."

How did she keep doing that? Twice the woman had chastened him as if he wasn't the educated man he was. Slipping his hands into his pants pockets, Dexter walked closer and towered over her. "Actually, it doesn't."

"Remember, I'm driving. You're just along for the ride," Jillian stated as if her words were some type of Morse code he had to decipher. She walked out a side door off the kitchen into the garage.

Not one to forego having the last word, as he strolled around to her driver's side and opened her door, he whispered, "When one driver gets tired, the backup driver takes the wheel. I'm your backup, Jay."

"Jay?" Jillian whispered.

"I hope my nickname doesn't offend you." He paused. "I see you as someone special, not as formal as others might consider Jillian Carter."

"My parents used to call me that when I was little. When I got my first job at seventeen, I insisted people call me Jillian because I thought it made me sound mature. I'm not offended."

He imagined she was probably as beautiful growing up as she was gorgeous now. And always a force to be reckoned with.

***

Special? Jillian liked the sound of that. Would she be vain to ask him to say it again? At least when he called her Jay she would know he thought she was special. She took deep gulps of air to calm her nerves, but his cologne just made her intoxicated. When Dexter strolled around to the passenger's side to get in, she shivered at the excitement of his closeness. Then she returned to reality.

First Alex and now Dexter was intruding into her orderly life. As far as Jillian was concerned, neither man better mess up the most important day of her daughter's life—besides the day Jesus saved her, of course. Jillian owed Shana that much.

"Okay," Jillian said, exhaling and gripping the steering wheel. She checked her rearview mirror a third time to keep from staring at Dexter. "Our first stop is the Top floor of Clayton Towers." Backing out the driveway, Jillian headed for Interstate 170.

"Did Shana ever tell you how she and Trent met?"

Small talk, she could handle that. Jillian smiled although she refused to look at him. She didn't realize until a few minutes earlier that his eyes were a striking shade of brown. "Of course. Every mother wants to hear about how her daughter fell in love with the man of her dreams."

Dexter chuckled. "I had flown to town that day for a conference and met my son there for lunch. Trent noticed Shana before I did. When I couldn't keep his attention, I turned in search of the distraction. When I saw the pretty young woman dressed in a smart white suit, I knew my boy was smitten.

"The emotions that played on Trent's face were clearly readable. It was fascination, hypnotic, determination, and a slight hesitation, but determination won out. When Shana dropped that orange card in the fish bowl for a chance at a free lunch at the restaurant, I never saw my son move so fast to pluck it out." He chuckled again. "As a cover up, Trent tossed in his card. Looking back, I would say it was love at first sight."

Jillian enjoyed love stories. She liked reading them and watching them on television. When she could listen to someone regale about them, Jillian experienced a feel-good moment. Although she accepted that love had passed her by a long time ago, she was willing to live vicariously through her daughter's happiness.

Keeping her eye on the traffic, her mind briefly wandered to when Shana first mentioned Trent's name.

"Mom, I got the strangest call today from a new client."

"How strange?" she asked. They had been waiting for the start of a fashion show, a fundraiser for their church.

"Well, this guy named Trent Harris is new in town and he wants me to decorate his place—two stories—with a crazy budget."

"Really?" Jillian had lifted her brows.

Shana leaned closer, so others couldn't get the full details. "He doesn't want to see my portfolio or contact my list of references. It's as if he has blind faith in my work. That makes me nervous."

"That is strange. How did he hear about you?"

"He said he saw one of my business cards." Shana's face brightened.

Jillian remembered when Shana had gotten two thousand printed and for weeks they had placed them in all kinds of businesses.

"Do you think he's legit and not a psychopath?" She had gnawed on her lips, concerned for her only child.

"Mom, you taught me well. I'm meeting him at a public place. Actually, it's at Maggiano's where I had lunch last week."

The rest was history as Jillian blinked and noticed her exit was coming up. "I thought what Trent did was romantic. Shana was so nervous the morning she was to meet him. We both were praying that the offer was the real deal. When she arrived at Maggiano's and saw this tall, dark, and extremely handsome man stand from behind a table and walk toward her, Shana said she thought she was going to faint."

Jillian sighed. "Anyway, when Trent presented Shana with the large check for the project, she almost passed out. When he revealed how he got her business card, Shana thought she was dealing with a stalker."

"Yes, I can see that, but my boy was sincere in his intentions and he won her over," Dexter boasted.

"Correct, but my girl gave him a run for his money. She cleared that check and did a background check on him and then took two of her coworkers with her to view the project."

"She did an amazing job with his place. Trent made sure he worked from home when he knew she would be there to oversee the work. Shana is not only beautiful, but incredibly talented with a heart to match Trent's. I hope they have a long, happy, satisfying marriage."

"I pray for that, also. Shana is all I have, and I want her to be happy. If they keep God as the center, they will enjoy many blissful years." *Unlike my past life as a single mom,* she thought.

"Humph. Life isn't promised."

"Neither is happiness, but I've struggled to learn to be content in situations and praise God for the unexpected blessings that come my way," she said more to herself than Dexter.

"You seemed to be at peace with the cards of life you were dealt. Any regrets?"

"I would have many if God hadn't forgiven me for

the mistakes I've made along the way, but since I'm living each day with a clean slate, no regrets."

"Not even for not being a wife?" Dexter seemed to press her.

She was not about to go there with this man she hadn't known for twenty-four hours. Jillian turned into a public lot across the street from the reception location and parked. Why not turn the tables on him? "I understand Trent's mother died when he was little. Why didn't you ever remarry?"

Evidently, Dexter was evading the question as she had or didn't hear her as he unbuckled his seatbelt and got out. She admired his confident stride as he walked around to the driver's side of her car to assist her. She could get used to his special treatment. "I can't tell all my secrets, or I would have to marry you." Dexter didn't smile or wink. Only a penetrating stare hinted he could be serious.

***

What made him say that to Jillian? Dexter saw that glimpse of surprise as if he had scared her. But she was the type of woman a man wanted to flirt with. Stepping back, he observed how she whirled the cape around her shoulders. A blast of a cool breeze danced with her shoulder-length hair.

Shutting the door, she walked like a model on a photo shoot. Knowing Shana's age and what Jillian had revealed, the woman hadn't hit forty yet. With her looks, Jillian Carter would make a worthy opponent of any woman in her twenties.

Although his mind drifted, he was very much aware of his surroundings, including the step off the curb Jillian was about to take at the same time a car was turning the corner. With little effort, he restrained her movements.

Startled, Jillian patted her chest and turned around. "Thanks for the rescue."

"Any time." Dexter winked. They waited until the light turned green, then he escorted her across the street.

Inside the building, they rode the empty elevator in silence to the top. The entire floor was designed for multiple functions. Dexter didn't like the feel—it seemed like a business dinner atmosphere—but he withheld his comments. Instead, he tuned out the guided tour's presentation and focused on Jillian. She caught him staring a few times and he held her attention until she broke away.

Thanking the representative, they left and agreed to scratch the place off the couple's list. Back in the car, Dexter relaxed. His mind revisited the question Jillian asked, but he hadn't answered. Why hadn't he remarried? He could childishly blame his nosy in-laws for ruining him for life, but that wasn't it.

As a physician, there was no shortage of candidates for the position of Mrs. In truth, only a handful of women seemed to be worth the effort of the pursuit. Yet, there was always something missing.

Jillian drove to their second venue, pointing out points of interest along the way. They were in and out of Clare's Classic Events in fifteen minutes. The place didn't look as if it was a throwback to nostalgia as advertised, but a place that should have been demolished.

If Jillian hadn't said they weren't interested first, Dexter was a breath away from voicing his concern.

Back behind the wheel, Jillian clicked her seatbelt and looked at him. "Are you game for the third and final? A Personal Touch by Jeanette was recommended by a church member, so I'm keeping my fingers crossed."

Dexter shrugged. "As long as it's in Trent and Shana's price range and better than the last two places."

"Is there a price on love?" Jillian asked, but Dexter didn't know if she was teasing or not.

He knew they were heading downtown when the Gateway Arch came into view. He glanced at Jillian. She had a faint smile.

"What are you thinking?" he asked.

"Good thoughts." She paused, and Dexter wondered if she would share. Jillian did without any prompting from him.

"You asked me earlier if I had any regrets. I wouldn't call it regret, but I always wanted a son, and in three short months, I'll have one. The bonus is I won't have to change any diapers."

He roared with amusement. He definitely wasn't expecting that. "Then I guess we're both getting what we want. I have a daddy's girl. When Shana first called me Dad, she stole my heart. It's a good thing she's marrying my son. I know he will treat her like a princess." Dexter gritted his teeth. He hoped Jillian had not picked up on his slip of the tongue. His heart pounded, hoping he didn't remind her that her ex was giving Shana away.

"I see the evidence that you were a great father." Jillian stopped and sighed heavily, "but as you heard last night, Alex appears to have no qualms about giving her away. God help me and him if he even thinks about bringing any drama to the altar..." She shook her head.

"I'm in."

"On what?" She glanced his way then exited off I-64.

"When my son proposed and she accepted, Shana officially became my little girl."

Jillian sniffed and whispered, "Thank you."

What had he just done? Agreed to be a part of in-law drama?

CHAPTER 5

Jillian's mind was playing tricks on her, or did her heart flutter, because it seemed to put more into Dexter's words rather than taking them at face value. He, like her, only wanted to ensure their children's wedding day went without a hitch. Thank God for that.

As she drove, she gave him the highlights about Forest Park being larger than New York's Central Park and described the doctors, lawyers, and politicians who resided in the large estates that lined the park. "Do you have a stately home in the suburbs of Atlanta?"

"I live comfortably with a housekeeper that comes in once a week."

"It must be nice."

"Things are always better when you have a person to share them with," Dexter said and looked out the window.

Jillian thought he would add more, but he didn't. The only person she had shared her life with Shana, and she was about to experience that loss in a few short months. She tried not to think about it when she turned off Kingshighway onto Maryland Plaza. A large water fountain held center court, directing traffic in a circle to the right.

She wished she could persuade Shana to reconsider a summer wedding where they could release butterflies and pose in front of a fountain. Jillian shook her head. She understood Trent and Shana's reasons. They were in love and they didn't want to sin against God. Kudos to her daughter who wanted to honor God.

"Hey," Dexter seemed to coo from the passenger's seat.

"Huh?" Jillian blushed. "I'm sorry. I didn't hear you."

Dexter lifted his brow and smirked. "I said I'm assuming we're here because you stopped the car and it seems like that water fountain has you in a trace."

Sticking out her tongue, Jillian grinned. "Yes, we're here."

Dexter released his seatbelt and got out. She waited until he opened her door and reached for her hand.

She graciously accepted his assistance. *Lord, thank You for blessing my daughter with a man who will love, honor and cherish her like this man. Amen.* Jillian blinked rapidly to keep from becoming teary eyed. What was wrong with her?

"Are you okay, Jay?" Dexter squeezed her shoulder as he shut the car door.

Gathering her thoughts, Jillian mustered up a genuine smile. "Yes, I'm okay." She waved him off to put some distance between them. "I get sentimental sometimes about water fountains and butterflies. Pay me no mind."

"A man never forgets what's important to a woman."

The sincerity shining in Dexter's eyes did cause a tear to escape. Before she could dab at it, Dexter's thumb was there on her cheek to catch it. Embarrassed, Jillian bowed her head. Too bad she and Alex had been too young to understand the difference between love and lust. To this day, Jillian still hadn't experienced love.

***

Dexter took the liberty of grabbing Jillian's hand. He squeezed it as if he was testing it for softness. "I see the Personal Touch sign. Come on. I'd better escort you across the street. You've already proven you don't look both ways."

Jillian laughed. "True." Within minutes, they passed under the archway entrance into another world. The majestic foyer had a marble floor that stopped at three steps that led to a carpeted platform.

A woman greeted them and had no problem giving them a tour without an appointment. She clasped her hands and smiled. "So when is the big day?"

"Saturday, April fifth," Dexter answered.

The woman congratulated them as if they were the happy couple. "Wow, it won't be long before you're husband and wife."

"Oh, it's not us. It's my daughter and his son," Jillian corrected, without making eye contact. Her blushing would remain stained in his image for a while.

The host's mouth dropped and she blinked wildly. She frowned and glanced at their hands before regaining her professionalism. "Well, love is always in the air, and sometimes people catch the bug at these events."

"I'm sure," Jillian responded, but seemed clueless to the lady's inference, but Dexter was in tune.

Following her up the steps brought them to the starting point of three marble archways going in different directions. She explained that each section represented a theme, such as elegant, whimsical, and eclectic, then asked which one they would like to see.

Dexter was surprised when Jillian suggested whimsical. He thought she would have chosen elegant. As they strolled down the hall, the majestic décor made Dexter feel as if he was about to enter the king's court.

Once the host pushed a button on the wall, a set of double doors opened to a world of soft colors and light decorations, which didn't overpower the room.

Jillian sighed. The scene was breathtaking, but Dexter was having a hard time taking in its ambiance. Jillian Carter was distracting him as she glided between the tables, fingering the napkins and scrutinizing the centerpieces. Her eyes sparkled as she admired the chandeliers.

She had the look of love, but instead of for a man, it was for the ballroom. He silently *tsk*ed. What a wasted emotion. Instead of the foolish notion that Jillian could be a subtle threat to Trent's marriage, Dexter was questioning whether Jillian was a major threat to his emotional stability.

Dexter cleared his throat and mind. He was not going there. Jillian was off limits, even if he did find himself unexpectedly attracted to her.

***

"This is perfect." Jillian whirled around and faced

Dexter. When she met his eyes, the raw desire scared her. She quickly turned to their host. "Is this room available on that date? If so, how much?"

Dexter whistled and Jillian cringed at the quote. The cost was twelve hundred dollars over Trent and Shana's budget. Jillian tabulated her money in her CDs, 401(k) and emergency savings. She could rebuild her accounts, but she could never remake the day. The big event would be worth every penny.

Coming to a decision, Jillian smiled. "Okay, let's sign the paperwork."

"Jay," Dexter said with caution, "let's not. It's too much. Plus, this place wasn't even on their list. We don't even know if they would like this."

"Seriously, what's not to like? Trust me."

"I don't—" Dexter seemed to catch himself from saying more.

"Excuse me?" Jillian's heart dropped. Surely, this man had not just insulted her. Why? She folded her arms. Their host distanced herself as if something across the room had gotten her attention.

"It's too much money...and I don't trust that you would know what they want," Dexter stuttered.

Jillian didn't know what that was all about. Before she could remind him that he could come out of his pocket, too, her cell rang. She pulled it out her shoulder bag and squinted at the number—unrecognizable.

"Hello," she greeted as Dexter watched her.

"Jillian, this is Alex...Alex Nixon."

The color must have drained from her face, because suddenly Dexter looked concerned, so she turned her back for privacy, stunned speechless.

"Hello?" Alex repeated.

"I'm still here, Al." She gnawed her lipstick off, getting dizzy from the questions racing through her mind.

"Listen, I know I haven't been around for Shana…and you," he said as if it was a second thought. "I regret that, but I want to be a part of her big day…"

"Is everything okay?" Dexter whispered as he came from behind and towered over her.

Recovering, Jillian nodded and took a few steps away from him. "Al, I'm sure Shana would appreciate your participation, but why are you calling me?"

Steadying her breathing, Jillian did her best to recall every scripture about forgiveness, revenge, and presumptuous sin. Although, Alex had not apologized for his neglect and abandonment, a simple sorry wouldn't suffice anyway.

"Shana asked me to get with you to help coordinate things. And the sky is the limit for my baby girl."

Jillian rolled her eyes and fumed. She trembled to keep from growling into the phone. Dexter returned to her side. His look of concern was fierce as he began to pace. "Listen, I'll make up a list and we can split the cost."

"No, send me the list and I'll pay for everything," Alex said. "Christ has redeemed me, Jillian. A few years ago, I repented and got baptized in the name of Jesus. I thought that was all to it, but a few hours later, a language I've near learned or heard exploded out of my mouth. The power shook my body."

Saved? She grabbed a nearby chair and flopped in it. His salvation had cheated her from giving the man a piece of her mind. All Jillian needed was sixty seconds to call him the names she seemed to have been practicing since she'd delivered Shana.

Ye ought rather to forgive him and comfort him, lest perhaps such a one should be swallowed up with overmuch sorrow. God spoke 2 Corinthians 2:7.

Lord, I know you're right, but what about my hurt and rejection all these years? She twisted her lips as if she were a scolded child. Alex's redemption canceled out any thoughts of revenge. He had repented, and the Lord had canceled out his debts, which meant Jillian had no choice as a Christian but to forgive his trespasses against her. It also saved her from having to repent after acting ungodly. *Jesus, help my heart because I'm not in a forgiving mood.*

"Ah, I'll get back with you," she said. "Good-bye."

"Wait," Alex shouted as she was about to push disconnect. "I owe you an apology. Please forgive me."

"I do," Jillian whispered and pushed End Call. Closing her eyes, she bowed her head. For the past twenty-three years, she had no man to contend with in regards to decision-making. Now she had two. Anchoring her elbows on the table, Jillian began to massage her temples to ward off a headache.

"Jay," Dexter's deep voice was soft and comforting. His hand rubbing her shoulders was soothing. "Is everything all right?"

As Jillian scooted back her chair, Dexter assisted her to her feet. *No,* was on the tip of her tongue.

"So, what did you two decide?" Their host reappeared.

"Yes, we'll take it. Her father is paying for everything." Jillian shrugged. "I'll give him your information to call you. Thank you for your time."

"What?" Dexter protested.

She ignored his roar and her head began to pound as she retraced each step back toward the entrance to her car. He trailed her, mumbling something.

Great. Maybe after the shock wore off, she would rejoice over Alex's blood-washed soul, but at the moment, all she wanted to do was be alone to cry, eat, and sleep, then she would pray. The beauty of salvation was it canceled out all sins. The disadvantage at the moment was she couldn't go off on Alex, especially after he called Shana his baby girl.

CHAPTER 6

What just happened? Dexter wondered. One phone call had changed it all. He never knew a woman could walk so fast in heels as Jillian made her escape. Dexter almost had to jog to catch up with her.

Once he reached outside, he didn't have to look far for Jillian. She had darted across the street without his assistance and was staring into the fountain. He approached quietly. Either she didn't hear him or chose to ignore him.

"Don't jump," Dexter joked, chuckling as he snuck up behind her. No response. "Do you mind telling me what's wrong?"

"Before you said you didn't trust me or after the phone call?" she said with her back still to him.

Dexter gritted his teeth. His frankness was costing him big time around her. "The phone call. I had hoped I cleared my name with my slip of the tongue earlier."

"You didn't. It's not about me or you—or Alex for that matter. April fifth is about Shana and Trent," she said with finality in her voice, then turned and headed to her car. Again, leaving Dexter to follow her.

"Agreed, but—"

"Dex, if you have any qualms about the expenses, you'll have to talk to Alex."

The electrifying mood in the car ride was gone. Dexter was glad when she opted to forego a lunch and drop him off at Trent's. The air was so thick, he was beginning to suffocate.

Alone at his son's condo, Dexter made himself a bite to eat and tried to relax. What was really going on? Did Jillian and Alex have any kind of cordial relationship at all? He had questions, but he had to wait for Trent to come home, which would be late because he was at Shana's house watching old movies. For some reason that irritated him because their days were numbered to when it would no longer be him and Trent. Shana's needs and wants would trump anything else.

Dexter was dozing when he heard the garage door activate. Adjusting Trent's recliner, Dexter scratched his beard. He didn't realize he was hungry until his son strolled in with a foil-covered plate.

"Hey, Pop. This is for you. Mom insisted I bring it as a peace offering, whatever that means." Trent frowned and laid it on the counter. Removing his blazer, Trent draped it on the back of a chair at the table.

"That was nice of her," Dexter said, joining his son in the kitchen. After washing his hands, Dexter unwrapped the covering on the plate; he salivated at the mashed potatoes and rich brown gravy, fried catfish, and collard greens.

She can be mad at me any time, Dexter thought.

Silently, he blessed his food and sampled the mashed potatoes first and moaned. "It was a rough day after Shana's father called. She seemed really upset."

"My babe has this fantasy that her parents might get back together. That's why she had him call her mother. I guess it's possible since he repented, got baptized, and Jesus filled him with the Holy Ghost. They are both unattached, so nothing is technically standing in their way."

Dexter decided to confide in his son. "That's not entirely true. My determination could be the size of a boulder if I decide to stand in their way. Did you forget that I am also unattached? I might be interested in your future mother-in-law, but one weekend isn't long enough to be sure." He eyed Trent as he forked off a bit of fish.

Shaking his head, Trent's expression wasn't encouraging. "Shana is on cloud nine. She's hoping that our wedding will bring them together."

Dexter wanted to demand whose side Trent was on, but he would lose. Trent's faithfulness should be with his future wife, which left Dexter on his own. "Well, I'm hoping love won't be in the air for anybody but you two."

Trent laughed. "My father who doesn't want anyone to interfere in my marriage is trying to interfere in someone else's marriage prospects. Pop, I know you loved Mom, and I know my grandparents were a thorn while I was growing up, but Shana's mom isn't like that. She's our cheerleader and would do anything in the world for us."

Shaking his head, Dexter recalled the sparkle in Jillian's eyes at the last stop. "I saw her in action this afternoon when she wanted to put money down on a hall that was over your budget."

His son's cocky grin reminded Dexter of himself. "If we didn't set a budget, Shana's mom would go overboard. She just can't resist giving us the world if she could. Jillian Carter is a jewel."

Yeah, it didn't take Dexter long to come to that same conclusion, he realized as he toyed with his mustache. He had come to St. Louis with one thing in mind: to make sure Trent's future mother-in-law would not be overbearing.

What he got, instead, was a bit of a crush on a very attractive mother-in-law to-be and an estranged ex. Dexter didn't know how much turmoil Alex would stir up, and unfortunately, Dexter wouldn't be there to find out. He was caught up in his musing until his son mentioned Shana's father.

"Anyway, Alex will be down, not this weekend, but the following weekend."

"Then so will I. Jillian was pretty upset after she got off the phone with him. I may not be a committed Christian, but I care about what happens to Jillian."

"Pop, let it go."

"You're not the only one who can be smitten at first sight, and I don't need to leave a business card behind to make my intentions known. This Alex character sounds like a real jerk who had his chance. I sure hope Jillian doesn't believe in second chances."

"God is all about second chances. A Christian man has the advantage with a Christian woman. Shana had no problem telling me that off the bat when I asked her out on a date." Trent seemed to take on a faraway look. "I fell hard for Shana. Since she was not impressed with

48

my bank account, only my life account, I asked God what I had to do to be saved completely. For weeks, the Lord directed me to the Book of Acts."

"I can't fathom why any woman would demand this water and fire baptism you've told me about in order to have a relationship. That's nonsense, son."

"I haven't convinced you yet, but the odds aren't in your favor. No one is going to tell you how to follow surgical procedures. You better believe nobody can tell God how to administer his plan of salvation."

Since Dexter had no rebuttal, that ended further discussion, but not his determination to foil any attempts Alex might have in his mind on getting Jillian back. Before retiring to bed, he booked a return flight for the following Friday. When he got back to Atlanta, he might start putting his affairs in order so that he could relocate to St. Louis before Shana and Trent tied the knot and Jillian was taken.

***

"Are there any more surprises you want to tell me about?" Jillian asked Shana sarcastically while she paced the living room. Jillian had been uptight all day since Alex called. She owed Dexter an apology, but she was too numb for small talk. The carryout she sent home with Trent was her offering.

"Since Alex seems to be footing the bill for whatever—which by the way, I'm still covering my portion—the only thing you need to do is give him a list."

"Mom, are you not in charge per se of my wedding planning? I simply asked him to coordinate things with you."

Lifting a brow, Jillian stared. Taking a seat in front

of her daughter, she looked into Shana's big, beautiful brown eyes. "I want you to have a relationship with Alex that does not include me."

"Yes, but he's a Holy Ghost–filled believer now. That has to count for something," Shana pressed.

"Absolutely. It's a prepaid ticket to catch the rapture. I've repented, too, so we'll be on that same flight. End of story."

"Hmm." Shana had a mischievous glint in her eyes. "Or it could be another chapter in your life. Mom, I've been praying that God would give you a companion. I didn't reach out to Alex because of that, but when he said he was saved, I just wondered if God had answered my prayers."

"I hope it's not with Alex," she mumbled as she stood to go to her bedroom.

CHAPTER 7

Early Sunday morning, Dexter was on the first flight out of St. Louis to Atlanta. Unfortunately, it was too early to call Jillian and make sure she was okay. When he landed hours later at Hartsfield-Jackson airport, his mind was already setting things in motion for a permanent move to the Midwest.

Jillian had enchanted him with her personality and blinded him with her beauty. Now, she was about to drive him crazy if she even considered reconnecting with Shana's biological donor. The man was scum to desert not only his child, but his responsibility. Of course Shana craved a father figure in her life, and Dexter was determined to be that man for her.

On Monday morning, Dexter shoved his personal issues aside when he walked through the door of his practice. He greeted his staff, then listened intently as the office manager briefed him on urgent matters, meetings, and medical supplies.

"Thanks, Mrs. Green, for holding the place together in my absence," Dexter said then strolled down the plush carpeted hall to his office. His upscale practice had been long in coming after his residency. He and another colleague had worked hard to stand out as top African-American internists and they succeeded. After putting in ten years at a family clinic in the inner city, Dexter branched out with his own private practice in the suburbs with regular biweekly visits to the same inner city clinic.

At forty-seven, Dexter was well established and highly recommended in the medical community. About five years earlier, he had welcomed two other doctors as partners. One had since retired and the other Dexter regarded as his protégé, who had hinted at buying him out in the future.

Dexter was about to call his bluff. If the price was right, Dexter would consider it before discussing it with his attorneys, then there was the matter of listing his home. It wouldn't be a hassle, considering home sellers usually got the asking price for property in Fulton County. Still, it was a lot to consider.

Those details were pushed aside as Dexter saw one patient after another. Plus, he had to write numerous appeals to insurance companies on behalf of a few seniors for medicine. By the time the office closed at five, he still was behind his desk updating patients' files. It wasn't until after seven when he locked up and headed to his silver Jaguar.

While he was on the road to his home in Sandy Springs, Jillian crossed his mind. Again, he wondered how she was faring. He had cataloged everything about her, which included her flawless skin, jet-black hair, lashes, lips and the list went on. How could he miss a person he had literally just met?

Almost an hour later, he exited off I-400 to Northridge. Dexter was minutes away from his Kenstone Place subdivision. Clearing the gated entrance, he slowed and assessed his story-and-a-half all brick and almost three-thousand-feet home in "Hotlanta". His life was in Georgia. He never gave serious thought to moving away and leaving his medical practice. His way of thinking changed drastically once he laid eyes on Jillian.

After parking in his three-car garage, Dexter strolled through the door of his garage to the laundry room before entering the breakfast area when his cell rang. He snatched it off his belt and hoped it wasn't the doctors' medical alert center calling about an emergency. The only thing he wanted was food, wine, and to relax.

He eyed the number. It had a St. Louis area code and it wasn't Trent. "This is Dr. Harris."

"Hi Dex, this is Jillian." Her soft voice was like a balm to his tense muscles.

"Jay, how are you?" Dropping his briefcase in a nearby chair, then kicking off his shoes, Dexter began a trail of discarded clothes that began with his tie.

"I'm sorry about snapping at you this weekend. I shouldn't have treated you rudely. I was going to invite you to dinner, but Trent said you left this morning. I hope it wasn't because of me."

Dexter smiled. It was all because of her that he was contemplating changes. "I decided to head home early and take care of some business."

"Oh."

She sounded disappointed, which pleased Dexter. "I'll be back sooner than you think."

"I can't wait."

"If you need me for anything, you call me. Southwest Airlines has non-stop flights to St. Louis hourly."

***

The work week proved to be challenging. Jillian smiled on the outside at the hospital where she worked as the human resources specialist, but alone behind closed doors and on the inside, she was emotionally tormented. A few times she thought about calling Dexter just to vent, but that wasn't her way of handling conflict. She had the Lord's ear at all times.

Only God knew she had silently resented Alex, but Jesus helped her heal. Surprisingly, God had given her strength not to bad mouth Alex in front of Shana. At least to her credit, she had reached out to him over the years to encourage his involvement in important events in Shana's life—nothing.

Now, the biggest day in any woman's life, Alex not only wanted to step up to the plate with a blank check, but he was untouchable in the Kingdom of God as far as Jillian's fury. She wanted to scold him, give Alex a piece of her mind and belittle him, but what would that accomplish, but make God ashamed? Jesus's love was amazing. It was a good thing for both of them.

"Lord, help me to bridle my tongue when I see this man," Jillian mumbled as she tapped into her computer in her office.

"What did you say?" Darla Bass, one of her two assistants, asked as she opened the door without knocking.

Shaking her head, Jillian gave the woman her undivided attention. "Nothing, I've just got a lot on my mind with Trent and Shana moving up the date and making some unexpected changes."

"Hmm…could it be?" Darla paused, gritted her teeth, and lowered her voice. "Is she expecting?"

"Don't make me hurt you. Why is it that some people think God's saints don't have the victory over sin? They moved the nuptials up to keep the victory. They really love each other. I'm offended you would not only think such a thing, but voice it." Jillian lifted a brow.

"I'm sorry. I just asked because your steadfastness in your faith is mind-boggling to me. No cursing, no drinking, no sex." Darla sighed. "What else is left?"

Forgiving the offense, Jillian took her cue as a witnessing moment. "Love—true love for a daughter, a husband, and Jesus. It makes for a pretty fulfilling life here, and when this life is over, Jesus has made reservations for the saints to have a mansion with a great view of God's glory. It's worth living for Jesus."

"Humph." Darla picked up some files out of a tray marked with her name and squeezed it against her chest. "You've scored two out of three. You've never had a husband, and it appears your daughter's father wasn't worth the love you shared," she said as if she completely missed the Jesus moment.

Jillian said, "I repented for my sins a long time ago. Shana's father, Alex, recently repented and experienced the water and fire baptism in Jesus' name, so we're even. God will work it out. You'll meet him at the wedding."

"You sure there won't be a double wedding?" Darla snickered and walked away.

"Positive," Jillian mumbled, having the last word.

On Friday, Jillian took off work to go shopping with Shana. Her daughter's smile was contagious as they headed out the door to visit the first of four bridal stores. "I hope you say yes to the dress," Jillian said from the passenger's seat of Shana's car, mimicking the lines from a popular show where the bride-to-be finally decides on "the" wedding dress.

"I'll know it when I see it." Shana grinned and checked the rearview mirror before backing up. "Are you ready to see...I'll have to figure out how to address Alex, Father or Dad. I already gave Mr. Harris my endearment as dad."

"Whatever feels right when you meet him. I'm sure Dexter will understand if you decide to use that term with Alex." Mixed emotions continued to plague Jillian. Why did her daughter have to mention coming face-to-face with a man who was her accomplice in losing her virginity and sinning against God. Of course, if he was overweight with a receding hairline, wearing thick lenses or anything that would distract from the handsome features she remembered, it would give her a sense of victory.

She didn't know how she felt about Shana calling any man 'dad'. The few male acquaintances she knew while Shana was growing up were forbidden from being around her child, so there wasn't a dad until now. Even Jillian's father had died the year after Shana was born, so they both had become fatherless.

Their first stop was Bridal Palace where they spent hours—they left the shop with a few "maybes" in mind. Next was The Ultimate Bridal near the Galleria and Clarice's Boutique. Great selection, but nothing seemed to jump out at Shana, where on the other hand, quite a few grabbed Jillian's attention.

By the time they arrived in Simply Elegance Bridal's parking lot, Jillian was famished after zigzagging across the greater St. Louis city and suburbs.

As they got out the car and headed to the entrance, the displays in the window were breathtaking. Jillian prayed Shana would connect with a dress and the price would connect with the budget Jillian had set as her wedding gift to her only daughter.

Tears filled Shana's eyes when she stepped into an Olia Zavozina gown. She paraded to the platform and modeled for Jillian. The fitted bodice was made of silk charmeuse that hugged Shana's small, but shapely hips. After that, yards of silk organza ruffles fanned out to form a dainty train. *Gorgeous,* Jillian thought as a sigh escaped from her lips.

"You're so beautiful," she said with such awe and sniffed to hold back tears. Now Jillian knew what she had cheated her own mother out of. The priceless moments of seeing her little girl grow up. Happy tears trickled down Jillian's face before tears of regret flowed. The sales representative and Shana thought she was overcome with joy.

However, joy had turned into regret as she pictured herself in a white dress. That window of opportunity had passed, and at this point in her life, she had to focus on becoming an empty nester and grandmother. "I can't believe you're a grown woman about to get married and leave me." She couldn't keep her voice from cracking.

"Mom." Shana wrapped her arm around Jillian's shoulder. "It's okay. You're not losing me. I'm not going away. We'll always be best girlfriends, and you'll have a son."

Through blurred vision, Jillian mustered a smile. She sniffed again and nodded. "Not only am I proud of you, but I'm happy for you, too," she whispered.

The sales rep handed her a bottle of chilled water, which Jillian accepted. "Sorry. Whew!" She fanned her hand in front of her face and took a deep breath. "So, is this yes to the dress?"

Shana cringed.

"What? How much is it?" Jillian braced herself.

"Six thousand dollars," her daughter said tentatively.

Immediately, Jillian grabbed a nearby magazine to fan herself. That amount was three thousand dollars over budget. And she refused to max out her two credit cards. *Lord, this is my only child. I saw the look on her face, and this is my gift to her,* she silently prayed. *Please give me wisdom with my money.*

"Mom, this is so beautiful, but this is more out of our league than the two I think could be runner ups."

The attendant intervened. "It's worth it for the one day you will always remember."

"Sweetie, it is beautiful, but we really need to talk about this. There was nothing else similar from another designer that was closer to our budget?"

For the next half hour, Shana modeled three more dresses. None of them had the oomph that the Olia Zavozina gown had on Shana.

Changing back into her street clothes, Shana returned to the showroom. "Can you hold this for a few days?" she asked the attendant and then faced Jillian. "Out of all the dresses I tried on, I really like this. Maybe we can go over the budget again and see what else we can cut."

Wrapping an arm around Shana, Jillian winked. "God will make a way."

CHAPTER 8

"Dr. Harris, are you serious?" Dr. Samuel Prentiss, Dexter's colleague, quizzed. "You're offering to let me buy you out of your portion of the practice so you can move to St. Louis? What's the real deal? Does this have anything to do with your untreated phobia about meddling in-laws? That's all you've been harping on since Trent became engaged."

"Watch it, son." Dexter had taken Samuel under his wing since Samuel's medical residency. Not only did Dexter serve as a mentor, but they had developed a father-and-son relationship. Even Trent considered him as an older brother. There were very few secrets kept between the two doctors.

"The real deal is I'm over my head. You've seen a picture of Shana." Dexter rubbed the waves in his hair, then started stroking his beard. He shook his head thinking about Jillian's brown eyes and smooth brown skin. She reminded him of brown sugar. "Well, her mother is even more beautiful. I knew she was estranged from Shana's father, but I didn't know the detail that they were never in a committed relationship. Miss Carter is very much available."

Samuel smirked. "Well, well, well. The widower doc is smitten. Any chance of a double wedding?" He grinned and wiggled a brow. Clearing his throat, he switched to a doctor mannerism. "This isn't part of a plan to rein in Shana's mother's interference as a conspiracy theory, is it?"

"Shana's mother is definitely not the problem." Dexter couldn't count Alex out until he met the man.

"Do yourself and Trent a favor, Dr. Harris. Don't become the monster you're trying to protect Trent from. Have you ever thought he accepted that position in St. Louis to have some space?"

"Trent is his own man. It was his idea that I move to be closer to him," Dexter defended. "I never gave it any serious thought until now."

Samuel stood and put his hand on the door handle in Dexter's office to leave. "I'll be praying for the best."

Dexter grunted. "According to my son, I'm going to need it because it appears Shana's long-lost father is back on the scene. It's him I'm concerned about interfering with my plans."

"Lord, help us all," Samuel said, shaking his head then closing the door.

Dexter never knew impatience until it was the night before his return trip to St. Louis. He was ready to get back to Jillian. He couldn't believe his attraction to her had grown while they were apart, but it had. Besides her call on Monday evening after his return to Atlanta, they chatted a few more times during the past few weeks.

But his time at home had been productive. Dexter had made an appointment to meet with his attorney to begin the process of selling his practice. He had his office manager juggle his schedule to where he would see his patients three days a week instead of five for the next month.

Before Trent and Shana said "I do", Dexter expected to be settled in temporary housing—an extended stay hotel or apartment. He fingered the small wrapped box in his hand. It was a gift to Jillian to make her smile. Did he have a chance at her heart? He was bent on finding out.

An hour and fifteen minutes later, his non-stop flight to St. Louis landed on time. Grabbing his luggage from the baggage department, Dexter headed to transportation to pick up his rental SUV. Once he was behind the wheel, he programmed the GPS to Jillian's Olivette condo.

Trent mentioned Shana would meet her father at Jillian's home. Trent was taking Shana to breakfast to give Jillian and Alex time to iron out rough patches from the past. Dexter grunted. When he arrived at Jillian's, Dexter wore a smug smile that he had beaten the competition.

***

The doorbell's chime echoed throughout Jillian's condo. She took a deep breath, but it didn't calm her nerves. It was like déjà vu. Unlike a few weeks ago when Jillian was pleasantly surprised by the handsome man on her doorstep, she was not looking forward to seeing Alex Nixon again.

She peeked out the window at the vehicle parked in her driveway as the bell chimed again. She positioned a smile on her face that she didn't feel and bowed her head for a quick prayer.

"Jesus, You said unless I forgive other's transgressions, You won't forgive mine. Help me to forgive the past hurts in my heart. Amen," she whispered as she turned the lock.

All things work together for good for those who love Me, God whispered back.

Opening the door, a few butterflies flew inside as if they were escaping the coolness of the spring. Delighted with the beautiful creatures in flight, she temporarily forgot about her guest. Turning back, Jillian's eyes widened with surprise.

"Dex?" she gasped. "Hi. What are you doing here?" She stepped back as her heart pounded with excitement. "What a wonderful surprise."

The build, the looks, and the cologne made a woman want to cry from appreciation. Dexter grinned as he removed his trench coat and hat.

"Well, considering I'm no longer a visitor, I decided I would stop by." He brushed a kiss on her cheek and gave her a loose but lingering embrace.

"Right, like you live down the street or around the corner." She closed the door and took his things. After hanging them in the closet, she turned back to him. He hadn't moved, but instead watched her.

"Seriously, what are you doing back in St. Louis?"

"How much time do we have for me to explain?"

Was he flirting with her or was that wishful thinking on her part? Looking away at her wall clock in the foyer, Jillian cleared her throat and led him back to the family room. "Not much. I'm expecting Shana's father any minute. That's who I thought you were."

Dexter made himself comfortable on the sofa and patted the space next to him when she was about to sit in the adjacent chair. She obliged, but hesitantly.

He reached for her hands and then squeezed them, as one of the butterflies landed on their joined hands then took off. She looked up at Dexter who was watching her.

"Thank you. They're beautiful." She eyed their joined hands again and her imagination took flight as if the butterfly had cast a magic spell on them. "Okay, they say the third time is a charm, so why are you here again?"

"Are you not happy to see me?"

"Dex, will you stopping asking me questions without answering mine." She couldn't help but giggle at their childish game.

Tightening his hold on her fingers, Dexter stared into her eyes. "The day Shana becomes Mrs. Trent Harris is the day she officially becomes my daughter and I will protect her—and you—at all costs. If her father is going to be upsetting you or her with his involvement in the wedding, then I'm willing to step in." He paused and played with her fingers. "The short answer is I missed you."

Jillian needed to fan herself, and it had nothing to do with menopause. She was far from that. "That's a bold statement after knowing the mother of the bride for all of fourteen days."

"And counting."

When her doorbell chimed, she broke free and hurried to the door. The loss of contact also meant the loss of feeling secure. She wondered at Dexter's words. Shana was getting a father and a father-in-law. What was she getting from all this?

***

Dexter was on her heels. Judging from Shana and Jillian's beauty, Dexter doubted she would have fallen for any plain-looking guy. Dexter's wish was the guy was a loser, but with an open-ended bank account, Dexter knew different.

Uh-oh. Alex and Jillian stared at each other a little too long for Dexter's taste. Clearing his throat, he reminded them of a third wheel in their presence.

"Jillian," Alex said, almost with a twinge of awe.

"Al." She nodded and bid him to come inside.

As he cleared the doorway, Dexter sized him up. Alex extended his hand. "Hello, I'm Alex Nixon, Shana's father."

Dexter accepted it with a firm grip. "Dr. Dexter Harris, Shana's soon-to-be dad-in-law," he said, putting emphasis on the word *dad.*

Alex seemed to relax. Jillian closed the door and directed him and Alex to the living room. "You and Al take a few minutes to get to know each other while I get refreshments for us."

"Jay, do you need any help with anything?" he called after her.

"No, I got it," she yelled from the kitchen.

"So, Alex—or may I call you Al? Where have you been for the past twenty-three years?"

***

Once in the kitchen, Jillian needed a few minutes for the shock to wear off at seeing Shana's father after so many years. He was still rather nice looking. Habit made her glance at his finger, no wedding ring. Surely, he was either married or had been married. She thought he was cute as a teenager, but the man at her door was handsome. *Don't go there,* she chided her mind. His marital status was not why he was at her house. It was Shana.

After scooping up the cheese and fruit platter she had prepared earlier, she turned and paused in her tracks. Two of the three butterflies were feasting on the fresh marigolds that were resting in a nearby vase.

Their grace and beauty seemed to have a calming effect on her racing heart. She would never see a butterfly again without remembering Dexter's thoughtfulness—unusual, but a sweet gesture. Taking a deep breath, Jillian continued to her living room. She was a few feet away from the doorway when she heard Dexter drilling Alex, as if he was counsel instead of a medical professional.

"Jay and I have already discussed our son and daughter's wishes. I hope you're not here to interfere."

"Actually, Jillian and I have a few things to discuss. I'm sure you can understand our need for privacy at this time. If you give us an hour or so alone, we would appreciate it."

"Okay, gentlemen," Jillian said, rushing in. She was still waiting for her nerves to settle. She had only been attracted to one man—Alex—and that had been a youthful infatuation.

However a few weeks ago, something within Jillian began to stir when Dexter gave her a compliment, then since he had returned to Atlanta, he had called three times to "compare notes" on the wedding, and they had touched on things from their past and sometimes the upcoming ceremony. Yet, he never mentioned his surprise visit.

Yes, Dexter was temptation dressed up in an expensive package, but Jillian had strengthened her faith in God to help her not to fall this time for another man. She had lasted twenty-three years with that resolve, but she always had Shana in the forefront as a distraction. Now her baby was getting married. What would be Jillian's excuse for not dating again? She was still working on an answer.

She eyed both men as she set the tray on the coffee table, then backed out as if she was a maid in her own house. Returning to her kitchen, her hands trembled as she reached for her decorative crystal bucket that held the miniature bottled water and juices.

Jillian needed to get herself together. With Dexter by her side, she did feel more confident. At least he was asking the questions she wanted to ask Alex. Only she would have more attitude behind her inquiries to him.

Plus, Alex's visit was not to rekindle what little attraction they had for each other. He was there to set the record straight with Shana—nothing more. She focused her interest on hearing his salvation experience.

Alex repeated his request to Dexter for privacy when she returned to the room. He wasn't budging until Jillian wanted him to. She nodded. "If you need me before Shana returns with Trent, you have my number." Dexter faced Alex with a slight scowl. "Jillian is family. I don't know where you will fit in, but I won't stand by and let your presence wreak havoc." He turned and headed for the front door.

Too late, Jillian thought. Chaos started the day Alex called her name after twenty-plus years.

CHAPTER 9

Dexter got behind the wheel of his rental, berating himself for issuing a threat to a man he didn't know. Was his attraction to Jillian that strong to cause him to break the Hippocratic Oath and hurt somebody? "I am losing my mind over this woman."

Punching in nearby attractions, nothing seemed appealing to spend an hour.

Swiping his smart phone off his waist belt, he tapped in Trent's cell number. His son answered right away.

"Hey, Pop. You made it to town."

"Actually, I've been here. I stopped at Jillian's first. Shana's father showed up and I left to give them some privacy—"

"Back up. You mean you've been in town and you didn't let me know?" Trent asked in a scolding tone.

"Son, you might almost be a married man, but I'm the father, remember? Anyway, there's a bowling alley around here. You and Shana want to meet me there for a couple of games?"

Trent laughed. "You're right, you are an old man," he teased, then relayed the invitation to Shana. She yelled in the background, "Hi, Dad."

Old. Dexter was far from old and the grave. Shana's endearment caused Alex's face to flash across his mind. Yep, Alex better not hurt his little girl's heart, or Dr. Dexter Harris would be a force to reckon with.

***

Jillian sat across the room, staring at the man who had brought heartache and joy into her life. She refused to speak first, and that seemed to make Alex uncomfortable.

Unscrewing the cap to the bottled water, Alex took a swig. He fumbled with the cap and then gave Jillian a look that reminded her of Shana when she was guilty of something.

"Jillian, you look well."

She nodded.

"I can't wait to see Shana."

"Her fiancé took her out to an early breakfast. They should return shortly. She's excited about meeting her biological father."

Her jab about biological seemed to hit the intended target of reminding him he had fallen short of being a dad. His handsome features seemed crestfallen. Jillian immediately felt condemned. "I'm sorry. I purposely said that. It was wrong." She moved closer to him and patted his hand.

He laid his hand on top of hers. "I deserved that and more. I was young, Jillian. We both were. I wasn't ready to father."

"I certainly wasn't prepared to be a mother at

sixteen." She regulated her breathing to keep from snapping. "I do have mixed feelings about you suddenly wanting to be a part of Shana's life on her big day. It was solely her decision to reach out to you. If it makes her happy, then I'm behind her, but why now?"

Alex shook his head. He lifted his hand and rubbed the back of his neck. Something across the room stole his attention. Jillian followed his gaze. She smiled at the distraction. One of the butterflies had landed on her ceiling. Briefly, she smirked, wondering if Dexter had bugged the gentle creature to be the fly on the wall.

"How did that thing get in here?"

"What, the butterfly? There are three of them, and they're a gift from Dexter."

"Humph." Alex grunted. "What an odd present."

"Excuse me?" Jillian silently fumed. Dexter's thoughtfulness had earned him brownie points that Alex would never be able to reach. "Why are you here?"

"One word—or person—Jesus. He has a way of taking an out-of-control person to hell and back in life. My lifestyle was anything, but perfect—the women, the drugs, the wrong crowd. I have two other children besides Shana." He held up his hand. "And before you ask, I was still a pitiful human being. I denied custody and spent time in jail for non-payment. Thank you for at least not sending the law after me."

"Don't think I didn't think about that and more." Jillian shrugged. "Sorry, I wasn't saved."

"I can imagine how your folks wanted to handle it, but while in prison, I had time to think. Two inmates talked to me about Jesus and how young I was and told me there was still time for me to turn my life around. Cocky, I dismissed them. They were hardcore. It wasn't until…I saw a guy get beaten to death that life started to mean something. In order not to return to jail, I had to find work. I got a job as an over the road truck driver."

Jillian didn't realize that her eyes had teared until she sniffed. "I'm sorry. I genuinely am. I always thought you got off scot-free. What about your other children?"

"Miranda put the girl up for adoption, and my son wants nothing to do with me." Alex bowed his head in shame.

Jillian felt sorry for him. How did God judge one sin against another? *Jesus, give him comfort,* she prayed silently.

Clearing her throat, Jillian changed the subject. "Okay, enough of darkness." She grinned. "Tell me about the new man through the blood of Christ Jesus."

With a source of renewed strength, Alex leaped up from his seat and began to pace the room. "God is awesome. When I was in prison, I began to ask myself how a promising All-American player wound up in a cell. I'm ashamed to say I cried, but a vision of God came to me. He made me a promise to save me from myself—and He did.

"Connecting with Shana was one piece in the puzzle of my new life. I was praying asking God to help me make it right, then I got her note in the mail about her wedding. I'm no longer a truck driver, but a successful business man in the transportation industry. Money can't buy happiness, but it's a start. I want to be a permanent fixture in her life and yours from now on."

Jillian was riveted as he explained the altar call during a revival service he attended with one of the inmates from prison.

"I remember every word that preacher said: That Jesus didn't deliver me just for the sake of doing it. He paid a high price for my salvation, and He was reaping what he sowed. I took the preacher up on his offer when he said, 'Come today and get the filth of your sins washed away in clear water that is the red blood of Jesus and He will give you a white garment of righteousness.'

"After I was buried in the name of Jesus, it took two ministers to restrain me as I shot out of the pool as if I was an Olympian. It was like an angelic out-of-body experience when I heard my lips move rapidly. I couldn't control my mouth or what was coming out of it. I was blown away. By the time they led me from the baptismal pool, I was physically weak, but my spirit was charged and ready for another angelic round."

Jillian's spirit began to bear witness to every word Alex told her. Standing, her soul began to rejoice for his salvation until the power fell in the room. They both began to rejoice. The tears flowed. Alex led them in a prayer of healing and thanksgiving.

Once they composed themselves, Alex opened his arms. "Friends and family?"

Jillian accepted the welcoming gesture and stepped into the embrace. She sniffed. Only God could mend a broken heart. "Yes."

"Mom? Alex?" Shana said as she entered the foyer and stared.

Dexter and Trent trailed her daughter. Jillian didn't even hear them coming in. A bewildered look marred Shana's face. It was a mixture of confusion and curiosity. Trent had a blank stare, but it was Dexter's nostrils flaring that caused her to push back from Alex.

Jillian made the introductions and left them to get comfortable as she went into the bathroom and patted her face with cool water. Staring into the mirror at her reflection, she whispered, "Jesus, I guess this really will be a joyous occasion."

***

Everybody seemed to be in a festive mood, but Dexter wasn't happy with all the new developments—mainly Alex. However, his daughter-in-law beamed as she sat between Trent and her biological father as they gathered in the dining room where wedding samples and other paraphernalia lay.

The scene earlier with Jillian in Alex's arms was ingrained in Dexter's mind. Her eyes were watery. Did that mean she and Shana's father had kissed and made up, or that he had delivered another blow to her heart? It didn't matter; the loser had his chance and blew it. Dexter never passed over a good thing.

By default, Jillian was situated between him and Alex. Dexter wondered at her thoughts. In his peripheral vision, two of the Monarch butterflies floated in the air before racing to a vase packed with an explosion of colorful flowers.

He glanced at Jillian to see if the creatures had caught her attention. Their movements had, and they shared a smile. She was so beautiful. After he pulled her into a brief trance, Dexter winked, causing Jillian to scrunch her perfectly shaped nose at him.

Their secret moment ended when she pulled away and refocused on the conversation. Dexter had no choice but to join her. That's when he caught Alex staring at them.

"Okay, the guest list," Shana rambled. "If you give

us names and addresses, we can send the invitations, but only about twenty."

"Twenty? Can't I have more?" Alex shook his head. "If it's a matter of money, I can foot the bill for that, too. I want to show off my beautiful daughter. I need at least fifty."

Dexter was about to protest Alex's late-on-the-scene interference, but Trent cut him a frown and discreetly shook his head.

"Alex—I mean Da…ah, Father," Shana said, struggling with what to call him.

Alex smiled tenderly at his daughter. "I'm Alex, and I'll always be your father. I would welcome the endearment, but I'm willing to wait to earn your trust and affection."

Shana nodded. "Okay, Alex for now. Anyway, Trent and I downsized our wedding because we moved our date up."

Alex pulled out the checkbook from his back pocket. "I will right this wrong, whatever the cost. As a matter of fact, I'll have my attorney calculate what I owe for back child support."

Jillian gasped in shock. Evidently, it was worse than Dexter had thought. The man hadn't even paid child support. *Pitiful.*

Shana patted the table and got Jillian's attention. "My dress, Mom."

"I don't know, sweetie. That was supposed to be my gift to you," Jillian said sadly.

"If you let Alex share the cost, then that will be the exact amount of what you planned to pay anyway."

All eyes were on Jillian as she gnawed on her lipstick. Dexter could see how much Shana wanted a particular dress and how badly Jillian wanted to buy it for her.

When Jillian nodded, everyone seemed to exhale. Dexter reached for her hand and squeezed it. "It's okay, Jay. Alex can never take away your special moments with Shana," he leaned closer and whispered.

"I know," she whispered back. "I guess I'm having mother withdrawal symptoms for having to share her with Alex."

"Dad?" Shana said, and both he and Alex answered.

"Sorry, I meant Trent's dad," she apologized to Alex who looked embarrassed.

Dexter wanted to rub the endearment in Alex's face. "Yes, daughter." He gave her his undivided attention.

"Thanks for being here. I see how much Mom needs you."

Dexter choked. He hadn't expected that. Stretching his arm on the back of Jillian's chair, he relaxed. "You're welcome."

"I know you've been a stickler about us maintaining our budget. What do you think? Do you and Mom feel like another field trip for a bigger reception hall?" Shana asked.

Alex attempted to jump in, but Dexter stopped him. "Jillian already chose one that could double the space if we call on Monday to book it."

Shana grinned, and it seemed to light up the room. "Well, Alex, give us your list as soon as possible and we'll add in your family—my family."

CHAPTER 10

Hours later after her guests were gone, Jillian relaxed in her bedroom. She stretched out her legs on the ottoman near her bay window. She stared at a butterfly that had made its way upstairs and was now roosted on a window.

Thank God she survived the day, because when she woke that morning, she was stressed about how things were going to turn out. Shana strolled into her room wearing a robe, a grin, and a dreamy expression. Until earlier that day, Jillian didn't realize how much her daughter didn't look like her. She favored Alex's lips, cheekbones, and nose. Their smiles were almost identical. At least Jillian could claim Shana's eyes, hair, and body.

Stretching across Jillian's bed, Shana chatted nonstop about her father, singing his praises. "Mom, you have good taste, and just think, my own father will walk me down the aisle. The bonus is he's now saved from his sins."

"That's the most important thing. God called Alex and he answered. "

"So, what do you think?" Shana lifted her brow mischievously and scrunched her nose. Shana might have her biological father's nose, but that gesture she got from her.

"About what?"

Shana began counting on her fingers. "Alex is saved, he's single, and it looks like he's still attracted to you."

Jillian squinted. "Excuse me, sweetie?"

"Is there a possibility that you and Alex could reconcile and get back together?"

"What?" Jillian's chuckled turned into an uncontrollable laugh. "We never were together. We were two teenagers experiencing puppy love."

"But what if he was interested in rekindling what you two began one summer?" Jillian shook her head, but Shana became relentless. "Don't you think God's in the plan? This was the first time Alex ever responded to our letters. Mom, he's saved now. You have so much in common, including me."

"Shana Nicole," Jillian said, putting aside the novel she'd never opened. "Need I tell you there also has to be attraction, which there is none between us. Al and I don't have the chemistry you share with Trent." *Or what I feel with Dexter.* Unfortunately, since they were about to become one family, those emotions couldn't be explored.

Her daughter sat up on the bed and wrapped her arms around her legs as she rested her chin on her knees. "I don't want you to be alone. It's been you and me for so long. You've sacrificed so much to give me all you could. I want you to be happy. Maybe Alex can be the one after all."

Jillian sniffed. Shana had been a blessing from heaven with a sensitive soul. "I'm happy watching you achieve things I haven't. You graduated from college, you repented and were baptized in Jesus' name and filled with the Holy Ghost as a teenager, you've kept yourself pure, and you're engaged to a man who adores you. If that wouldn't make a mother happy, then I don't know her definition."

"Mom, don't you think you'll ever get married?"

Jillian didn't want to think about that. "There's wants and there's reality. I'm thirty-nine years old. I think I'm considered an old maid on the dating scene. Men are marrying young ladies. I can focus on completing my degree and going on to get my MBA."

Neither said a word for the next few moments, lost in their own thoughts. Finally, Shana stood and headed for the door, then glanced over her shoulder. "Now I know what to pray for: a sweet love for my mother." She disappeared down the hall.

Jillian's eyes teared. Besides Jesus, Shana was a mother's love. It was too late for her. Jillian wasn't about to compete with two or three women for one man or whatever the ratio was to get a man. She thought about Alex again. Maybe, if he was interested in her as a woman and not as Shana's mother only, she might be willing to explore his intentions.

As she sighed, feeling like she was settling for any man, a butterfly stole her attention as it danced in the hall. She thought of the giver—Dexter. She exhaled. Whatever she felt around him, Jillian wasn't at liberty to divulge. There were too many odds stacked against them. She was a practicing Christian; he was a closet Christian, if that. Dexter was highly educated, she was still struggling to get her bachelor's degree.

Along with education came money. She assumed he had plenty. Jillian was frugal, so her money came from pinching pennies, cutting corners, and paying her tithes and offerings down through the years. She had received quarterly bonuses, steady raises, promotions, and was taught how to invest within her 401(k).

The bottom line was Dexter was off limits.

CHAPTER 11

The next day, Dexter gripped his son in a bear hug good-bye. He had more mixed emotions about his two-day stay this time. The nagging question always returned: would Alex stay out of his way?

"I love you, Pop."

"Me too. Take care of Shana and Jillian. I'll see you soon," Dexter said as he walked out of Trent's condo to his rental car to return to the airport. Trent was on his way to pick up Shana and Jillian and escort them to church. Briefly, he wondered if Alex was also attending.

Dexter was a man who was always sure of himself, so he wondered why he felt threatened by Alex. Plain and simple, the man was in the way. He learned from his interrogation of Alex that he had rebounded from his past mistakes and was doing quite well for himself. Dexter forgot the name of the business he pioneered and helped flourish.

Once he had checked in at the airport, cleared security, and not long after that settled in his window seat, Dexter wondered what attracted Jillian to a man besides butterflies. He chuckled, recalling the look of pleasure when they practically kissed her face when she opened the door. He had momentarily become invisible.

Three weeks. That's how long Dexter would have to wait until he could return to St. Louis. Still, he refused to let five hundred miles keep him from wooing Jillian.

Later that night, alone in his spacious home, he phoned her. She chatted mostly about Sunday's sermon, but he patiently suffered through it just to hear her voice. Finally, seemingly out of wind, Jillian opened the floor to Dexter.

"Jay, when was the last time you were out on a date—I mean pampered from the front door to dinner, play, whatever and back to your doorstep?"

The line was silent until Dexter thought she might not answer. "I was a teenage mother, and when Shana became a teenager, I kept a close eye on her. A social life wasn't an option... I did go out with a few brothers from my church, but let's face it, why get involved with a woman with a baby when there are plenty of childless ladies to choose from?"

"I know a beautiful woman such as yourself wasn't completely homebound, so how long has it been since you had a date?" Dexter smirked. "And no long explanation. This is a numbers question."

"Okay, six months ago. Are you satisfied?"

"Very."

Eying the time, Dexter knew he should get ready for work the next day. At the moment, he wished they were silly teenagers who would fall asleep on the phone while waiting for the other to disconnect.

"I know you like spinach. How about we set up a Skype later in the week and we can prepare a dish together."

Jillian chuckled and then took her time answering, "Different, but it sounds like fun."

He smiled at the excitement in her voice. "I'll call you tomorrow or the next day with a recipe and the ingredients you'll need."

"I can't wait."

He couldn't either as he imagined her eyes bright with anticipation. Skyping was only one of many ways he planned to remind Jillian of his presence while he was away from her. For the next few minutes, he conjured up ways to pull out the stops: flowers, more butterflies, and gifts.

"Dex?"

"Yeah, baby," he answered before he could catch himself. He held his breath, waiting to see how she would respond to his endearment.

"Ah..." she stuttered. "You're so sweet. I'm so glad Shana not only will have her real father, but a man she feels comfortable enough to call Dad."

He could only grunt. Dexter didn't want to be reminded of that loser Alex. "At the moment, I'm interested in what you want me to be to you."

"A great in-law."

Wrong answer, Dexter decided before disconnecting.

***

On Thursday, Dexter's heart pounded with excitement about the Skype call with Jillian. Although he wasn't able to call until the night before, she had reassured him she didn't mind the last-minute request. She understood about his schedule and would be ready.

He made a quick call that morning in between patients. "Hi, Jay, are you all set for our dinner date this evening?"

"Absolutely. I have all my ingredients. I told Shana what we were doing and she thinks it's romantic that her dad—you— would do such a thing. "

Was he getting help from his daughter-in-law? Great. "You'll never be bored or lonely once I move to St. Louis—"

"Wait a minute. You're moving to St. Louis? When did you decide this?" Her questions were endless.

Dexter vaguely answered them. He didn't want to give too much away yet. He was close to finalizing things, but everything wasn't wrapped up yet. "I'm sure we can entertain each other." Dexter couldn't stop the naughty thoughts from coming, even though they would never happen with the church woman Jillian was.

"Contrary to what you and my daughter may think, I do have an active life, too," she said then changed the subject. "So you're really going to uproot your life and relocate here? Do you plan to set up a practice?" She returned to the subject.

Encouraged by her inquisitiveness, Dexter taunted her. "I'll share more about that later. See you at sixty-thirty my time," he said, hurrying off the phone.

Dexter grinned. Whether it was two or twenty minutes talking with Jillian, she made him feel content, and he hadn't had that feeling since his wife passed away. Yes, women had made him happy, but the contentment he searched for always seemed to elude him.

His office door opened, and Samuel stuck his head in. "Whenever you decide you want to come back to earth, I have a patient's treatment plan I want to discuss with you."

Waving his partner into his office, Dexter didn't hide his smile. "Dr. Prentiss, I suggest you hurry. I have a dinner date in the next few hours, and I don't intend to keep a pretty lady waiting."

"Jillian is here in town?"

"No, she's in St. Louis. Technology is a wonderful thing."

Samuel shook his head and chuckled. They shared a laugh, then got down to business. Dexter was determined that not even Atlanta's traffic would delay him getting to Jillian.

Soon enough, Dexter arrived at his house with an hour to spare. He surveyed his state-of-the-art kitchen that his cook/housekeeper, Miss Roberta Flack—not the singer, but claimed to be the original—raved about. As requested, she had set up everything for the night's date.

The woman always fussed that she needed a family to really cook for and he needed a family to thrive. Dexter finally admitted Miss Roberta was right. That was a good reason to make a change.

Eyeing the clock on the microwave, he knew he better hurry if he was to make himself presentable, even if it would be via computer. Taking the back steps two at a time to his master bathroom, Dexter showered and shaved. Miss Roberta had even bought him a white chef's shirt and cap for a special touch. "Why not?"

Back downstairs, Dexter counted down the minutes until he logged onto his laptop. He snickered to learn that Jillian was already online. As he came into her view, she chuckled at his getup. "Hey, I take my dinner dates seriously, Miss Carter," he told her winking—a habit he was developing with her, whether she saw it or not.

"You amaze me. You're so adorable, Dex," she teased, peering closer into the monitor. "Nice kitchen."

Dexter lifted the computer and performed a three-sixty of his cooking area. He smirked at Jillian's *ahh*s and wows.

"Okay." He set it down again. "Hungry?"

"I am." Jillian nodded.

"Then let's get started. How many chicken breasts did you buy?"

"Six. Your son and my daughter—"

"There is no my son and your daughter. They are ours. Our son and daughter," he corrected. Dexter noted the same whimsical expression that crossed her face when she saw the butterflies. Although he had every intention to woo her, Dexter meant what he just said. Shana was his and Trent was Jillian's.

"Yes, sir." Jillian giggled, leaned close to the monitor, and scrunched her nose. "All right, our children may stop by and taste our masterpiece."

Rubbing his hands together, Dexter grinned in triumph. "Let's get started, babe." The endearment didn't slip that time. Staring at Jillian, he waited for the reaction that he was denied while they spoke over the phone. He wasn't sure, but she seemed to blush. Good, she wasn't going to fight him.

Grabbing a remote, he programmed a music station and began the preparation. In sync, they boiled water in a two-quart saucepan for their brown rice. Next, they diced pine nuts, garlic, and spinach leaves. As an attentive student, Jillian patiently waited for his next instructions as if the meal was so complicated she couldn't proceed without him.

Halfway through the meal, Jillian's doorbell chimed. "Hmm. I wonder who that is." When she disappeared out the kitchen to answer the door, Dexter paid close attention to what she was wearing.

He could tell by her skirt and low heels that she had dressed as if they were going out instead of wearing sloppy clothes and house shoes. Since he had dressed for the occasion too, they both appeared to be on the same page.

She returned sniffing flowers and smiling. Dexter waited impatiently as Jillian opened the card to see her reaction.

"Oh, Dex, these are beautiful. Thank you," she gushed.

"Not as beautiful as you. Dinner with you wouldn't be complete without flowers."

She sniffed again, and this time it wasn't from the flowers. Jillian was becoming emotional before his eyes.

"You're so thoughtful. You're indescribable."

"I'm sure the words will come, but for right now, you better check on the chicken breasts before they burn."

While the rice simmered and the chicken baked, Jillian updated him on wedding plans. If she mentioned

Alex, he changed subjects. After preparing their Greek salad, each fixed their plates. "Ready?"

"I am," she answered and carried her laptop into the dining room where a sole placemat was waiting for her. Nice touch.

Dexter grunted as he transferred his laptop to his table. Miss Roberta should have thought of that. Next, he returned for his glass of iced tea and plate, making sure the stove and oven were off.

When he situated the computer and then sat, Jillian was waiting for him with her arms folded. "I'll say grace," she volunteered, bowing her head.

Closing his eyes, Dexter listened.

"Oh, Heavenly Father in Your name, Jesus, I thank You for waking me up this morning and the blessings you have bestowed on me and my family. I ask that you bless my daugh…our children, and bless Dex. Please give him the desires of his heart, as well as a desire to grow with You…"

Was a laundry list necessary to bless their meal? He didn't dare voice a complaint as she continued.

"Jesus, thank You for this moment I shared with Dexter and sanctify this meal. Help us to bless others who are hungry in Jesus' matchless name. Amen."

"Amen," he happily repeated. "Bon appétit." He dug in and she followed. He stared at her while she chewed then sipped on her ginger ale.

Although her skin was flawless, he admired the eyeliner on her eyes, which gave her a more dramatic look. Her lips were glossy before the first bite and her hair was combed to perfection. It just made him wish he could reach out and touch her.

There was very little conversation, just smiles and moans of delight. Dexter reflected on Jillian's prayer, which was disguised as saying grace. She had mentioned desires. "What would you say if I told you that you are the desire of my heart?"

Sucking in her breath, Jillian stared at him first and then looked away. "I would be speechless as I am now. Dex, we're practically family."

"Yes, we could be—"

Laughter and voices in the background grew louder, cutting into their ambiance. He recognized Trent and Shana. Bad timing on their part, but there were a few more unfamiliar voices. Jillian stood and momentarily blocked his view.

"Hi, Pop," Trent greeted, peering into the monitor. As expected, Shana was by his side.

Shana leaned closer to the monitor and waved. "Hi, Dad."

Jillian seemed preoccupied, so Dexter chatted with them until he noticed Alex in the background with a man and woman. "What's going on?"

"Oh, that's Alex's brother and sister. They all flew in from Kansas City on business. I now have an aunt and uncle," Shana said.

Despite his culinary skills, Dexter suddenly lost his appetite. He seemed temporarily forgotten until the group gathered in the dining room. It seemed as if Alex noticed him at the same time Jillian must have remembered him.

"Dexter." Alex nodded. "Interesting set-up."

"Dex." Jillian rushed back to the computer. "I'm so sorry. It seems like I have unexpected guests, I guess this ends our dinner date. It's been so much fun. We have to do this again."

"Dinner date?" Alex balked in the background. "How about going out to a real dinner with me tomorrow? I'll be here until Saturday."

Instead of allowing him to hear her answer, she bid him goodnight and signed off. Dexter snarled. He hated cliffhangers.

CHAPTER 12

Jillian used all her restraint to keep from pouting. She was really enjoying herself during the video chat. She admired how engaging Dexter was from his home as if distance and a monitor didn't separate them.

Plus, when he called her babe, the word flowed so smoothly from his lips; Jillian did her best not to sigh and command him to call her that again. She liked Dexter's familiar endearments with her.

Although she had perfect hearing, Jillian pretended she didn't hear Alex's snide remark about dinner. Shana's father was handsome enough, charming, and now saved for Christ's purposes, but she would take a virtual dinner with Dexter over a real one with Alex any day.

"I have a meeting late tomorrow at church." She was not about to tell him it was a singles ministry and all were invited. She felt no guilt with the look of disappointment on Alex's face.

"That's okay. It will give me more time to spend with our daughter and her fiancé."

How come when Alex said "our" daughter, she wanted to cringe and when Dexter said it, her heart melted. Maybe because Alex had been out of the picture for so long—like Shana's entire life.

Since Jillian cooked more than enough, everyone converged in the kitchen to sample what Jillian dubbed as Dexter's "masterpiece" recipe. The mood was light as everyone got to know one another better.

Later that night after everyone had left, she and Shana straightened the kitchen. Once she was in the bedroom and alone with her thoughts, she considered her first impression of the Nixons. Oddly, they embraced Shana as if years had not separated them. Jillian wondered what their reasons were for not reaching out to Shana beforehand. But to dwell on those thoughts would only bring resentment, and she was praying for neutrality as best she could.

All evening, Jillian felt Alex's eyes on her. Although she smiled, Jillian still was working through mixed feelings about their past.

Shana leaned against the door frame in her pajamas. A yellow comb was dangling from her thick hair. "Mom, I think two men are after you," she teased, "I can't believe it. My mother is still a diva at thirty-nine."

"You're too much of a romantic." Jillian tried to dismiss her remark.

Pushing off the door, Shana sauntered into the room and flopped on Jillian's bed. "What are you going to do about Trent's dad? I know you don't want to encourage him when Alex's interested."

"I don't want to encourage Alex, either. If I saw him on the street, I might give him a second glance because he's good-looking." Jillian paused and squinted at her daughter who was all smiles at the compliment she paid her biological father. "Sorry, but there are no sparks. I want to be friends with your father, nothing more."

"This could be your second chance to make it work."

"There is nothing for us to work on. At fifteen, I was clueless at the repercussions of my actions. I was a virgin experimenting with a crush. I'm not a teenager anymore."

"I don't want you to be alone," Shana said with the saddest expression.

Jillian's heart sank at her daughter's concern, but it was unwarranted. "I have you and Trent. Live your life. I'm living mine." Would it include a companion? Only the Lord knew.

Recognizing her daughter's stubborn lift of the chin, Jillian knew they would revisit the topic again soon. It didn't matter. At the end of the day, Jillian was the mother, and her decisions were final.

"You can't be serious about Trent's father. He's almost family."

Jillian stood and shooed her daughter out of her bedroom. "Goodnight, almost Mrs. Trent Harris."

Shana grinned. "I know, and I can't wait."

Alone, she thought about what Shana had said about Dexter. Jillian had the same internal argument, too, but her heart did things when Dexter was near, on the phone or like tonight on a video chat.

He was the one who stole her breath away when she opened the door more than a month ago. And again when he released butterflies on his last visit and that night with the 'cooking with Dr. Harris' demonstration. Those feelings she kept hidden in her heart. She had a wedding to plan, and it wasn't hers.

CHAPTER 13

It had been days since Dexter's dinner date via the internet when Jillian had been abruptly interrupted. He thought she would have called him by now. Not a man prone to jealousy, he couldn't help but wonder if Alex made good on his offer to take Jillian out.

Dexter had golfed practically all day with fellow colleagues at the nearby country club. No doubt, Jillian was in church. Hopefully, she was praying for him not to lose his mind with the distance between them.

While warming up leftovers that his housekeeper had prepared to last the weekend, he grabbed his cordless and punched in her number. His heart pounded when she answered. It took him a few moments to get his bearings. "I missed speaking with you."

"It's been crazy around here as we get closer to the date. How are you?"

"Fine. Did you enjoy our dinner?"

"I did. That was the most fun I've had in a long time. Sorry about the interruption with Alex and his siblings. I'm really beginning to think Alex can make up for lost time with Shana. I can see the man is trying."

"What about Alex making up with Shana's mother?"

Jillian didn't answer right away, which caused Dexter to think about obstacles to get Alex out of his way.

"We already have. I'm glad God has saved us both from our sins so we can be a united front for our daughter. As a matter of fact, he and I are going to check out a musician and videographer on his next visit. Shana has a very demanding high profile client she is trying to please. I want to keep my baby from stressing out as much as possible."

Dexter sighed heavily. "I had assumed you and I were covering all bases."

"We still are. With Alex, we now have a third baseman. He's Shana's biological father and she wants him to be a part of her life. I'm just going along with the flow."

"I'm all for peace, but all I ask is that your heart doesn't become a casualty for going along with the flow. I'm very interested in getting to know you, and not as an in-law.

"But that's our connection, Dex."

"On paper, perhaps, but if you put your heart on the line, then I believe you'll chose me to protect it. Guaranteed," he confidently said before ending the call. Whatever else that needed to be said in regards to wooing her, Dexter would do it in person.

***

Jillian had grown accustomed to Alex's weekly appearances. Kansas City was only three hours away from St. Louis. What projects she had started with Dexter, she completed with Alex's help. Still, her heart fluttered in anticipation of Dexter's pending visit. He had texted his flight information to her, and Jillian guessed his plane had landed.

It had been seventeen days and she was counting the minutes until she saw him. Shana was leaning against Trent, teasing him about their honeymoon destination, which he refused to divulge. They were all supposed to be working on wedding stuff, but the couple continued to be slackers for their own nuptials.

"Where do you see your life after our baby girl is married?" Alex asked while placing address labels on wedding invitation envelopes.

Ours. Would she ever get used to him saying that?

Alex didn't wait for an answer. "Do you plan to wait to be a grandmother or consider getting back in the market to become somebody's wife?"

"She's too young to be a grandmother," Shana said smugly as she started stuffing invitations with tissue sheets again.

"Then she's still young enough to start a family," Alex said.

When the doorbell chimed, Jillian jumped up and excused herself to get it. She appreciated the old adage, 'saved by the bell'. She didn't like the feeling of being double teamed. Her sweet son-in-law-to-be hadn't said a word. She opened the door, hoping it was Dexter, and she wasn't disappointed.

His eyes sucked her into a trance first, then it was his cologne. She should have backed up to allow him inside, but she couldn't as he inched closer. They stared at each other until laughter jolted them from their private moment.

"Hi," Jillian said, finding her voice.

Dexter responded with a gentle smothering hug. "I don't do drugs, but I could get high on your beauty. I've missed my new family." He gave her a final squeeze before clearing the opening. Jillian shut the door and playfully nudged him toward the dining room where boxes of invitations, envelopes, and labels sat in piles.

Trent stood and greeted his father with a hug while Shana waited her turn. "Hi, Dad."

"Hungry?" Jillian asked, but was already heading to her kitchen. She wasn't surprised that Dexter was following.

"If it will give us some alone time, then definitely," he said as he removed his light jacket. Walking to the kitchen sink, he rinsed his hands.

Jillian watched and admired his movements around her kitchen, which seemed small compared to what he showed her of his place during the Skype call. Still, Dexter seemed comfortable as he located a plate and glass. Unlike Alex, Dexter fascinated her. An eligible man—good-looking man—who had remained single for almost twenty years, and no love child that she had heard of.

Taking a seat on her stool, she leaned her elbow on her counter then rested her chin in her cupped hand. "Dex, what's the real reason you never remarried?"

He pivoted, and in what seemed like slow motion, walked over to her. Leaning closer, he was inches away from her face, and she thought he was about to kiss her. Jillian willed herself to push back from the counter, but it appeared her heart overruled her command and didn't budge.

"I was waiting for that real woman to come into my life," Dexter whispered as his nostrils flared. As if to make sure there was no guessing on her part, he added. "I've opened the door, Jay, but you have yet to enter."

Jillian swallowed and did push back. She was not about to go there with a pending in-law, yet the vibes continued to get stronger. She bowed her head, but Dexter reached out and lifted her chin with his thumb.

"We can have this discussion before the kids get married or after. The sooner, the better for me, but when a man knows, he knows what and who he wants." Dexter turned back and walked to the stove and started lifting pot lids.

Jillian exhaled slowly as Shana strolled into the kitchen with Trent not far behind. Not to be left alone, Alex followed them.

"We're heading out to the all-night prayer shut-in service at church, Mom," Shana reminded her.

"Okay, sweetie. Pray for me. God knows why. " Jillian stood and hugged her. Since she felt Alex didn't make the cut on her attraction list, she needed direction about Dexter.

"Hey, pray for your old man, too," Alex added.

"Any special requests, Pop?" Trent prompted his father.

"Surprise me," Dexter said with a slight shrug.

"Pray for God's will in his life," Jillian blurted before she could catch herself.

Shana and Trent mumbled, "Amen."

Dexter stared at her. "I'll second that."

CHAPTER 14

Alex didn't get the clue that it was time for him to leave. That's what Dexter should have prayed for—that Alex would go back into hiding as he had for the past twenty-three years. Jillian and Shana may have forgiven him, but too easily by Dexter's way of thinking.

Dexter didn't know Alex's real motives nor did he trust them, but if the man hurt Shana in any way, once Trent got through with him, Dexter would finish him off.

Dismissing Alex, he turned to Jillian. "They actually stay awake and pray all night?" He shook his head as he made a beeline to the stool next to Jillian before Alex could sit.

"They are young and have the energy. I took Shana a few times when she was a teenager."

"I attended one myself after the Lord saved me," Alex added as he took a seat. "Doesn't your church in Atlanta have them?"

If the man was trying to front Dexter, it wasn't going to work. "Actually, I don't know. I attend a very large church, and I'm not familiar with all its programs. Since I'm relocating to St. Louis, I'm sure my church attendance will be up." He grinned as if he gave Alex a checkmate.

"Jillian, are you going to be okay here all night by yourself?" Alex frowned.

Bobbing her head, she seemed clueless to the male hormones raging for dominance around her. "Sure. I have an alarm and they should be back by sunrise. Plus, I might as well get used to being an empty nester."

Jillian flashed a pensive look before batting her lashes. Dexter wanted to say she wouldn't remain in that status long if she would open her eyes and heart and test the waters with him. As Alex discussed more in detail about his trucking business, Dexter ate silently and listened intently. By the time Dexter cleaned his plate, he was impressed. Anyone who had the drive to work their way up in any business to the top or ownership deserved his respect. Alex just wasn't getting it that day from him.

"Well, I guess it's time to bid the two men in my daughter's life goodnight." Jillian stood as a signal for them to fall in line.

Dexter didn't move toward the door as he began to wipe off the counter and put away the pots. "Do you have any plans in the morning?"

"Just some errands." She shrugged and slipped on her shoes, which Dexter didn't know she had kicked off. He smirked when he got a glimpse of her neon green toe nail polish. Butterflies, crazy nail polish, and a single mother. What else didn't he know about her?

Now that Trent was gone, Dexter conjured up more prayer requests, like convincing Jillian to give them a chance.

Since it didn't seem like Alex was going to leave them alone, Dexter dried his hands then strolled to Jillian. "Goodnight, Jay," he whispered in her ear. He brushed a kiss on her cheek and smiled.

Her eyes twinkled at him and she returned his smile. "Call me. We'll do something together."

They were getting lost in each other's eyes when Alex cleared his throat. "I'm here all weekend, so I'll call you, too."

Dexter pulled Jillian closer to his side. After squeezing Jillian's hand, Dexter delivered another kiss to her cheek and then turned to Alex. "Come on, let's walk out together."

It was time for them to have a little talk. Once they were outside, Dexter made his position clear. "Alex, I know your intentions are to be a part of Shana's life. What I don't know is what they are concerning Jillian. To be clear, I'm very interested in Jay, so I would appreciate if you don't interfere."

Alex snorted and stuffed his hands in his pockets. "I already have a head start. In case you forgot, we share a beautiful daughter together. Plus, we're spiritually in tune. We're both walking down the same path."

Dexter regulated his breathing. Hard-headed people annoyed him. Dexter was trying to be cordial with his request. Maybe he needed to rephrase his demand. "I welcome you as Shana's biological father and nothing more. As soon as she says, 'I do', I will become her dad, and Jillian and I will share a daughter." He thumped his chest. "So there will no misunderstanding between us, I'm in tune with Jay. As far as your other concern, I'm a quiet man who worships the Lord in my own way."

"Okay, brother, make sure your way is the right way, or Jillian will have nothing to do with you. Goodnight." Waving Dexter off, Alex walked to his car with a cocky gait.

That annoyed Dexter, too. Determined to have the last word, Dexter said firmly, "Your mistake with letting Jay go won't be my mistake." Whistling, he deactivated the car alarm, got in, and drove away.

Alex's words seemed to taunt Dexter on the drive to Trent's place. Stopping at a red light, he glanced at his watch. It was almost eleven. Dexter took a chance that she might still be awake; he tapped her name on his smart phone and waited.

"Hello?" Jillian answered on the second ring.

"Are you asleep?"

"Are you kidding, with you and Al going at it outside my door?"

Dexter cringed at being caught with his hand in the cookie jar, but he would not apologize for his feelings for her. "This is strictly a yes-or-no answer. Do I have a chance with you?"

"Yes."

Biting his bottom lip, Dexter nodded. "Even without this spiritual commitment Alex referenced?"

"No," she stated quickly.

"When I said give me a yes-and-no answer, I didn't mean in the same sentence. What do I need to do to be on the same level with you?"

"That, my dear, is what you should have asked your son to pray for tonight. You need to be saved. We all do, not partially, but completely. I have major objections about a man who has not completed his salvation check."

Dexter hated when women made demands on a man, but in this case, he was willing to compromise. "What about Alex? Does he have a chance?"

"With Shana, a million, but history will not repeat itself with me. Goodnight."

"Oh Jay, what a great color on your toes."

She giggled. "That was Shana's idea."

"What's not perfect about you?" Dexter chuckled.

"Ah, that's one more thing you could have added to your prayer list. It seems like pretty soon, you and Jesus are going to have a lot to talk about that might also include me. Drive safely."

CHAPTER 15

God, I'm trusting You to protect my heart, Jillian prayed Friday night before getting in bed and again on Saturday morning when she woke. With Shana's wedding a little more than a month away, she never imagined this type of emotional drama—two unexpected men wanting to pursue her. Unfortunately, disregarding them was not an option. She would be bound to them forever.

Sitting up in bed, Jillian reached for her Bible. Her stomach growled, but she was determined to search the scriptures. Opening her Bible, she flipped through the pages.

Dexter took her breath away the moment she opened her front door, but she had tried to ignore those emotions, feeling guilty about her attraction to a man who would be considered family. She could be swayed on that way of thinking, but not on his walk with God. There was no compromise.

Alex Nixon. She sighed. She really didn't know the man. As teenagers, they thought they were in love—

correction, she thought she was in love. Shortly after Shana's birth, Jillian admitted to her mother and grandmother that it was nothing more than infatuation.

Shana was just as surprised as she was when Alex responded to her note telling him that she was getting married and would like for him to attend. He came into their lives like a storm with glue to fix things, but Jillian couldn't be fixed. God had already made her whole.

Despite forgiving Alex for his transgression of deserting them over the years, deep down inside Jillian knew she would make him work too hard for her affections. It wouldn't be worth it for either of them. Her mind shifted back to Dexter.

She had to refocus. Twice she had stopped at the Book of Ruth. She already knew the familiar story about Ruth's faithfulness to her mother-in-law, Naomi. How was that applicable to her? Jillian tried to find some similarities. Naomi brought Boaz and Ruth together. Dexter again popped in her mind. *Were there any similarities to piece together?* she wondered.

Shana was the glue that brought her and Dexter together. Boaz was older than Ruth. She was thirty-nine. Dexter was forty-seven. That wasn't a big deal. Boaz was considered wealthy in his time. Dr. Dexter Harris definitely wasn't lacking in financial security.

She began to earnestly pray until the tears fell, knowing that despite all that Dexter possessed, if he didn't have Jesus, then he was like a poor man. "Lord, lead me so I'll know Your will. Amen." Jillian was sniffing as Shana walked into her bedroom.

"Good morning…" Losing the bright smile Shana wore every morning, she rushed to her side alarmed.

"Mom, what's wrong? Did someone die? Is Alex okay?" she continued to bombard her with questions.

"I'm seeking God about something." Although she and Shana were close, Shana was too close to this situation to be a neutral sounding board.

"About?"

Jillian looked into her daughter's eyes, which she now associated with Alex. She decided not to share her thoughts.

"Mom, you can trust me." Hugging her, Shana kissed her and smiled. "I love you."

"I know, but I have to depend on Jesus for this one."

Shana nodded. "I respect that. After God gives you the answer, you'll let me in on it, won't you?"

"I will." They hugged again. *Jesus, Your Word says You'll give me the desires of my heart. Will You give me a hint of what that is?*

Believing God for an answer, Jillian got out of bed and began her day. After breakfast, Jillian dressed to run errands, which included a manicure and pedicure. She wiggled her toes. So Dexter thought she had pretty feet. That thought made her blush.

She also had a hair appointment. Afterward, she would go shopping for some type of tokens to give Shana's three bridesmaids while Shana and Trent were doing other wedding-related things.

When the doorbell chimed, Jillian didn't rush to get it. Shana was downstairs, and it was probably Trent. It chimed a second time. By the third ring, Shana frowned and hurried downstairs barefooted to get the door. Maybe Shana was in the bathroom, because she never left without telling her goodbye.

Opening the door, it was becoming déjà vu with Dexter standing there. This time, rather impatiently. "You can give a doctor a heart attack worrying about you." With a flirtatious smirk, he gave a slow appraisal of what she was and wasn't wearing—shoes. "You have the most beautiful toes I've ever seen on a woman."

Jillian peeped over her shoulder and saw Shana in the garage, rambling through her car. She probably didn't know her future father-in-law was there. A burglar could sneak up on her child, but Shana passed her self-defense class and would probably welcome the challenge.

"Thanks, but I'm on my way to get my fingers and toes done." Jillian was a bit disappointed that she wouldn't be able to entertain him, but one thing she didn't do was show up late for her appointments. The penalty would be all day at the place.

"If you're hungry, there are still some pancakes left that Shana made for breakfast. Help yourself, but I'm leaving in about five minutes. Sorry."

He patted his stomach. "That's enough time for me to help myself. Since you have a busy schedule, I'm sure you could appreciate the services of a personal chauffeur at no charge to you.

Jillian shook her head. "And the women in Atlanta couldn't snag you, huh?"

"Neither will any woman in St. Louis once I move here, except one," Dexter said with a cocky swagger toward her kitchen. She raced upstairs, shaking her head. Back in her room, she pushed her belt through the loops, slipped on her flats, and brushed her hair into a ponytail, all while wondering if God was orchestrating the day with Dexter.

***

Dexter wolfed down the pancakes. He had purposely not disturbed Shana so he could have a few minutes of alone time with Jillian. Dexter had no idea what Jillian had planned to do for the day, or if Alex would be there, but he wanted nothing more than to spend time with her alone. Jillian was an attractive woman—from her wild hair to her bare narrow feet. Pleasing to the eye couldn't begin to describe her.

Dexter quickly cleared his mess and headed back to the living room where he could have a direct view of Jillian coming down the stairs. She was already over her five minutes. As he made himself comfortable, the front door opened and Shana stuck her head in. "Hi, Dad. Tell Mom I'm gone with Trent."

"Will do, sweetheart." He stood and walked to the door. Trent had just pulled up and parked his vehicle. Getting out, Trent walked around and helped Shana inside. Dexter nodded at his son. 'Always treat a woman like a lady,' he often told him, 'and a man would have a queen for life.' Unfortunately for him, his idyllic life was short lived with Marsha's illness, but he was ready for another empress.

He shut the door as Jillian breezed down the stairs. Dexter had to pat his chest. His blood pressure was under control, but that didn't stop his heart from pounding wildly.

With her hair brushed back, Jillian looked years younger than she was. Yes, he could see any man falling in love with her at first sight, including Alex and himself.

"You want to be my chauffeur, huh? And what do you plan to do while I'm getting my toes and nails done?" Jillian scrunched her nose at him, flirting. That would have earned her a kiss, but Dexter didn't dare. Kissing was serious business for him, and he had to woo her first.

"Real men are groomed too," he said.

"Then I guess we should go."

After she gathered her purse and jacket, Jillian activated the home alarm and followed Dexter out the door where he had the car door open, waiting for her. She whispered her thanks.

Jillian gave him directions to Diva's Hair and Nails in Westport. They chatted about their childhood and life before children. He downplayed his medical education when Jillian mentioned she had another year and a half to get her bachelor's degree in business management.

"Shana is not only the love of my life, she's my protégé. She beat me getting her degree. She's also the first to get married—"

"That can change," Dexter interrupted, glancing at her before checking his speed as they cruised down Page Boulevard.

"Not in four weeks, it can't." She laughed in a sing-song medley that he had never noticed before. "The bottom line is I'm so glad she didn't follow in my footsteps."

You want to place a bet on four weeks? Shaking his head, Dexter couldn't contain his thoughts. "Baby, I'd say Shana has the best example. If you don't pat yourself on the back, I will."

Jillian turned in her seat and smiled. "That's so sweet of you to say, but it's God I have to give a high five to because Jesus forgave me and then I had my mother's guidance until she passed away."

When they arrived at Diva's, Dexter parked. Activity came to a standstill when Dexter escorted her inside, but he was not one to be intimidated around women. He asked if there was time for him to go in with her and they obliged him.

Sitting side by side, Dexter watched in fascination as the technician massaged and pampered Jillian's feet. She giggled as her heels were scrubbed, which made him chuckle when his technician started her ministration on him.

Since Jillian had grabbed five colors and had a hard time deciding, she asked him to choose and Dexter picked a grape color. He got the nod from Jillian and both technicians. Once her polish dried under the light, he escorted her to the manicure table and they both received service.

Leaning closer, Jillian whispered. "I'm giddy with you here. I can't believe you're doing this. I wonder if Trent has ever gone with Shana."

Dexter shrugged as the manicurist manhandled his nails. "I seriously doubt it. Trent has boundaries. Let's just call this our first."

Jillian's eyes sparkled as she agreed. They discussed various topics that always seemed to come back to Jesus and foot washing services.

"I don't recall seeing that done at church before."

"That's a shame because it was one of the most humbling acts Jesus demonstrated for us to follow and many churches don't honor it. Almost every denomination obeys the Bible with communion, but not the foot washing," Jillian got on a preaching binge.

"What's the real purpose?"

"Humility. You can't be a Christian without it. "

That gave Dexter something to think about while their nails dried. Once that was done, they strolled out the door and headed down a short hall to the hair salon.

The building seemed to contain full services to keep a woman there all day. There was also a spa and a women's fitness class.

"You sure you want to wait while I get my hair done? I know this is backwards, but Bettie didn't have any openings until after my nails were done."

"I have nothing to do today but watch a beautiful princess be transformed into a striking queen," Dexter told her and watched her blush before she recovered.

"Okay. Don't say I didn't warn you. Are you flying out early in the morning like you have been?"

"Not this time." Folding his arms, Dexter stared into her eyes. "What do you want me to do?"

"Escort me to church and enjoy yourself like you did today," she said as the stylist called her back to the shampoo bowl. Jillian left him in the lobby to ponder her request. Or maybe it was a dare.

CHAPTER 16

When Jillian's hair was styled and Dexter complimented with a genuine awe expression, she did feel beautiful. She felt like a teenager as they had lunch and shopped for gifts for the wedding party.

With those errands out of the way, they took in a movie, then enjoyed a late dinner. Late that night, Dexter walked her to her door. The moment seemed magical as Jillian braced herself for the kiss on the cheek she had come to expect. However, Dexter advanced his cause with a brief sweep of his lips against hers.

Wow was stuck in Jillian's throat. She blinked rapidly to regulate her breathing. Was she a princess in a fairytale? The way Dexter treated her made Jillian not want to wake up. She swallowed. "Ah, service is at ten, so breakfast is at nine."

"I'll be here at eight fifty-five. 'Night." Dexter had backed away, then watched until she was inside the house and waved.

Once she closed the door, she leaned on it and sighed. Her heart fluttered. Maybe this was how Shana felt when she knew Trent was the one. Jillian smiled and strolled farther into her room as her phone rang. She grinned, thinking it was Dexter.

"Hello."

"Jillian, I tried reaching you earlier, and even left a few messages." Alex paused as if he was waiting for an explanation.

She shook her head. If she was in the middle of a sweet dream, Alex would probably pop up for a commercial break. He really wasn't that bad. Alex just seemed to always be in the way lately. Pulling her cell phone out her pocket, she realized she had not taken her phone off silent since leaving the movie theater.

"Sorry about that. What's the emergency at this hour?"

"Well, I would like to visit your church with you tomorrow before I drive back to Kansas City."

"Sure. The more the merrier." Jillian never turned anyone away who wanted to attend church.

"What do you mean?"

"Service starts at ten, so I'll be waiting for you in the vestibule."

"Oh, I was hoping we could ride together. I could pick you up," Alex offered.

"That won't be necessary. Plan to meet me and Shana tomorrow at nine-fifty, and don't be late. There's nothing worse than interrupting my praise and worship time."

"Amen."

***

The following morning, Jillian rose earlier than usual. On her knees, she praised Jesus for His blood on Calvary, thanked Him for her blessings, then ended her prayer with, "Lord, help me to see what You see in Dexter, in Jesus' name. Amen."

Later, in the kitchen Jillian gave Shana an update. "Dex is attending church with us today."

"That's great!" Shana beamed.

"But so is Al. I hope there won't be any tension in the pews. Although your biological father is sweet, I think his motives toward me are strictly because of you. Otherwise, I don't think he would be interested. Dex…" She grinned. "My feelings for him are strong, and it appears neither of us is letting the fact that we'll be in-laws be a deterrent, which is causing me to boost my prayer time with Jesus. I hope God will show me something today."

"God knows I want you to be happy, Mom. To be honest, I was hoping you would rekindle what you had with Alex, but I can tell Dad really likes you and would make you happy." She stood from her stool when the doorbell rang.

"That's our men," Shana teased and left to answer the door.

Jillian whirled around and busied herself with buttering the biscuits. She didn't know how to interact with Dexter after the kiss the previous night. She didn't care how brief the touch, the match was lit and the line crossed.

Dexter strolled into the kitchen before Shana and Trent. "Good morning, sunshine. Something smells good. Why don't you sit? I can take it from here and serve you."

Facing him, he offered her a warm smile that relaxed her nerves. He always seemed ready to pamper her, which was flattering. "Who am I to argue with my blessing?" she said off-handedly, then wondered if Dexter truly was her blessing.

Good naturedly, Dexter wound up serving all three of them. Afterward, they quickly tidied the kitchen, and within minutes drove two separate vehicles to Bethesda Temple, which was right off the interstate and minutes from the airport.

Inside Dexter's rental, they were preoccupied with their own thoughts as gospel music floated around them until they pulled into the church parking lot.

"Thanks for coming."

"I can't be a part of your world without you sharing it with me. Thank you for inviting me," Dexter replied tenderly.

By the time they had parked and walked to the entrance, Shana and Trent had beaten them inside. Alex was already there. He greeted Trent with a handshake, Shana with a kiss and hug, Dexter with a blank expression, and Jillian with a perplexed look.

"Right on time," Jillian said and led the way. Neither man knew about the other attending. God would handle any mess the devil wanted to stir up.

Dexter whispered, "Did you know he was coming?"

"Yep." Jillian didn't stop until she found a pew with enough room for all of them.

There was a quick debate about who should sit next to the other. In the end, Dexter took the aisle seat, planting Jillian between him and Alex.

As the musicians and praise team warmed up, Jillian stood. She refused to let either man's presence deter her from turning her mind to Jesus. Alex was on his feet in a matter of moments. She spied Dexter, wondering if he would follow suit. He didn't, but his shoe tapped to the beat. The praise team began singing, "Glorious Day," which brought the congregation to their feet, including Dexter.

She hoped the lyrics would penetrate his soul. Too soon, the singing ended followed by a group prayer, then Pastor James Johnson's booming voice welcomed guests as everyone took their seats.

"My subject today is simplistic," Jillian's pastor began. "How do you know when your turkey or chicken is done? It may appear to be fully cooked on the outside, but is it still raw on the inside?" Pastor Johnson opened his Bible to Jeremiah 29:11. "You see, God knows what temperature to bake you until you're done. Don't be fooled by the outside. God is judging the inside. If your heart is frozen, God can thaw it and cook it to perfection."

As far as Jillian was concerned, Pastor's analogy should have hit home. Alex was definitely rooting her pastor on, along with Shana and Trent with their Amen's and Hallelujah's. It was Dexter's quietness that concerned her. She wondered what he was thinking.

"You may be put together and packaged nicely on the outside, but you know whether you are done today. What temperature does your soul need to completely surrender to Jesus?" Pastor continued preaching until a short time later, when he concluded with the altar call. Throughout the sanctuary, everyone got to their feet to pray for God to call and save souls.

Jillian reached for Dexter's hand, and he didn't hesitate to grasp hers and then squeeze it. She began to pray that God would reveal to her Dexter's level of doneness. She desperately wanted to know.

"Friends, God is the master baker. He has created masterpieces to perfection, but something may have happened along the way where you need to be warmed up, reheated. His Holy Ghost power will stir you up! Come to Jesus now. Repent from where you are, ask the Lord to make you whole, then walk out to one of our ministers who will listen to you and pray.

"Let God save you today by washing your sins away in water baptism in Jesus' name. Once you're empty, let God fill you with His precious spirit—the Holy Ghost. How will you know if you have it? You'll experience power with the explosion of speaking in unknown tongues. Come and receive salvation today..."

Dexter didn't budge, which caused Jillian's spirit to drop, but in the end, salvation was left up to the Lord and the individual. Once the benediction was over, Alex praised the service and the message while Dexter remained silent. When Alex offered to take her home, Dexter didn't argue. Something had happened between them, or maybe it was between him and God.

"Are you sure? You don't want to go out to dinner with Trent, Shana, and me?" Jillian schooled her tone to keep from sounding as if she was pleading with Dexter. She really wanted to pick his brain.

"No, Jay, go ahead. I'm flying out tomorrow to finalize everything at home. When I return right before the wedding, then I'm all yours."

Twisting her fingers, Jillian nodded as he shook hands with Alex and Trent and kissed Shana. Jillian was rewarded with a crushing hug with no words, whispers, or soft kiss to the cheek. Within moments, he disappeared into the crowd.

While Shana and Trent were conversing with others, Alex scooted her to the side. "Jillian, how he could not be affected by that message is mind boggling. I don't think he's ready for a commitment to God or you."

Gathering her Bible and purse, Jillian didn't comment as her mind said the same thing, but her heart told her to trust God. "Then I guess it's our responsibility to fast and pray. Come on. Let's go. I'm hungry."

***

The sermon shook Dexter up, and he needed space to reflect on the message. Why did it seem as if Jillian's pastor was talking about him? There were literally a few thousand people in the audience.

Dexter left church more confused than when he arrived. Dexter lived right and had upstanding morals. When it came to God, he didn't saturate his mind with scriptures, nor make a big production of being a Christian.

How could such a simple message perplex him? Back at Trent's condo while others were at dinner, Dexter picked up an extra Bible Trent had laying around and began to flip through the pages.

On Monday morning, he called Jillian from the airport. More than once she asked if he was all right.

"I'm fine. I've just got a lot on my mind: selling my practice, making sure my patients are comfortable,

selling my house, getting other local affairs in order..."
What he didn't say was the sermon seemed to be
gnawing at his insides—something Maalox couldn't
settle. The question Dexter couldn't answer was if he
was fully baked inside and out.

"I'm amazed you're really willing to start over here
and you're not a spring chicken," she joked, which
made him chuckle.

"Allow me to prove how wrong you are about the
last part." When Jillian didn't respond, he baited her.
"Nothing to say?"

"I dare not, but seriously, what will you do? I can
see if my hospital is recruiting physicians."

Besides his housekeeper and office manager, it had
been a while since a woman looked out for his well-
being and wanted nothing in return. "Sweetheart..." he
called her as if he had the full right to do so, and Jillian
didn't object. "The world of medicine is changing. The
cost of running a practice is more expensive and less
lucrative today. Thank God I don't have any student
loans."

Jillian laughed, and he joined in. "But seriously,
office visits are becoming a thing of the past. Home
visits are on their way back. That's why I applied and
have been accepted to come on board with the Visiting
Doctors Association. It will allow me to maintain my
lifestyle without skipping a beat."

"Okay, if you say so."

"I say so. See you soon." They disconnected.

For the next few weeks, Dexter's spiritual senses
seemed to be heightened. He never realized how many
times he heard God's name mentioned in conversations,
posted on billboards or splattered on bumper stickers.

When did his colleague, Samuel, start wearing that small silver cross that dangled from a chain around his neck? Had their office manager always had a scripture-a-day calendar on her desk? Did he even pay attention when some of his elderly patients left his office with thanks and "God bless you, Dr. Harris"? Had he become that immune spiritually?

Dexter was having such a Jesus overload in his brain that when he spoke with Jillian, he didn't cringe when she shared a scripture or two with him. He didn't actively participate, but he was no longer bothered by it.

Finally, his parting from Georgia was bittersweet. His staff gave him a going-away party attended by some of his lifelong patients. They brought cards and small gifts to show their appreciation for his dedication to them over the years. Jillian was thoughtful enough to send him flowers.

When the well-wishers were gone and the staff had restored the office, Dexter sat in his empty office one last time and reminisced not only about his life as an internist in Atlanta, but on his marriage, being a father, and finally, becoming a widower.

It was after Marsha passed away that Dexter started shunning God and told himself that he had justification for doing it. Now, it seemed as if God was finding him at the same time he was about to lose his son—at least it was not in death.

"Dr. Harris, it won't be the same without you. Who will I consult when I treat difficult patients?" Samuel asked, walking farther into the room. He angled his body in a nearby chair. His colleague didn't bother to hide his sorrow. "I will miss you," he choked, then regained his composure.

Dexter folded his hands as he leaned on his desk. "Technology, son—Skype, phone, email, or text, I'll always be close by if you need me. It's time for a new chapter in my life."

Suddenly, Dexter's cell chimed with the tone he had assigned to Jillian. He grinned as he reached for his phone. Samuel stood and pointed.

"And that, Dr. Harris, is going to be the woman who'll change your life." Laughing, the other doctor saluted him and walked out the office, closing the door.

CHAPTER 17

Three days before the wedding and Jillian was a nervous wreck. It also marked three weeks since she had last seen Dexter, and she was anxious. They had spoken often—practically every day—and each time she felt like some whimsical teenager. But she had already been there once and done that.

She didn't believe in fairy tales, but Dexter made her wish she did. Jesus was her godfather and He alone bestowed the blessings on her life. Jillian had hoped Dexter would be the one. Although he wouldn't discuss the sermon her pastor preached the day he attended church, he did listen patiently when she shared testimonies about what God had done for her one day or another.

Jillian and Shana were back at Diva's Hair and Nails getting pedicures. Jillian couldn't help but remember her last visit when Dexter tagged along. It was a romantic moment she would keep close to her heart like the love she felt for him. *Love.* Oh, Lord, she was in love with him. Did he know? Did it show when she smiled? She could admit the love to herself, but never to him if he didn't embrace God's salvation completely. They would remain nothing more than in-laws.

Shana interrupted her musings. "In less than seventy-two hours, I'll belong to someone else." Her face glowed, then her smile faded. "Do you think I'll be a good wife?"

"Absolutely. First Peter 4:8 and Proverbs 10:12 say love covers a multitude of sins. You and Trent's love is solid as his abs," Jillian joked to put that smile back on her daughter's face. "If you start crying, we both will be boo-hooing. Tomorrow night will be the last time you will sleep in your bed." That meant Jillian was about to lose her baby—her first love. She sniffed.

As the nail technician engaged Shana in lively chatter about nail designs for her wedding, Jillian regained her private thoughts. The day Shana experienced her first moment as a wife; Jillian would experience her life alone for the first time.

This didn't compare with Shana going away to school. Jillian knew her daughter would return to her old bedroom. Fighting off a bout of melancholy, Jillian mentally stumbled through several worship songs until her heart settled on, "When You Want to Talk to Jesus." At the present time she had a mouthful that she was ready to unload to Him.

***

Dexter couldn't believe he had actually poured out his soul on the last night he slept in his house. *Jesus, I realize I've been going through the motions all these years. To some standing on the outside, I might have appeared to have moved on, but Marsha's death left me empty, half-baked inside. I've been ashamed of You, God. I know my limitations as a physician, but I know You have no constraints, but you allowed Marsha to die.*

God, I'm sorry for my wayward thinking. I acknowledge that anyone who is healed under my care is healed because of You. I...

Dexter was on his knees so long that night that they cracked as he stood. He chuckled. Now that he had repented, what more could Jillian want?

It's what I want. God's voice was like the sound of thunder and Dexter shivered as He continued, *Have you not read Acts 2:38–40? Repent, and be baptized every one of you in My name, Jesus Christ, for the remission of sins, and ye shall receive the gift of the Holy Ghost. My promise is unto you, and to your children, and to all that are afar off, even as many as I shall call. Save yourselves from this untoward generation.*

God's presence left him numb. A while later, lying in bed, Dexter still hadn't really recovered after what he had experienced. God had plainly told him what was required to be saved.

The memories faded as his name was called during the rehearsal, but Dexter couldn't keep his eyes off Jillian. She glowed with happiness, but at times, he connected with her hints of sadness.

If Jillian would give them a chance, she would never be alone. Where most women just wanted a man to commit, Jillian wanted it all—a man committed to God, then her. Dexter smirked. He and God had had some in-depth, heart-to-heart discussions.

Two hours later, they cleared the chapel en route to Bistro for the rehearsal dinner. Once there, Dexter gave himself ten minutes and that was his limit to keep his hands off Jillian. There were at least thirty people present, but he was about to have his moment with her with or without an audience. As she mingled with Alex's friends and family, Dexter trailed her. When she whirled around, he was there.

"I see you putting up a brave front, Jay, but I know you're scared," he whispered.

She didn't deny it, but nodded. That was permission enough for him to wrap his arms around her as she released tears. Dexter rubbed her back and whispered soothing words in her ear. Concerned, guests came to her aid, but Dexter waved them off, including Shana and Trent.

"A mother's losing her baby," he explained.

Some nodded and smiled while a few shook their head in sympathy. He led her outside to Bistro's patio away from their party inside the restaurant. Ensured of some privacy, Dexter lifted her chin and began to smooth away the tears. "You have me."

"But you are not enough. I need a whole man, spiritually—"

Dexter kissed her and it wasn't a quick brush of the lips. He didn't mean for their first kiss—real kiss—to be witnessed by prying eyes. He stared at her. "Babe, you have no idea what has been going on with me lately, but I have repented. How can you think that sermon weeks ago didn't affect me? I had to dissect the message by myself."

She squinted. "What are you saying?"

"If there was any way there could be a double wedding tomorrow, there would be."

Before Dexter could say more, the bridal party had made its way outside in search of them and dragged them back into the festivities. Alex eyed Dexter, and he challenged the man's stare. Jillian was spoken for. Period.

CHAPTER 18

The big day arrived the following evening. Dexter had an unobstructed view of the aisle as Trent's best man. The wedding processional started on time. While his son waited for his bride, Dexter watched the door for the mother of the bride.

On the arm of a young usher, Jillian glided down the aisle as the candlelight flickered around them. She was too beautiful not to be a bride—his.

While the bridesmaids stepped in sync, the flower girl pranced and the ring bearer marched to the altar, Dexter only focused on one woman until the music stopped.

All conversation paused as the dimmed lights blinked off. Seconds later, a spotlight danced against the back wall until it found its target—double doors. When the trumpet sounded, they slowly opened.

Shana was already pretty, but in the gown, she was a vision of loveliness. Glancing at his son, he saw that Trent's eyes had glossed over. It was the same look of love Dexter had possessed on his wedding day.

Alex beamed proudly as if he had watched his little girl blossom into a beautiful woman. Dexter was still dumbfounded how Jillian and Shana could forgive the man so easily.

I forgave your sins, God whispered, commandeering his thoughts.

Dexter swallowed, then nodded. Apparently, Alex thought Dexter's gesture was toward him, so Alex nodded back before taking his seat next to Jillian.

Moments later, Pastor Johnson asked, "Who gives this woman away?"

Alex stood and helped Jillian to her feet. With hands linked, they said in unison, "We do."

As Shana and Trent began reciting their vows, Dexter was transformed back twenty-plus years ago when he thought he had a lifetime of love. He fought for mental control. Dexter refused to go down that pity party road again that seemed to lead him into a bitterness dead end and thwarted his relationship from thriving with the Lord.

Barely listening to his future daughter-in-law's vows, Dexter perked up when his son's voice raised. "Shana Nicole Carter, I promise you my love, honor, faithfulness, and protection until I take the last breath in my body. I will forsake all others..." Trent stared into Shana's eyes, then repeated. "I promise, baby."

Pastor Johnson asked everyone to bow their heads, and he offered a prayer of blessing and unity in their marriage. "Let no man, woman, or outside influence separate you in the name of our Lord and Savior Jesus Christ. Give them patience and help them to be kind to one another...Amen."

Trent held the edges of Shana's veil, waiting for the signal. Dexter chuckled at his impatience, but he understood. He was ready to make a commitment to Jillian and lay a kiss on her she would soon never forget.

"You may now salute your bri…" Pastor Johnson began, but faded off when Trent crushed his lips to Shana's, barely brushing her veil out the way. The applause was deafening and the couple turned around and faced their witnesses.

A while later after the pictures, well-wishes, and carriage ride to the Central West End, the bridal party entered the reception at A Personal Touch by Jeanette.

Dexter had the waiter switch seats so he was next to Jillian instead of next to Trent. One wedding down, the making of wedding two was about to get underway.

***

Jillian tried her best not to cry throughout the ceremony. Alex patting her hand helped. However, the tender glances Dexter sent her way were her undoing. Now that the nuptials were over and everyone was officially family, Jillian relaxed as a string quartet serenaded the guests.

Sandwiched between Alex and Dexter, Jillian tried to balance the conversation with both of them until Alex leaned closer. "Jay, as Dexter calls you, since it appears I don't have a chance with winning your affections, I hope you won't be offended if I mingle with the guests and see what blessings God may have for me."

Jillian mustered a smile. "Al, you don't owe me an explanation, but I'm flattered at your respect." She giggled. "Please pray for me and Dexter. I don't know what God is going to do with us, but I'm hopeful."

"You've got it." Alex winked and pushed back his chair. Standing, he reached behind Jillian's chair and shook Dexter's hand. Also getting to his feet, Dexter accepted the peace offering.

"Guard her heart, Dr. Harris. I'm sure she already had suffered a major heart failure because of my actions in the past to last a lifetime," Alex said and walked away.

Reclaiming his seat, Dexter scooted closer as the photographer snapped a candid shot of them.

"Everything was beautiful, wasn't it? My daughter and Trent look so happy."

"What about my baby girl's mother? Is Jillian happy?" Dexter's baritone voice sent a shiver through her. She swallowed to remain mentally in control, but as she began to fumble with her fingers, Dexter suddenly grabbed them and squeezed them.

"How about we go and introduce ourselves to our guests and make sure they're enjoying themselves?"

"Good idea."

With their hands linked—Dexter's idea since he wouldn't let her go—they strolled up to the pastor and the first lady.

Jillian thanked him for conducting the ceremony before Dexter took over the conversation. "Pastor Johnson, you may not be aware that I've permanently relocated to St. Louis from Atlanta."

"Welcome, Dr. Harris."

"Also, I have repented of my sins, and I'm ready to be baptized at your earliest convenience."

Jillian gasped. Had she heard correctly? She couldn't stop her eyes from blurring.

"God grant you favor until in the morning," her pastor said, delighted.

Squeezing Jillian's hand, Dexter stared into her eyes. "After that, how soon can you perform another wedding ceremony?"

"Dex," Jillian gasped. Not only did he want to get baptized, but he wanted to get married, too, immediately? *Jesus, You were definitely working behind the scenes on this.*

Pastor looked from her to Dexter and chuckled. "Maybe you should ask her first and then we'll talk."

First Lady Johnson exchanged a knowing smile with Jillian as Dexter tugged her away. He located a secluded area away from the height of the celebration.

On a bench, he faced her. "Jay, I have a son and now a daughter. The only thing missing in my life is a wife. My strong attraction to you has developed into these overpowering feelings until I've reached this point where I can profess my love. My son is not the only one who can vow his faithfulness to one woman. I love you, Jillian. Marry me, and you can wake up to butterflies every morning."

Marriage? Jillian never thought a wedding proposal was in her life plan. Still, Dexter's repentance was the first step; he needed to complete his salvation process.

"Fulfill your commitment to God first, then ask me again." *Please God, let him ask me again.*

Huffing, Dexter appeared frustrated as he glanced around the room. "You mean to tell me out of all the churches in this city, not one of them is having church or a shut-in service tonight?" He stood with a frown. "This is unacceptable. I thought the church doors were supposed to always be open." His gaze swept over Jillian, which caused her to blush.

"Come on, sweetheart. A man's got to do what a man's got to do."

Although they were congratulated along the way as parents of the happy couple, Dexter seemed to be on a mission. Once again, they came to her pastor. He made sure Jillian was seated this time, then he sat next to Pastor Johnson.

"I don't want to put it off. Can't someone baptize me tonight?"

Her pastor's expression was unreadable. After a few minutes, he nodded. "Dr. Harris, I will make some calls to have a deacon open the church and have a minister meet you there to baptize you. He'll make sure a church mother will be on hand to pray with you until the Holy Ghost fills you.

Dexter physically exhaled. "Thank you, sir." They shook hands. "Come on, baby. We'd better tell our children."

Jillian was in awe at what was going on. When he told Shana and Trent, they were so excited, Trent took the microphone.

"May I have your attention, please? May I have your attention?" Trent respectfully demanded. "I have some breaking news. It appears another party is about to go down tonight." He chuckled. "My dad has repented and as we speak, our pastor is putting things in motion for someone to meet him at the church to have his sins washed away."

Cheers and applause exploded around them. Shana opened her arms, and Jillian walked into them.

"Dad's doing this because of you, isn't he?" Shana teased.

"Yes, no…I hope not," Jillian said, still amazed.

"Finally, Mom, you'll have another love besides me."

CHAPTER 19

Dexter didn't expect the bride, groom, and a handful of the guests to leave the wedding celebration to follow him to the church for the baptismal, but that's exactly what happened—limousine and all.

The church was indeed opened and the minister and altar workers to assist in the baptism were waiting on him.

Minister Michaels shook his hand. "Since it appears you came with many witnesses, I feel compelled to hold an impromptu altar call. In Matthew 25 in the Bible, Jesus speaks through the parable about the ten virgins who knew Christ the Groom was coming. Five were ready with their temple filled with the Holy Ghost power. The foolish virgins put off getting filled. We know how the story ends. It was too late.

"Verse thirteen says, *'Watch therefore, for ye know neither the day nor the hour wherein the Son of man cometh.'* It's not a coincidence that some of you are here tonight. Instead of being a witness of one soul repenting, join in this kind of celebration for your own soul.

"We have a change of clothing for your baptism. The only thing that is required of you is to repent of your sins. The Bible says in Acts 2 to repent and be baptized in the name of Jesus for the remission of your sins. Join the celebration and confess your sins to the Lord. Minister Saunders and I are here to pray for you. Is there anyone else who will come?"

"Acts 2," Dexter whispered. It was the same scripture God had given him.

Someone stepped from the group and started toward Minister Michaels. Dexter had to do a double take. It was Dr. Samuel Prentiss, his protégé from Atlanta. Pleased, Dexter exchanged nods with him. What better person to be his partner in baptism than the man he considered his partner in medicine.

The two shook hands and Dexter patted him on the back after Minister Michaels prayed for them. They were led through a side door to a changing room. Dexter exchanged his tux, tie, and other clothing for a white T-shirt, pants, and socks, then altar workers ushered them to a huge pool. As Dexter ascended the steps to the platform, he looked out into the sanctuary where Shana and Trent held center court, watching with their hands folded.

"We love you, Pop," Trent shouted, sparking applause and hallelujahs around him.

Dexter descended, stirring the warm water, then Samuel. The ministers instructed them to fold their arms over their chest.

Suddenly, the booming voice of Pastor Johnson was heard in the background. He had come. He had set everything in place for others to perform the baptism, so he wasn't needed per se, but he had come.

"Lord, we ask that you bless these young men…"

Dexter smiled. Although there was a gap between his forty-seven years to Samuel's thirty-one, he heartily accepted the compliment.

The pastor continued, "Your promises are sure, for Your Word says it is for generations, we ask in Your name that You fill them with Your Holy Spirit and send them on their way rejoicing." Pastor Johnson paused. "Amen. You may proceed."

With one arm up in the air and the other one gripped on the back of Dexter's T-shirt, Minister Michaels lifted his voice. "My dear brothers, upon the confession of your faith and the confidence we have in the blessed Word of God concerning His death, burial, and grand resurrection, we indeed baptize you two in the mighty name of Jesus for the remission of your sins. For there is no other Name under heaven whereby anybody can be saved, and the Word says you shall receive the Holy Ghost. Amen."

Dexter wasn't dipped but dunked under the water. He didn't completely understand how God could blot out his sins with water, but he came through the threshold, believing God. Applause erupted from the small gathering in the sanctuary as Dexter lifted his hands in praise.

Suddenly, Dexter felt the same presence he had experience that one night in Atlanta. Then it was as if he possessed bionic hearing when the sound of a powerful wind seemed to be heading toward him. Samuel had already stepped out of the pool. Dexter was almost at the rail when he was struck by an unidentifiable force that propelled him out the water and on his knees as he heard words coming out of his mouth that he couldn't control.

This was it. This was really it, his spirit told him. The speaking in tongues as mentioned in the Book of Acts. It was real. Dexter couldn't stop as tears poured out of him.

Ask and it shall be given, God spoke through his tongues. *Your sins are now forgiven and you are a new creature. Walk in My name and I will bless you.*

Dexter didn't know how long he was stretched out on the floor or how he made it back to the changing room, but he was exhausted by the time he regained his strength and his words. The first recognizable word out his mouth was *Hallelujah.*

When he opened his eyes, Trent, the pastor, and Alex were by his side. They were clapping and praising Jesus. Somewhat embarrassed that others had seen him in such a humiliating state, he latched onto a chair and sat in it. He shivered from the wet clothes. The altar worker ushered him into another room to dry off and redress in his formal attire.

Glancing in the mirror to straighten his bow tie, Dexter scrutinized himself minutes later. On the outside, he couldn't see a difference, but he knew now, without a doubt, that he was well done on the inside.

"Congratulations, Pop." Trent hugged him as soon as he returned to the group.

Dexter patted his back, then cleared his throat. "Don't you have a bride waiting for you?"

"And Mrs. Harris is waiting to see you, too." Opening the door to the hall, he was greeted with cheers and whistles.

Chuckling, Dexter nodded as he searched for Jillian. Once he had locked onto his target, the crowd parted until he reached her. Tears were streaming down her face, but she was still beautiful. He bent on one knee and reached for her hand, which trembled.

"Jillian Carter, I am a man God has made over with your specifications for a husband. I've been baked through and through. Will you do me the honor of marrying me? I promise I'll love, honor, and respect you. Please, baby."

"Yes," she barely whispered as he stood and lifted her off the floor in a hug. More applause encouraged them on until Dexter stole a kiss.

"Okay, Pop, let's take the limo back to the reception. We still have a lot of celebration left."

"Amen," Dexter said, pumping his fist in the air.

EPILOGUE

For the next ninety days, it was like déjà vu for Jillian and her fiancé. Dexter insisted on an outdoor wedding in a flower garden for a butterfly release. They chose the Botanical Garden. On the morning of August third, Jillian Carter uttered her wedding vows to become Mrs. Dexter Harris. He had truly given her the gift of love.

On Christmas day, she gave Dexter the biggest present: She was pregnant with twins.

"I told you this old man got game," Dexter teased his wife who rewarded him with a breathtaking kiss.

Immediately, Shana switched roles and took on the role of an overbearing mother. Seven months later, Dr. Dexter and Mrs. Harris welcomed a boy and girl.

Recovering in the birthing room, Dexter smothered Jillian with kisses. "I always wanted a daughter—thank you."

Shana walked in the room with one hand on her

hip. "Hey, I heard that. What am I? You can spoil Victoria and Dexter Jr. if you want, but they better remember that Trent and I were first."

Dexter barked out a laugh as he reached for Jillian's hands. With Shana and Trent and the babies in the room, they prayed and thanked God for the family that God had planned for them all along.

MAKING LOVE WORK

Prologue

Call it old fashion, but Simone French was smitten with a love letter. Not a text, email, or Facebook post, but a love letter sent through snail mail.

The prose wasn't the corny roses-are-red-and-violets-are-blue stuff. The first letter contained short accolades for a job well done. Soon after, the missives were filled with passionate words from a man who confessed the hidden secrets of his soul. He revealed his unspoken weaknesses, listed his uncompromising desires, and unapologetically noted his subtle strengths.

Rice Taylor was ready to surrender to love.

Whew. Closing her eyes, Simone inhaled the faint lingering smell of roses on the beige plain stationery. She had a testimony. If anyone would listen, she would proclaim that love was truly blind.

CHAPTER 1

Seven months ago

Beware, not be careful, of what you ask for because you just might get it, Simone French thought. As a hot upcoming St. Louis radio personality, she was surprised how much her listeners took what she said literally.

What person was bold and gullible enough to go on a blind date anymore? At twenty-six years old, Simone was single and trying to convince herself that she was satisfied. Only she knew the truth. And God, which makes two.

Every morning on KXNG-FM, Simone's radio show, "Don't Get French with Me" dominated the airwaves. Sipping on a glass of pineapple juice, Simone adjusted her headset, then she re-positioned the microphone inches above her mouth. The countdown to her segment had begun.

It was Monday and open line. Simone dreaded the combination. She assumed some listeners still had pent up frustrations left over from the weekend and her show was the venue to dump their laundry. That was a waste with so many strong topics to discuss. Simone never understood the station's decision to have an open forum twice a week for trivial things people could bore their mother, a therapist, or stranger on public transportation with.

When some callers became unruly, she did have recourse. They were subject to her tag line, "don't get French with me," and then the call was dropped.

Simone swayed her shoulders as she hummed along with her theme music that was blaring from the overhead speakers. Although the station was popular, the owner was slow to embrace the new millennium way of running a business. Basically, he didn't consolidate job duties and lay off staff.

That was one reason why Simone didn't have to multi-task and work the controls, answer the phone lines and be the talent. Thank God for Glen Howard, her technical board operator and senior engineer.

When he cued her, Simone took a deep breath and commanded a bubbly introduction, "Heeeeeeey, it's Monday on 'Don't Get French with Me', comin' at ya in three, two, and one."

Just as Simone's energy kicked into high gear, Glen yawned. *Pitiful.* Her show was the first of four Glen engineered daily, and he looked as if he'd already worked a twenty-four hour shift and wouldn't stay awake much longer.

He wasn't happy that he had to put in the extra effort to answer the phone. Glen preferred engineering shows where the hosts were so boring, the phones hardly rang. He reminded her of a Maytag repairman.

"Welcome, St. Louis," she purred. "It's open mic. Give me a call and tell me what's on your mind." Simone gave the number.

Although the station used a three second delay feature, no one screened her calls. If management decided to further stimulate the economy, she would put her request in for a screener.   All   seven   phone lines lit up and Simone took the first caller. "Good morning, Patrick. What's on your mind?"

"Besides you and me and—"

Simone rolled her eyes. A Beyoncé or Halle, she was not. As a matter of fact, very few people even knew how she looked. She refused to have her picture posted on the station website. At first management bucked, but then they decided with her voice, why not create a mystique about her. That was all well and fine with her.

"Keep your clothes on or in five seconds, you know what you'll hear."

"No harm, Frenchie, no harm. I called to talk about materialistic relationships."

Really? Although she could somewhat relate to the topic, she hoped Patrick's point of view wasn't about berating   women.   Thanks   to   disingenuous   ex-boyfriends, Simone seldom dated anymore.

While her guest ranted, her mind drifted back to some of her own disappointing fiascos: David Knight had   no   problem   insulting   her   by   stating   their relationship was less stimulating than her talk shows. He wanted the radio sex kitten he heard on the air every morning. Before him, there was Calvin Kane. Although the brother was fine, the "snake' had his own agenda: to use her to increase his personal contacts within the radio industry.

Whoever said that a woman could have it all—lied. She had yet to become that woman, considering she was living a double life. Men described her radio voice as sultry. One time she was teasingly told she could turn a simple, *hello* into a five-minute pillow talk.

She couldn't take credit for a voice God gave her. That asset aided in her show's popularity and paid the bills. Otherwise, she had no problem being soft spoken.

Simone was nothing like the image she portrayed over the airwaves. As a Christian who believed in practicing what her pastor preached, Simone longed for a deep, meaningful and committed relationship. She preferred a Christian man, but she was open as long as the date was respectful and willing to attend church. Who knows, the sermon might lead him to repentance.

As Glen eagerly signaled for her to take a break, Simone realized that she had given her caller more than his one minute of fame. It was also time to air a goofy car dealership commercial Glen had recorded. Although her engineer was a media tech guru, he couldn't buy a broadcast voice.

"Thanks Patrick," she disconnected. "You're listening to 'Don't Get French with Me' on KXNG. When I come back, I want to hear from you. There's got to be some love out there!"

It was the first time she had zoned out during one of her Monday open mic shows. Maybe she was becoming immune to gripers. Soon enough, Glen tapped on the glass partition, and then counted down the seconds before she was live on the air again.

Simone punched the second line. "We're back. Let's welcome Gina to the show."

"Frenchie, I don't know why the brothers are complaining. The guy before the break, Patrick, and other men are only after one thing—make that two, physical gratification they call intimacy and a hot cooked meal.

"Sisters are tired of being used and discarded. It's a new day. When the break-up occurs, we can walk away with compensation for a broken heart."

She was not about to play referee. Withholding her sigh, Simone responded, "Hmm, games people play, just roll the dice and you might get love, or a once-scorned companion. C'mon, somebody out there has to have a true love story. Make me want to use this box of tissue."

For the next hour, Simone's show was inundated with calls about busted, shaky, and unfulfilling relationships. Women described themselves as bitter and broken. Men characterized their former girlfriends as gold diggers.

Finally, a sixty-five-year-old retired bus driver phoned in, describing the perfect love affair that bloomed into a forty year marriage. "Stop playing games. I think people know instantly if he or she is the one."

Simone had faith in God, but wasn't completely sold on the 'love at first sight' thing. There were too many unknown variables. Basically, like the man being a jerk. "Okay, I'm out of time," then without realizing what she was saying, Simone tossed out a challenge, "Go out on a blind date. Close your eyes and open your heart. You might find the love of your life."

Removing her headset, Simone stood and gathered her papers to make way for the next host behind her. Without asking for one, she strolled out the studio with a headache. Simone liked her job, but it was the crazy people who called who challenged her patience.

CHAPTER 2

Rice Taylor was a first time listener to "Don't Get French with Me" and he had every intention of being a first time caller. As luck would have it, the show concluded before he could get through to the host from his cell phone. He rarely listened to his local stations anymore, especially talk radio.

Normally, he preferred smooth jazz on his satellite radio. But the woman's voice demanded his attention, which almost caused him to run into the back of a Cadillac as he sat in traffic, hoping he wouldn't miss his flight.

It was Frenchie's sensual voice that made him pause, but it was his ex-girlfriend, Regina "Gina" Larson's comments that made him pump the brakes.

"How dare she call a radio station and publicly justify her actions," he spat out his disgust. Initially, his mind had been stuck on stupid. Rice credited God for opening his eyes before he got any deeper into their six-month liaison.

Physical—ha! That was a two-way street. Gina had only been interested in receiving lavish gifts from every destination his plane touched down while he was away on business. He spoiled her with expensive dinners at exclusive restaurants and supported her financially when she quit her job. Rice's nostrils flared. He did not want to think about Regina Larson anymore—ever.

Rice squirmed in his leather seat to shake any lingering memories of Gina. His mind fast-forwarded to more pleasant thoughts like the host, Frenchie, who exhibited such a great sense of humor and intellect. He bit his bottom lip laughing. *The sista did a great job of holding conversations with the craziest callers.* Frenchie definitely kept the flow balanced between male and female comments. It seemed she even saw through Gina's shallowness.

Taking a deep breath, Rice smiled. Frenchie's voice was intoxicating, unique, and very, very sensual. He would never forget how her huskiness lowered to a whisper right before the commercial breaks. Umph, umph, umph, he bet she was drop-dead gorgeous. Suddenly Rice envied the man who dominated Frenchie's thoughts and shared her special moments.

One thing's for certain, he would never subject himself to a blind date. His eyes were wide open and Gina had still fooled him. When women learned he was a senior sales rep at a pharmaceutical company and earned a good income, they stopped focusing on him and saw the dollar signs. The next woman he chose had better have a chisel handy to break the ice around his heart.

As traffic began to pick up, Rice steered his SUV around a minor fender bender in hopes of making his flight. He would give anything to hear Frenchie's voice and show again. It wouldn't happen any time soon with scheduled early meetings the next couple of weeks on the East Coast.

Frenchie. Did she earn that nickname because of her sassiness or because of an alluring appearance? Either way, the sister earned his respect. "Ah, and to think I was complaining about running late this morning. Well, thanks to the host, it looks like I'm going to have a great day!"

When Rice pulled into the Park and Ride Garage, his silly fantasy about the radio personality didn't dissipate. He briefly thought about sending an email or text to the station telling them that Frenchie had picked up a new fan, but that seemed so impersonal. A quick handwritten note would be a nicer gesture.

***

On Friday morning, Simone slid out of bed and said her good morning prayer of thanks to the Lord. Before she even got to work, she contemplated what she wanted to do after she got off. Simone thought about enjoying a leisurely bike ride through Forest Park alone or taking in a matinee—alone. *Who needs a man?* To be honest, she would rather have someone to do something with or to go someplace for something exciting, but the next best thing for loneliness was self-pampering.

As she padded her way into the bathroom, Simone showered and then stared in the mirror. She wouldn't consider herself naturally beautiful like her older sister,

Hershey, but people constantly complimented her about her smile. Braces paid off.

She chose black as her choice of attire from her leather ankle boots to her turtleneck, all in an effort to appear thinner and give the illusion of added height. Other women would probably call the attire sexy and dangerous. She couldn't identify with either.

An hour later, Simone arrived at the station in an extremely good mood.

In the studio, Glen cued her with a nod as her theme music faded. Taking a deep breath, she spoke into the mic, "Heeeey, it's Friday. You're waking up to 'Don't Get French with Me' coming at you in three-two-one..."

"My guest today is an authority on the real estate market. Teresa Cain is here with valuable tips to keep you in your homes and avoid foreclosure," Simone said. For the next hour, the phone lines were jammed as desperate homeowners inquired about her agency and the programs.

The second hour proved just as informative with a representative from Mothers Against Drunk Driving, MADD. When Simone removed her headset and thanked her guest for coming in, she had a one track mind: to get out the door to start her weekend.

Payday and the end of another work week was a wonderful thing. On her way out, she greeted Annette Truman with a smile. Not only was Annette her best friend, but she was also the station's program director.

Tall and graceful, Annette could strut the hallways as if it was a runway, with long steps and her head held high. When male guests came to the station for an interview, Annette had been known to add an extra amount of sway to the hips. "Hey, girlfriend."

"Hey, yourself. That was a great show on the real estate market. Something's got to give soon. There are at least four houses for sale on my block. Anyway, good info. You're hot, girl. Just sizzlin'," Annette hissed like a snake before grinning. "Oh, by the way, pick up a couple pieces of mail on your way out, and have a great weekend."

"Thanks, Netta. I'm indulging for the next two days. First, a full-body massage at the spa, a new hairstyle, shopping, and then to be counter-productive, I'm pigging out on everything high in fat, sodium, and carbohydrates. It'll be the best of both worlds."

"All this before you go to church and repent for abusing your body." Annette laughed.

"Don't make me feel guilty before I actually commit the act." Simone feigned a pout.

"Okay, don't come wobbling in here on Monday, whining about how you have to go on another diet because your clothes shrunk."

"Do I do that? Don't answer." Simone hugged her friend, dismissing her comment. She admired Annette, who had been recently promoted to management and used a no-nonsense approach to solve personnel disagreements.

Without skipping a beat, Simone swooped up the mail off the desk near the door and continued to the bank of elevators on the fifth floor. Once she stepped inside and pressed L, Simone examined the three envelopes as she rode down to the lobby. One letter was handwritten—fan mail. She opened that first, hoping it wasn't a complaint.

Dear Frenchie:

Monday was the first time I've ever listened to your show. You made my day. Boy, you're good! Your conversation is lively, but I also heard your gentleness. I agree with your thoughts about relationships. If we could love what's in a person's heart rather than material things, economic status, appearances, and education, then maybe love will find us.

You suggested a blind date. What a challenge! I'm laughing just thinking about some disasters my friends have experienced from them. I regret I may not have a chance to listen again soon because of my work travel. But, I cherish the thought of knowing there's somebody else out there who's trying to find the deeper things in life.

Sincerely,

Rice Taylor, your one time fan

Simone folded the letter with an audible sigh. "How sweet." When the elevator doors opened, she stepped out with a smile. "Fan mail that inspires. Yep, it's going to be a great weekend."

CHAPTER 3

One letter lead to another and before Rice knew it, he and Simone had kicked off a month long writing campaign. They were a throwback to pen pals in another millennium.

It had become, of sorts, a friendly sparring of thoughts. After the second letter, curiosity got the best of him when he tried to find what she looked like on social networks and the station's personality profiles. The best he came up with was a group picture with Frenchie hiding in the back row.

When he mentioned his efforts to her, Simone asked that he curb the urge to judge her by her looks and let their friendship be blind. Although he was still a bit curious, he reluctantly agreed.

Rice,

Your letters are like a bowl of double-dip chocolate ice cream on a hot summer night. Believe it or not, you inspire me. I feel that I can really get what I want in a relationship. Sometimes, I think we ladies don't know what we want or expect from a man. Rice, be honest with me. Are women the only ones who want to feel special? Don't men want more than a hot meal, a clean house, and physical pleasure on demand? Your letters are an insight into a man's heart. I don't want just a man. I want his heart.

Can't wait for our next heart-to-heart,
Simone

He had somehow become obsessed, not with the radio personality, but the woman. As Rice relaxed in his seat in the business class section on the plane, he stared out the window. He surrendered his mind to float effortlessly with the clouds.

Usually, his work-related travel throughout the week was the downside to his salary, but that changed. Thanks to his pen pal, Rice welcomed the trips that allowed him more time to daydream about Simone and write her about things he hadn't shared with another woman.

A jet soaring in the distance drew Rice's attention. Suddenly, he wondered if he and Simone had ever crossed paths from a distance, held a conversation, or made eye contact. He was so tempted to Google images for Simone, but Rice didn't want that. He enjoyed back-to-back banter about things most men and women wouldn't discuss while dating.

Plus, when she wrote, Rice no longer heard her sultry voice, but her heart.

He must have spoken his thoughts out loud, because an elderly woman sitting beside him nudged him.

"I don't know, most people describe my voice as raspy, but if you think it's sexy—" she flirted and batted her lids. "I've never been picked up on a plane before."

Rice cringed from embarrassment. It was a long flight and he didn't want to offend somebody's grandmother figure.

Reaching over, she patted his hand. "Ah, young love. When you have the right woman," she advised, squinting through her thick glasses, "you'll find your heart uttering all of its secrets."

"Oh, I'm not in love. I haven't even met her yet."

The passenger adjusted her glasses and peered at Rice, giving him a once over before turning back around in her seat. "Then, you're one sick puppy."

He resisted laughing at the woman's comments. She had no idea how deep he was falling. As a matter of fact, he had written Simone back to back, not waiting for her to respond.

Dear Simone,

I'm flying to New York again, and of course, I was thinking about you. Wondering if you're okay, are you smiling, or if your day is going well? I know we've discussed so many things over the past weeks. I guess you can say we've been comparing notes. Can I get personal? What makes a woman stay in love with her man? Think about it and share your thoughts with me in your next letter. May your days be as lovely as you and your thoughts be filled with the passion of life. Sincerely,

Rice, your number one fan

He spied his seatmate and when he felt the elderly woman was engrossed in her e-reader, he reached into his pocket for Simone's last letter, which left him dumbfounded. Something wasn't right. Up until now, she had been chatty on paper, sometimes filling up two to three pages. Carefully, he unfolded it and reread it.

Up to this letter, Rice knew they had been completely truthful with each other. That was the basis for their continued correspondence. Now, Simone's honesty disturbed him.

Dear Rice:

I've never been in love.

Until next time, may God bless you with the woman of your dreams.

Simone

Two lines, few words, yet Simone was sending him a message. What was she not saying? Rice closed his eyes. *A whole lot, that's for sure.* It was unbelievable that a woman as genuine and passionate as Simone had not found love.

CHAPTER 4

"Okay, sister," Annette said, marching to Simone's desk like a military soldier performing drill. "I can understand pen pals from around the world, but around the neighborhood is a bit much. He's even thrown in a few postmarked letters from the East Coast. Email is cheaper." Resting her rump on the edge of the desk, Annette folded her arms and lifted a brow.

Shrugging, Simone didn't say a word as she tried to ignore her.

"Come clean. What's going on with you and this guy?" she asked, shoving a stack of letters in Simone's face.

"Nothing." She sniffed her recent delivery of pink roses. Every Monday, fresh roses arrived, and then on Fridays, he sent a mixed floral arrangement for her to take home. How could a man pamper her from a piece of paper? She was too happy, flattered, and preoccupied reading Rice's current letter.

Simone,

Our day is coming. Personally, I don't think special women get enough flowers. Some receive them for the wrong reasons like after a big fight, or a guilt trip on their man's part. But I want you to be surrounded by beauty because that's the way I see you. So that's my reason for the flowers today and every time in the future.

May you have the sweetest day,
Rice

His words made her light-headed. He didn't pressure her when she stated she wasn't ready to meet yet. That endeared him to her even more. And yes, Rice made her feel wonderful every day.

"Wipe that smile off your face. What aren't you telling me?" Annette demanded.

"The brother and I are just exchanging the written word," Simone defended innocently.

"Yeah. You and Mr. W-R-I-T-E have been exchanging a lot more than ink. You've been sniffing correction fluid?" Annette accusingly pointed her red-hot polished fingernail. "This week alone he's sent, including the stack that I've just handed you, about nine letters! Girl, this ain't the post office."

She continued her ranting as she gripped her spiked hair as if she was about to yank it out. "What's gotten into you? What has this guy been slipping in these envelopes? Please tell me you aren't serious?"

In order to put an end to her friend's hysteria, Simone simply replied, "His name is Rice Taylor, and we're just friends."

"Hmm-mm. Frenchie, who you kiddin'? This is me, White sista-girlfriend." Annette arched her eyebrow. "I hope he hasn't been sending drugs through the mail. What's going on in that hyperactive mind of yours?"

"This isn't a terrorist plot. We're simply exchanging letters filled with words that are funny, sensitive and thought-provoking. This is not an intimate relationship."

Retreating to a nearby chair, Annette collapsed and gave Simone an I-don't-believe-that's-all look. "Let me bring you into the new millennium. Ever heard of email? You're planning on getting involved with this Rice-a-Roni brother, aren't you?"

"I won't respond to your name calling, but I'm enjoying this—" She paused and frowned...how would she describe what she was doing? "Put it this way: We're just bouncing our thoughts off of each other without any commitments."

Smirking, Simone lowered her voice. "Rice and I have made up this game called *Find Me*. Every day, we search the crowd, trying to find each other. Since we agreed earlier not to disclose any of our physical descriptions, we're supposed to imagine what the other looks like from the words we've expressed in our letters.

"For instance, once I wrote, 'I saw you today, reading the newspaper at Starbucks. Your expression was serious as you wiggled your thick mustache against your nut brown skin.'"

Annette shook her head. "Well, that's worth staying up all night and reading again. I think both of you need to enroll at Forest Park Community College in Love 101. I'm surprised he hasn't contacted Miss Cleo, that old psychic woman, for the answers. Just be careful, Frenchie. Please."

Simone carefully modulated her voice to sound unaffected. "I'll have you know, Rice is strengthening his Christian walk—no demonic consultations. Since we started corresponding, he even stopped buying lottery tickets. So don't you even think about drizzling on my parade. I think he is searching his heart and making me look into mine. "

"He just better not hurt my girl. That's all I've got to say," She threatened as she stood and strutted away.

Me too. Simone sighed and rested her chin in her palm. Annette just didn't understand. Rice wasn't a threat to her on paper. *It was the ones that smiled in your face that could be deceitful.*

Later that evening, locked away in her bedroom with smooth gospel jazz serenading her, Simone leisurely read through the stack of fresh new letters. His words were so inspiring. "Rice, I wish I could hear your voice."

Was it a deep, rich baritone that would mesmerize her as he spoke the very words he wrote? Caught up in a whirlwind of questions, she drifted off to sleep.

***

Three weeks later…

"So, Frenchie, how is lover boy?" Annette asked minutes after Simone finished her show and strolled into the break room.

Washing her hands in the sink, Simone glanced over her shoulder at her friend's curious stare. "Well, he must be moving up in your book. No more, Rice-a-Roni? Well. He's wonderful."

Despite what Annette probably believed, Rice didn't occupy her thoughts all the time. She did have a job and a life. As a matter of fact, Simone was still riding high from her first hour show on the state and future of historically black colleges and universities.

"Well, actually, I was thinking of switching to Rice Crispy Treats. Get it?" Annette released a body-shaking laugh. She fanned herself as her face turned red. "Okay, okay girlfriend. I admit, Mr. San Francisco Treat has been sounding more interesting lately. So when is the big day?"

Rice had been asking the same thing. "Netta, I may talk the talk, but girl, I can't even begin to take baby steps on this walk. I don't know if I can do this."

"Trust me, you can. And I want to be there, too."

Ignoring Annette, Simone began pacing around tables and chairs in the empty break room. "Can you believe our attraction is growing? Our innocent letters have suddenly become romantic, sometimes mysterious, but our words are always honest."

"I don't know anything about Rice-a-Roni being romantic on paper, but the man is definitely a mystery."

Simone stopped and stared out the window, amused by the antics of two blue jays chasing each other on tree branches. "Wouldn't it be something if Rice was incredibly irresistible, and devastatingly handsome?"

"Yeah, that would be something." Annette threw up her hands in frustration. "You're starting to lose it. H-E-L-L-O? Let me burst your bubble. This brother could also be a loser. There is no way I believe he doesn't know what you look like. Have you ever heard of Google search? Even the people on eHarmony have a composite picture. It may be from childhood, but at least you have an idea. The sooner you can dump him, the better."

Or be dumped, she thought. No one would ever believe she had self-esteem issues. Simone chuckled as she sauntered out of the break room. But this was her fantasy, and she would live in it as long as she wanted. She stuck her head back in the doorway. Annette was rinsing out her coffee cup. "I don't know, Netta. He could turn out to be the sexiest man alive."

She thought back to letter number twenty-three:

Simone...

Whatever you want in a man, I can be that man of your dreams. I would become putty in your hands to mold and shape to your heart's content.

Trust me. Trust your heart.

"And I bet the suspense is killing you," Annette whispered as a guest for another host's show passed them in the corridor. "It's definitely killing me."

CHAPTER 5

I saw you today, Simi. I hope you enjoy my nickname for you. From afar, I watched you scan the shelves at Barnes & Noble. At first, you didn't notice me, but slowly you must have felt my presence. When our eyes met, I was instantly drawn to your luscious lashes.

Your skin was the color of cinnamon, your hair swept off your neck and held by a gold clip. Your height was perfect, standing over five feet. You are just perfect.

If that had been you, I know you would've run into my arms. Instead she asked someone to call security because I looked suspicious and was possibly stalking her. I'm releasing a heavy grunt. This Find Me game is going to get me hurt or arrested. I'm missing you.

Rice, more than a fan.

He sealed the envelope to mail it on his way out the door. It was two weeks before Christmas, and Rice was dying a slow death with these letters to and from

Simone. If he forced her into a meeting before she was ready, would he lose her? If Rice held out any longer, he would lose his mind. He was a flesh and blood man, not a paper boy doll.

Rice dressed in a chocolate-brown designer suit and accessories for the annual 100 Black Men's banquet held at the Hyatt downtown. He would've given anything to have Simone accompany him tonight instead of being around a bunch of men.

Every brother who attended was either well connected professionally and/or socially, or waiting in the wings for the right opportunity to shine with their skills. As he mingled with old friends and associates, one person caught his attention, Allan Martin, the station manager for KXNG.

Before Rice could get to him, the master of ceremonies asked everyone to be seated so the program could begin. Although the guest speaker entertained the audience with his witty sense of humor and political insight, Rice's mind was on his friend on the other side of the room.

During a brief intermission, he tracked down Simone's boss. "Hey, Allan, what's up man?"

They exchanged a handshake, a measured hug, and the pat on the back. "Rice...how have you been, man? Still traveling and making all the money?"

"Right. You're the one running the show. How many more stations has Clear Channel purchased?" Rice easily made eighty thousand a year in salary and bonus, but Allan commanded six digits.

The station manager shrugged as he rubbed his clean-shaven head, frowning as he curled his lips. "A few." He was a tall imposing, rugged-looking dark-skinned man.

Years ago, they were considered a good catch by women, attached and single. Allan had played the love games. Rice retired before he graduated college.

Doing a quick sweep of the room, Rice nudged him aside. "Look, man. You've got a female host..." his voice faded. "I was wondering if you could help with an introduction."

"I have twelve on-air personalities. Do you have a name?" Crossing his arms, Allan seemed amused.

"You're probably going to think I'm an idiot."

"Probably, but try me."

"For the past few months, Simone French and I have been exchanging letters. I know, a little prehistoric in the age of texting, but I have no idea what she looks like."

Allan squinted and twisted his lips. "A blind date would have been easier. I'm not comfortable getting in the middle of what you and Simone have or don't have going on." He chuckled, making eye contact with passers-by. "There must be a reason why you two haven't met, and I don't even want to know. In Simone's defense, she's extremely talented with a sharp wit. She should be taken very seriously." He paused. "Remember that. I don't want one of my frat brothers messin' with her head and crushing her heart."

"I have a clean record when it comes to women, except for the last disaster that rolled into my life."

Allan appeared to be thinking as he massaged his black beard with specks of gray. "Simone usually doesn't attend station events unless it's mandatory. How about our annual station Christmas party? I'm willing to make an introduction. After that," he said, folding his arms, "let's just say, you're on your own."

"I'll be there." Hopefully, she would be too.

***

Despite Simone's bold and quick witted personality that she demonstrated on the radio, she was a private person and Allan knew it. He didn't know what to think about what Rice confided in him. Allan's only question was, "Why the game?" And this had been going on for months. "He's a better man than me," he mumbled to himself.

Simone was somewhat of a recluse when it came to public events. If she wasn't ordered to go, Simone opted out, which added to her mystique. She was nothing like the showgirls Rice had dated in the past. Allan's employee possessed a sweet innocence about her that was hidden behind the microphone.

Every male who listened to his station wanted to know, "Does she look as good as she sounds?" He usually gave a brief physical description and dropped the subject. But he had a hunch with Rice that his request was genuine.

Shaking his head, Allan drummed his finger on his lips, thinking as he scanned the stack of resumes, audition tapes, and other mail scattered across his desk. This was going to be interesting. He pressed the intercom alerting the control room. "Glen, ask Frenchie to come to my office after her show."

Her engineer's monotonous voice suddenly became perky. "She's in trouble, ain't she? I knew that slave reparation was too controversial."

"Religion, politics, taxes, and even death are controversial. Japanese-Americans and Jews were compensated, so should African-Americans. Through open dialogue people will have an opportunity to hear both sides of the argument. Now, just have Simone come to my office." He disconnected and waited.

A half hour later, Simone breezed through his door. Her choice of color that day was red, including the cap, hiding the mystery of her hairdo. He had become accustomed to seeing her in black.

"Allan, you wanted to see me? Did you have a problem with the show?" Simone bowed her head, smiling. "The phone lines jammed as racial lines were clearly divided today. I never heard so many angry people."

He waved her in. "Heated dialogue is good. I noted you had to hang up on more than one irate caller. It comes along with the territory."

Simone sat in a brown leather seat, facing his massive desk and crossed her legs. Allan gave a brief recap of his conversation with Rice. Then he watched Simone's reaction to Rice's invitation to the station holiday party. "As your boss, the last thing I wanted to do was ambush you."

"I'm not going!" Simone blurted out as she leaped out of her seat with a stricken expression across her face.

Concerned, Allan told her to calm down as she began to pace the carpet in his office. "Rice isn't stalking you, is he? You haven't missed the Christmas party in four years."

"If we meet, then it's over."

"I'm confused. What's over?"

Simone was slow to make eye contact as she explained, "My escape, and our fantasy. It's the special something that has developed between us." Suddenly, she spun around and faced him. "Allan…" Her voice dropped to a sexy undertone.

He was amused. She knew her charm only worked on listeners who couldn't see her. Simone's magic spell had no power over him. He leaned forward, speaking in his own husky voice. "Yes?" he whispered teasingly.

"Tell me something about him," Simone pleaded. "Like the shade of his brown skin, the color of eyes, height, weight, and social security number." She grinned. "I'm kidding on the last part."

Leaning back in his chair, he folded his arms. "Who says he's brown? And I don't stare into any man's eyes." He was tickled by her antics.

Simone chewed on her bottom lip. "Okay, so he's not a shade of pecan. Anything. What about his cologne? Of course, whatever you say will remain strictly confidential. Is he nice looking?"

Allan barked out a laugh and pushed back from his desk. "That's it! I'm not sniffing behind any man." Standing, he pointed to the door. "Don't you have a promo or something to record?" They were not about to get him in the middle of their love fest. Although he wished he could be a fly on the wall when they first meet, if they ever agreed to stop paying postage. He was aware of Simone's tactics in trying to pry information out of him, but he wasn't having it.

"You're not going to tell me anything, are you?"

"If you came to the Christmas party, you could see, touch, and sniff for yourself."

CHAPTER 6

With the station party just two days away, Simone's heart ached to go. She hadn't slept well since Allan mentioned Rice's intention. She chided herself for her behavior, but her vulnerability was raw. *Just go, and get it over with*, a brave voice within her challenged.

"Oh, I want to go," Simone spoke aloud as she headed toward the studio. If she bailed out, she would sorely miss the camaraderie with her colleagues and their families. Simone tapped the wall in frustration.

"Hmm, writing to imaginary boyfriends, arguing with invisible people, and now you're boxing. The true signs of a woman in need of therapy," Annette taunted from behind her.

"Would you stop sneaking up on me." Simone snarled.

"Still debating whether to come to the party or not? You're supposed to be ecstatic about seeing the man you've dreamed about all day and read his letters every night."

"I do want to meet Rice, but I feel like the lion in the Wizard of Oz. I've got no courage," Simone whispered, avoiding Annette's eyes.

When Simone slumped against the wall, Annette scrutinized her. "Girl, look at you with dark circles under your puffy eyes—I've shown you myself how to apply make-up."

"Not now. I've got five minutes to get into the studio."

"I only need one of those minutes. Have you looked at yourself lately? You usually take the time to artistically curl your hair every morning and your clothes, whew! Black and orange only match on Halloween," Annette advised her.

"I just haven't been in the mood."

"Why are you allowing yourself to go through these changes?" Annette reached out and fingered Simone's scarf. "And, red definitely doesn't enhance your outfit."

"I can't concentrate lately."

"I don't know, maybe Rice is starting to brainwash me too, but honey, are you sure you don't want to go? I could pretend I'm you while you check out your knight in writing hardware."

"You're so corny." Simone laughed and sniffed. "It's knight in shining armor, girl. I'm not ready to lose this wonderful friendship with him."

Simone heard her theme music. "Gotta go." She raced inside the studio, collapsed in the chair behind the microphone, and assessed her attire. Her feelings about Rice were as mixed as her clothes.

Today, Simone felt the way Glen looked, like he didn't want to be there. She took a series of deep breaths as he cued her three seconds. She perked up. *Time to put on a show.* "Heeeey, it's Friday, and that means open line. It's the end of the workweek, close to the holidays, and maybe your payday. Talk to me in three, two and one."

Punching in the first line, Simone welcomed a female listener. "Good morning, Gina."

"Hi, Frenchie, I called a few months ago about being materialistic."

"Yes, I remember."

"Well, the spirit of Christmas has made me re-think some things that I've done in the past. I'm going to turn my life around and get my man back; the one I hurt the most with my selfish ways."

Well, praise God for Gina's reflection. Because Simone didn't work for a Christian station, she dared not utter any praises over the air. "Reconciliation—that's a wonderful way to close out the year. I wish you much success and all the happiness in the world."

Gina sparked a line of callers with confessions, declarations, and happy holiday wishes. The show went smoothly with callers commenting about what they planned to do for others for Christmas instead of focusing on themselves. Simone was exhausted as she pulled off her headset by the time her show ended. Exercising her witty persona over the air was mentally draining at times. She did her customary bow to Glen and strolled out of the studio.

When Simone reached the reception area, a FedEx deliveryman was clearing the doorway, struggling with a large package. He gave her attire a strange look and then nodded. "Ladies," he greeted, placing the box on the receptionist's desk.

Annette signed his clipboard and read the sender's name. "Either Rice-a-Roni is using larger paper, or it's a laptop to bring you two into the new millennium."

Simone accepted the package with thanks. "His name is Rice Anthony Taylor. You're close to being at the top of my list of ex-friends."

"Humph, even his initials spell a rat. Now, open the box. I'm nosy, and you know it."

She did so with eagerness. Inside there was a meticulously wrapped gift, and a sealed envelope Rice had taped to the present.

"Skip the letter, girl. Go for the present!" Annette clasped her hands. "Hurry up, because I'm not going anywhere until you do."

"Don't rush me." Simone stomped her suede boot as she tore open the envelope. "I sense this letter is very special even without the gift."

She slid into the chair behind the desk of the receptionist who always seemed to be in the bathroom or getting another cup of coffee. Fingering the envelope, Simone debated whether to read it now or later.

Annette sucked her teeth and without shame boldly peeked over Simone's shoulder. "Will you open the gift, or do you want me to do it?"

Her voice faded away as Simone gasped after removing the lid off the box. Smiling, she followed Rice's instructions and pulled out a bracelet covered with tiny birthstones. Next was a lead crystal 5x7 picture frame with a magazine photo of an attractive black couple.

"Wow." Annette whistled and folded her arms. "Okay, so Rice-crispy has good taste."

Ignoring her silly remark, Simone stared at a rhinestone-covered key-shaped brooch. "What does this mean?" she whispered as a tear fell.

Pulling a tissue from a box on the desk, Annette feigned a sniff. "These gifts are so beautiful."

"They're also private, so if you don't mind, I'm going to read my letter at home." Simone collected her goodies and grabbed her black and brown leopard swing coat and put it on. "Good-bye. Have fun at the party this weekend," she said with a sorrowful smile.

"I still wish you were coming." She pulled back and shook her head at Simone's clothes. "Girl, please go home, and color-coordinate your life, your man, and your wardrobe."

***

Rice Taylor had complicated Simone's life on paper. Saturday night, an hour before the company Christmas party, reality set in. "I can't believe I'm really not going for the first time ever." She laid her gifts across the bed, and stretched out on top of the comforter. She reread Rice's letter again.

Merry Christmas, baby,

First, he gave her the nickname, Simi, and now she was his 'baby'. She would probably like the sound of it from his lips.

I still want to be a part of your holidays, since you've decided against going to the party tonight. This is madness. The picture frame is for us to imagine our future together. Listen to your heart. It knows how we feel about each other. The bracelet is for you to wrap around your wrist since I can't wrap my arms around you.

Tears filled her eyes. "Who needs a good romance novel when I've got Rice's words that reach out and grab me?"

Finally, I want you to know that only you hold the key to unlocking the dreams of my heart. The rhinestone pin represents the way you have covered my heart with warm words and bright promises.

Baby...

Simone's heart pounded faster at the sight of his endearing word again. Rice's words had the power to possess her body and soul. She could almost hear his voice whisper in her ears.

She smiled, imagining the sound of his voice. Was it strong and deep? Would it soften whenever he said baby? She gritted her teeth and screamed out her frustration. "Ahhh!" Deep down, Simone wanted to see him badly as she continued reading:

I do respect your decision to wait for now, but I want more, so much more for us. I pray you'll feel the same way eventually. Again, Merry Christmas, sweetheart.

Here's my phone number, 314-313-5081 in case you want to talk...about us.

I'm Yours,

Rice

Tears trickled down her cheeks. With blurred vision Simone closed his letter and placed it over her heart. "I'm addicted to you," she confessed. "Lord, give me the courage to receive my blessing, if he is it," she prayed. If not, then he 'Won't get French with Her' because she could disconnect him from her life. Unfortunately, she was too far gone to act tough.

CHAPTER 7

One day after New Year's Day

"Special delivery for Mr. Rice Taylor." A goofy-looking, gum-popping, and impatient deliveryman stood on Rice's porch, eyeing him. "You him, man?"

Rice didn't answer when he eyed the flowers. He reached for them with one hand and dug into his pocket for a tip with the other.

The older teenager nodded after stuffing the bills in his pocket. After jumping off the snow-shoveled stairs, he went on his way.

Only one person would send a man flowers. Rice massaged his chin. "Maybe I didn't strike out after all." He was about to rip open a large purple envelope. Suddenly, his smoke alarm went off at the same time he smelled his sausage burning.

Irritated more by the interruption than the incineration of his breakfast, Rice rushed to the stove and turned off the burners. He transferred the skillet to the sink and then opened a window. As he fanned the remnants of smoke from his face, he sat at the table with Simone's card in his hand.

His stomach could wait. For five long days, Simone hadn't written him back or used the phone number he gave her. Rice had begun to second-guess himself, misreading Simone's words as someone who indeed only wanted friendship.

Hi Sweetie,

Rice snickered. Interesting salutation and the first time she didn't call him by his name.

Sorry it's taken me so long to gather my thoughts. Rice, you're a special man. I'm blessed to have you dominate my thoughts, dreams, and yes, my life. I'm constantly wondering if you're everything I've dreamed. I just don't know if I'm ready for us to meet.

Anyway, each flower you see, I handpicked for the arrangement because the bright and soft colors remind me of how your words make me feel, alive and happy. Your emotions saturate my mind each day.

As our relationship changes, I admit I want more too. I want you to hold me when you call me baby. I long to hear your voice, but my feelings aren't stronger than my fear of losing what we have. I know I'm not making sense. Don't try to figure me out. No man has yet. I can't even figure myself out. I need a little more time.

I'm yours too,
Simone

Rice groaned in frustration as he pounded his fist on the table. This had to stop. "We're falling in love on paper. I'm setting a date." First, he had to pack for a three day regional sales conference.

The next day while he waited in the airport for his flight, he pulled a sheet of stationery from his briefcase and began writing as soon as his pen touched the paper.

My Love,

I agree that we do have a good thing going. We've both opened up and shared some private things about ourselves. The best Christmas present I could've had would've been wrapping you in my arms, looking in your eyes and bringing in the New Year with you. It's time. Will you allow me to pick a date? I can't hold out any longer. I need more than paper and a pen when I'm thinking about you. I need to touch you. I need to understand your moods and see you when you're happy or sad, my paper doll. I want you to hear me say, I love you.

I'm yours,

Rice

P.S. Simone, I'm your friend first and I can give you more friendship than any person alive because I love you. That will not change. I know you love me. I can feel it

CHAPTER 8

Can I flirt on paper? Simone wondered. As an avid mall shopper, she couldn't resist the after-Christmas leftovers and the end-of-the-year clear outs, but then she strolled into Papyrus.

She ignored shoe and clothing sales, and went crazy in the stationery store. She snatched up solid, textured and water stained, and scented paper. She even tossed satin ribbon, and raffia ties in her basket.

Later that night, she couldn't sleep. Why did it seem so easy for Rice to disclose his feelings without knowing if she would be physically attractive? Sitting up in bed, she turned on the light. Her stomach was twisting just like her heart. She grabbed her scented stationery and started scribbling.

Dear Rice,

You're my love too. Yes, it's time. Okay, it's past time, but why do I feel like I am losing here? Stupid question. Don't answer that. I can do this. I can, but I 'm scared. Can we be as happy physically as we have been on paper? Don't answer that. I'm falling apart. I need more time.

Yours,

Simone

A few days later, Rice surprised her with a letter written on mint-scented green water-stained parchment. They had advanced from notebook paper to designer sheets of stationery. She smiled until Rice insisted on Valentine's Day for their very first rendezvous, which was less than six weeks away. He said it was plenty of time. She disagreed. It wasn't enough to collect her courage.

I'm craving your voice, your touch, and your smell like an addict. I want to put a stamp on my forehead and deliver myself to your station. I am beyond ready. You asked for time. You have thirty-eight days until I sweep you off your feet.

Our first date will be everything it should be for two people in love, special and romantic. Simone, I'm going for the gold. You are the prize I seek, not as a trophy, but as a best friend, special companion, and...I'll whisper the rest when I see you.

Rice

Simone inhaled the peppermint fragrance of the stationery. Her vision was blurred, her heart heavy, and her mind scared to death. "Whoa. Am I ready to accept my fate?" She was asking herself more questions than she had answers for lately.

Her nerves were frayed. She couldn't eat, sleep, or concentrate. She should be happy that a sensitive man was in love with her, sight unseen. Wasn't that her prayer to God...a man who could see her heart first?

That thought took her back to the conversation at the table for Christmas dinner at her parents' house with her older twin brother and sister. Hershel was named after football great Hershel Walker.

When her mother learned she was having twins, Evelyn French scrambled for a second name. Once they were born, she picked Hershey for her sister because of her silky milk chocolate skin. Simone took after her mother's side of the family, because she looked nothing like her siblings.

Hershey, a former runway model, was very tall, almost six feet. She was blessed with glowing flawless skin. She possessed multi-cultural features with her slanted hazel eyes; long slender nose; and short Halle Berry haircut. Plus, Hershey had an outgoing personality.

Hershel's looks were a masculine carbon copy. He stood six-foot five with an athletic body. Besides good-looking, he was also caring. Both siblings grabbed attention with their bright photogenic smiles, outstanding looks, and sex appeal. They were gorgeous, but Simone could only claim her voice as her best asset, which helped with a radio career. She looked nothing like them in skin color, height, or weight.

As the youngest, she felt the love, but not the closeness since they were eight years older than her. Besides Annette, no other person knew of her love-letter affair, not even her family, which was one reason they asked about her dating prospects at the dinner table. She declined their offers for a physical blind date. She could barely handle the one on paper.

At work, she caught Allan watching her a few times, but he never asked about her situation with Rice.

Did her boss know something that she should know? Was she was making a big mistake, or would she eventually find happiness?

In the following weeks, Rice held nothing back in his letters, which became more personal and romantic, penned on different colors and types of stationery. Each never failed to mention a *Find Me* scenario. He was becoming so intense; it was almost giving Simone a haunting feeling.

Simi,

I saw you today. I was riding up the escalator at Nordstrom's. The harmonious sounds of the piano player soothed my mind. I was caught up daydreaming when I passed by the women's shoe department. I smiled when I thought about how you mentioned you enjoyed shopping for shoes.

You were very tall with shapely long legs with skin the color of mocha. I just froze in the aisle and watched how you gently guided your feet into low heels, no heels, and tall heels. I envied the shoes and the salesman. My heart dropped when you winked and waved me over.

Swallowing, I walked toward you. I almost knelt down and slipped a pair of shoes on your feet until a deep voice spoke behind me calling you, Janise. Needless to say, I turned like a military soldier in the opposite direction. Whew! I told you this game might get me hurt. Simone put your man out of his misery.

I'm counting the days, hours, and minutes until I see your lovely face. But, I'm worried about you. For the next month, I want you to focus on yourself and enjoy shopping, movies, or parties until we meet.

Maybe, we'll find each other at one of those places.

Love,
Rice

***

Days later, Simone planned to do just as Rice had suggested. She enjoyed herself at her siblings' thirty-third birthday celebration. The French twins resided in the posh middle-to-upper class area of West County in Creve Coeur.

Replicas of old-fashioned gaslights lined the streets, and saluted the occasional Rolls Royce, Benz, and BMW. The luxury vehicles paraded the neighborhood taking its occupants to nearby gated eateries, exclusive shopping, and secluded homes. Populated with less than fifteen-percent minorities, those Blacks who could afford the exorbitant home prices were successful as entrepreneurs or in upper-management positions in Fortune 500 companies.

Hershey had recently purchased a large condo that was ten minutes away from Hershel's split-leveled townhouse. Both were at least ten miles away outside St. Louis' city limits. Preferring city living, Simone opted for a small one-bedroom apartment in the pricey Central West End. It was minutes away from downtown and close to her job.

Before Simone could ring the doorbell, Hershey opened the thick Maplewood door and embraced her in a bear hug. "Hey, girl, what's up?" Hershey displayed a dazzling smile.

Simone sniffed Hershey's expensive sweet perfume, sensuous. She always felt inferior around Hershey. Regardless of how well Simone dressed, Hershey always did it better with a flair.

"C'mon. I thought you would never get here. I don't want to be late for my own birthday party. You'll see some old and new faces, but there'll be plenty of men for both of us." Hershey's waxed eyebrow rose with mischief gleaming in her eyes as she slipped into a white leather jacket with its reddish-brown fox collar.

The only man I want to see is Rice Taylor, and God knows I would barely keep myself composed if I saw him. Simone cringed; she didn't want to be bothered. She would have been satisfied to stay at home and talk to Rice—correction—write to him. "Doesn't matter, Hershey. I'm very content with the man I have at the moment," Simone replied softly.

"Whoa. Really?" Hershey reached over and finger-combed Simone's curls, always trying to improve what she felt was out of place. "All this since Christmas? Wow, I can't wait to hear about him on the ride over to Hersh's place."

After strapping on her seatbelt, Simone took a deep breath. Sooner or later, her family would know and if they met Rice, they would want to know how they met. "He's so deep; he could write a love song with Baby Face."

"Ooh, a man who knows how to express himself. I love it. Okay, so what does he look like, decent, fine, or gorgeous?"

Here I go. "Funny, you should ask. Remember when you told me that looks aren't everything?"

"Yeah, and I should know. Some of the best-looking models can't hold a conversation."

"Well, I've never met him. I mean, I don't know how he looks. We've been writing back and forth for months."

Hershey squinted. "You're a pen pal to a serviceman. That's noble." She frowned. "But how do I say this…isn't that rather desperate? You need a man who is stateside."

Simone felt deflated. *Oh well, forget the family support.*

"That doesn't sound good. You remember Marie?"

"What about Marie?"

Her sister barely waited for Simone's acknowledgment. "Well, the same thing happened to her. She fell in love with a guy she had been writing to for months. I can't remember the details on how she came about writing the loser, but girl, it turned out to be a nightmare."

Simone's heart dropped. "What happened?"

Hershey made a *tsk*ing sound. "Brother turned out to be an inmate at the state prison in Jefferson City. He had seen her picture in the paper when she got her job promotion and instantly fell in love with Marie."

A convicted felon? *Oh no.* Simone held her breath. She asked Rice not to Google her, maybe she should have done a background check on him instead. Before her mind got carried away, she had to assure herself God wouldn't allow her to be deceived like that.

Simone began to chew the lipstick off her bottom lip. Rice said his travel schedule gave him plenty of time to write. Was that true? She wondered.

"Sis, you better nip that in the bud," Hershey counseled.

She had to believe in what they had. "I'm in love."

"What!" Hershey stopped at a green light, causing tires to squeal behind her. "Not with an invisible man? Are you crazy? You are my sister, right?" Silence filled the car before Hershey cleared her throat. "Girl, put the paper man away and go for the flesh and blood man who you can see. Don't forget about touch, talk to, and kiss."

Kissing. Simone blushed like she had tasted one of Rice's kisses. Their letter writing had made her bold. Never had she told a man how she liked to be kissed! Rice insisted a passionate kiss couldn't be controlled. *Kisses will replace our words of love,* he had said. It was going to have to be. Suddenly, she wondered if Rice's kisses would be strong and intoxicating.

Hershey nudged Simone's leg for attention. "All men aren't looking for a model-type to love. You're a big shot radio personality."

"Don't remind me. I've attracted some real losers because of that."

Hershey's voice softened, "I wonder what your pen pal is hiding."

Simone gripped the door handle. "It's not him. It's me. He's been trying to see me since Christmas, but I'm chicken. We've set a date...no, Rice has picked Valentine's weekend."

"That's a few weeks away. Maybe some smart brother will change your mind tonight at the party."

She hoped not. Clearing her head, Simone banished the issue until she was alone and prepared to have a good time despite her sister's dire predictions. Blinking, Simone couldn't believe the number of cars that packed the cul-de-sac.

Then she smiled at the orange cones Hershel had placed in his driveway to reserve a space for his sisters. Simone smirked, wondering what construction site her brother had hit.

"Well, don't sit in the car. We're here." Hershey jumped out and walked to Hershel's door like she was on a runway. Suddenly, Simone wished Rice was a guest at the party.

Hershel opened his door with a crowd standing behind him. Some faces Simone recognized, others she hadn't seen before and greeted as they walked in the foyer. Simone watched a very tall, dark-skinned, and very handsome brother check out Hershey in her body-fitting black leather pants, black sweater, and black boots. He didn't waste one glance at Simone.

Hershel, dressed in a denim shirt and jeans, engulfed her in a tight hug. "Hey, shortie, you're looking good, but a little tired. Have some fun tonight." He smacked a juicy kiss against her cheek.

She teased, "You think you invited enough people?"

"Nah." He grinned, shrugging. "It's our birthday. Hershey and I felt like doing it up. I could've crammed in another fifty or so."

Hershel made introductions, but Simone quickly forgot names and faces as she strolled toward his kitchen for a soda. She wished Rice was there, and then she chided herself. It was up to her to invite him.

Downstairs in the lower level, an even bigger party was underway. The enormous three-room area was designed for entertaining, complete with a surround-sound home theatre section and a half a dozen tall marble tables with matching bar stools.

A sliding door led outside to a patio. Despite the chilly temperature, it was cracked open to cool the heated air from so many bodies. On the other side, guests were shooting pool while others tested their ability at darts.

Suddenly, a heated dispute between two rowdy couples seated at a makeshift card table drew Simone's attention. She chuckled at their intense argument before laughter erupted. In the midst of the activity, without warning, Simone sensed someone following her movements, as if she was the highlight of the party. *Could Rice be here? Don't be silly.* Rice would have mentioned if he knew any Frenches.

Maybe she had played too many *Find Me* games and now her mind was playing tricks on her. Therefore she ignored the tumbling jabs in her stomach and the raised hairs on her arms, warning her something was about to happen.

Moving to a vacated barstool, Simone waited her turn for a new round of darts when Hershel caused a stir. He treaded down the stairs, lugging a stack of pizza boxes with a trail following the aroma like the Pied Piper's spell.

"Hi," a deep voice whispered close to Simone's ear.

Startled, Simone jumped and then gripped the counter. Afraid to move, she held her breath. Slowly she turned and met the softest brown eyes she had ever seen. *Whew!* She almost slumped to the floor.

Were these the same warm eyes following her earlier? He wasn't as tall as Hershel, but the brother was definitely inches taller than her. He was casually dressed in an oxford shirt and jeans and was definitely a looker.

"Sorry, I didn't mean to scare you. I'm also waiting for a turn. Would you like to play a round against me?"

His smile was so mesmerizing Simone could only nod. He grabbed a stool and scooted close to Simone. "I'm Anthony."

Rice's middle name. Simone didn't realize she had been staring until she heard him clear his throat. Anthony gave her a wide smile that stretched his thick mustache.

She blushed from embarrassment as she lowered her head. "Sorry, I'm Simone."

He curled his lips. "I don't have a problem forgoing a dart game if you want us to stare at each other all night. Plus, I love the sound of your voice."

Most people did, which was why she was such a success in radio, but unless someone asked, she never freely gave her profession. She made the mistake of taking a deep breath to calm her nerves and that's when she got a whiff of his spicy cologne. It was a nice fragrance.

"Simone is a beautiful name."

"So is Anthony," she whispered.

Anthony lifted a brow. "Really? Hmm." He chuckled. "I thought it was pretty common. Nobody ever said that to me before except my mother who named me. My first name is a bit unusual, so I go by my middle name. You know, the one you like," he joked.

They shared a laugh.

Her curiosity was piqued. She leaned closer, wondering if he fit the profile of the Rice she had conjured up in her mind. "Tell me your first name."

Anthony chuckled and winked. "It begins with 'r' that's all I'll divulge." He looked around the room. "Say, can I get you a drink?"

Surely, she mentioned that to Rice in one of her letters. *Didn't she?* Simone questioned herself. "No, thank you. I don't drink."

Anthony tilted his head. "Oh, is it a religious thing or something else?"

"No, it's because drunk drivers kill about three-hundred people every week of every year."

He frowned. "Whoa. That seems a bit excessive. Are you sure?"

Glancing over his shoulder, she met Hershey's eyes as her sister nodded her approval of Anthony. From the looks of a man clinging to Hershey's side, she might want to handle her own business; Simone withheld her smirk.

She refocused on Anthony. "I'm a radio talk show host and it's my job to know the latest news and information. Mothers Against Drunk Driving just released its figures a few weeks ago."

"I'm impressed. I'll have to start listening when I'm not traveling with my job." Anthony paused, smoothing his silky mustache. "Hey, wait a minute, you're not Simone French a.k.a. Frenchie, the sassy sister on the radio, are you?" He then proceeded to scrutinize her face from the silly auburn wig she was wearing, which Hershey had raved about after Simone refused to try coloring her hair.

Hershey had insisted the color enhanced Simone's skin. His eyes swept over her attire: a bulky sweater and then her maybe-a-little-too-tight jeans, the evidence of too many scoops of ice cream while reading Rice's letters.

"Yeah, that's me."

He pointed his finger in the air. "You know, I did catch the tail end of your show months ago when you challenged listeners to try the blind date thing. Remember that show?"

"How could I forget?" she chuckled. "My life hasn't been the same since."

"Hmm," Anthony responded as if a great revelation hit, but he wasn't sharing.

After a few moments of awkward silence, the mood changed. For the rest of the night, they observed one another. Simone was feeling good vibes.

Anthony seemed relaxed in his surroundings. They competed with other couples in darts, high-fiving themselves every time they won and childishly pouting together when they lost. Simone wondered more than once if Anthony was *her* Rice Anthony.

If it were Rice, wouldn't he identify himself once he found out who she was? *Unless she didn't meet his expectations.* She had seen the scenarios countless times in movies where people on blind dates act as if they were having a good time. When the night ended, one or both decide it wasn't a love connection.

After the guests concluded a second round of singing Happy Birthday, Simone gathered her coat to leave, when Anthony linked his fingers through hers. "I would like to see you again."

Simone's body froze. All night Anthony said the right words, acted like he was her escort to the twin's party, and made her laugh so much, her cheeks ached. Simone stared again into magical brown eyes, deciding what to do.

If he were Rice, she would see him again. If not, then Rice would have a hefty price to pay for making her miss out on a handsome and interested brother. Was this a test of love?

Anthony squeezed her hand. "You've talked to me all night, now you're speechless?" he teased, offering an enticing smile and his one-of-a-kind dimple. "Simone," his voice called softly. "I really enjoyed tonight. I don't want our great time to end here. Say you'll see me again."

"Maybe, you will see me again," Simone said confidently, but inwardly she hoped she wasn't passing up a good man, especially after what Hershey said. She walked to where her sister was waiting. Her legs were shaking and her heart pounding. That could have been from the stupid tight wig. *R-i-c-e…you better not be playing with my head!*

CHAPTER 9

The *Find Me* game was starting to affect Rice even when he wasn't playing. His secret desires had actually brought Simone to Rice's front door. He rubbed his tired eyes. *Now I'm hallucinating.*

When Rice steered the SUV into his driveway, there was a gorgeous woman waiting for him. *It can't be.* It was—Gina Larson. Rice snarled. What did she want? Gina had the nerve to show her face at his house and then dress in that dark-brown designer suede outfit he bought her for a birthday gift. The form fitting pants and the short faux fur and brown-suede jacket still looked good on her.

Enticing—yes; beautiful—no doubt about it. Then Rice added cunning, deceitful, and shallow—and then some. Methodically, Rice turned off the ignition, retrieved his briefcase. He took his time getting out his car. He swaggered up to his front door as if her presence didn't unnerve him. At one time, he really cared about her. Rice nodded. "Gina, why are you here?"

Her professionally applied make-up demanded she be noticed. Her face brightened with a smile meant to please. "To say, I'm sorry."

"Accepted." Rice purposely stared into Gina's hazel eyes that tightly held its secrets and kept the windows to her heart closed. Eyes that at one time had him enthralled. He had felt lucky to be in the presence of such a rare beauty.

Not anymore, beauty can be bought, applied surgically, or blossom from within. He desired the latter. "Good bye." He moved to step around her.

Gina blocked his front door and waved an envelope in front of his face. "I knew you wouldn't take my calls, so I wrote you a long letter and delivered it myself."

"Helping the post office deliver mail? What could you possibly say?" He folded his arms and waited impatiently, occasionally peering down the street, searching for a distraction. "Gina, I'm glad you saved the stamp, but you could've saved your gas. You can't push my buttons anymore."

As her seductive expression registered the shock, the moment was comedic. "Rice," she whined. "I poured out my heart. I searched my soul. I confessed my faults to you in this love letter."

Rice huffed. He was tired, irritable, and just wanted to relax and write Simone. "Gina, what we had ended months ago. So again, I ask, why are you really here, today, now? Wait a minute. Valentine's Day is coming…expecting more sweet treats? There will be none forthcoming."

"I deserved that, especially after the stunt I tried to pull—it was stupid and childish. I know it went against the brotherly bond thing of trying to date best friends. Chalk it up to vanity. When I recently saw you at the movie theater by yourself, I was also there, suffering through my loneliness. I thought or rather hoped we could salvage... Here, it's all in my letter." She pressed the envelope to his chest.

"I only read love letters from one woman, and you could never be her. She's everything you're not, including faithful. Your letter isn't going to change how I feel about her or you."

Gina lowered her lashes shyly. In the past, the gesture would have caused him to succumb to her requests. What a fool he had been.

"If you just read it, I know it will."

"Not this time. I'm already too deeply in love with my lady."

***

A few weeks later in New York, Rice was doing his best to keep a straight face. Three women dining in the same restaurant as he and a client were putting on a show. Body language: a silent, but active form of expressing sadness, anger, or...seduction, Rice recited his own definition.

They were sitting in a corner booth table across from him, giving free lessons, as if Rice was sitting at the head of the class. When his client excused herself to go to the ladies room, their attempts became bolder.

One woman kept puckering her fire-engine-red lips. Rice gave her the benefit of a doubt, hoping she was sucking food from between her teeth. The second woman was blinking wildly as if a lash was caught in her eye. The third woman just posed seductively with an enticing smile that lifted her cheeks to her eyes. Where he was confident Simone was a class act, the trio lacked class.

Rice glanced around. Their antics had caught the attention of several willing patrons. His main concern was flying out of LaGuardia with the blizzard-like snow falling outside.

With the meeting over, he and Mrs. Carson enjoyed a meal while waiting for the company driver to pick them up and hopefully drop Rice off at the airport.

His thoughts drifted to Simone as his client returned just as their food arrived. With little conversation as they ate, Rice picked at his steak and salad meal. He was restless in the crowded hotel-dining lounge. The soft music drifting in the background did nothing to soothe savage travelers.

A group of stranded business airline passengers huddled around a television monitor and listened attentively to the forecast. Great, LaGuardia had suspended all flights. Mrs. Carson declared her meal finished when the driver arrived. Rice checked back in to his suite and phoned his parents' house.

"Hi Mom, I'm just letting you know I'm stuck in New York, maybe for an extra night. At least my meeting went great."

Sharon Taylor gasped. "Oh, that's too bad. I just made a big peach cobbler."

"Thanks for making me homesick, Mama. I'm so ready to get back to St. Louis."

"I hate it when you travel so much and alone."

When would his mother stop worrying? "Well, three women tried to pick me up a while back in the hotel restaurant. Does that make you feel better?" he teased.

"You were wearing that blue pinstripe Christian Dior suit, weren't you?"

Rice squinted in his closet and chuckled. "I was."

Sharon snorted. "Those little wenches smelled money."

"I thought I was at a sleaze bar. It would have been hilarious if it wasn't such a big turn off," he said disgustedly.

"Well, you're almost wealthy, making near a hundred-thousand a year, you're still cute as a button like the day I brought you home from the hospital, and need I remind you? You're single and very available."

"Not really."

"You've met someone?" his mother asked excitedly.

Suddenly Rice heard the phone shuffling as his older brother, Winston came on the line. His questions were rapid and non-stop, causing Rice's mind to recall Simone's last letter.

Rice,

Last night I met you, R. Anthony. Your seductive brown eyes and slow smile captivated me all evening. Rice, were you playing with me last night? If yes, you're in big trouble. If not, you still could be in big trouble—competition.

I desperately wanted him to be you.

Simone

Rice stared out his hotel suite window. He replayed the words of Simone's letter again in his mind. Should he be worried? When he suggested a harmless game of *Find Me*, he really didn't expect Simone to find someone else. He had crushed her letter in his fist. "I must have been crazy to let this go on this long."

"What has gone on this long?" Winston queried.

Rice ignored him. Simone's letter still rattled him. Although his trip was productive, and his client was pleased with the recent sales figures for the new cancer drug, he couldn't focus. Rice was close to forgoing their special date and showing up at her job.

But after he coaxed himself to calm down, he responded with words of love, passion, and hope. God had to help him on the patience part.

Sweetheart,

There is no other woman my heart craves. I believe you, Simone French, were made just for me. Although our relationship has been based on the written word, it has withstood four months of soul searching.

We've shared secrets of the heart, our eyes have searched for the images we've created, and soon we'll erase all the loneliness we endured apart. No, Simi, if I were at the same party, I would have made my presence known. Our hearts would've beaten as one. So close your eyes and count down the days and I'll be there.

Rice, your genuine love

Of course, he didn't mention his ex-girlfriend resurfacing at his house and coincidently, Gina was at a gathering he attended on the same weekend as Simone's siblings' birthday party. The real coincidence was they both were at a party, but not the right ones.

Flames suddenly roared in the fireplace, jolting Rice back to his conversation with Winston. As his brother complained about his job search in the economy, Rice's thoughts drifted involuntarily to

Simone and her interesting relaxation techniques—fireplace therapy.

Dear Rice,

Most people don't like the cold weather, but I enjoy the brisk winds, chilly temperatures, and heavy snow. I'm in awe of the warmth from sitting in front of the fireplace, the glowing embers gently ease my stress away as I relax, and begin to pamper my mind and body.

I know some people call a fire romantic. I call it my quiet time therapy. I have my soft gospel instrumental music playing in the background. No television or phone is competing for my attention, just my mind meditating about all the blessings in my life. It is an activity I don't rush. Plus, this is my time with God to work out my problems. So when you see a nice warm fire, think of me.

Simone

That's all Rice could do was think of her. What he wouldn't give to be with Simone at this very moment. Well not in a hotel room, because he assured her he was strengthening his walk with the Lord.

He loved Simone senseless, if that was believable. And just think, before her, he was like any other red-blooded man. Rice had been drawn to women based solely on looks. How stupid! It was as if a gorgeous woman validated his manhood.

Most women had told him his looks didn't matter. He chuckled. His mother would beg to differ. In all honesty, he learned after the fact that his dates sniffed out money, noted his car, and scrutinized his suits. They proved to be heartless when it came to possessions.

Rice had accepted months ago that Simone might not be a looker, but was someone who filled his heart. He had to bring his paper doll to life soon. *She had to be beautiful*, he thought, *because beauty was in the eye of the beholder.* Simone's passion ignited a fire within him that could not be extinguished. Whenever he wrestled with the doubt, the love for her overpowered him.

"Hey…bro, are you listening to anything I've been saying?"

"Sorry, Winston, man. My mind is elsewhere."

"Or on someone. Mom told me your business trip went well, so who is she?"

Had Rice been that zoned out? "That bad, uh?"

"I hear it in your voice. This time, keep your wallet until you find out where she's coming from. And, watch out for the 'Ginas' out there. I ran into her and her brother. I still can't believe she tried to hit on me while you two were dating, saying we were more compatible. You know it was because I was the better-looking brother."

Rice threw his head back laughing. "Oh, I thought it was because you were pulling in six figures."

"At the time, I was."

Suddenly, Rice heard the ruffling sound of the phone receiver. His mother's voice returned to the phone. "Son, you haven't told me about a new girlfriend."

"Well, we've been writing each other several times a week, sometimes I wrote more than once a day. Mom, I'm in love with her. There, it's out. I've said it. I don't know what she looks like—"

"What made you decide to pursue this young lady in this manner? It's almost my bed time so get to the point." Sharon yawned without trying to hide her fatigue.

"Our relationship has been honest from the very first letter. We had nothing to lose by sharing the truth about ourselves. We've become addicted to each other. Our first date is Valentine's weekend."

"A lot of couples have found happiness after a blind date. Remember, you've invested your feelings, so what you see is also what you get. Still, be on guard and I sure hope you two don't have ugly kids."

CHAPTER 10

In one day, Simone would come face-to-face with Rice. With that on her mind, Simone woke anxious. She slid to the floor. "Lord, help me not to be afraid of the unknown. You gave me the Holy Ghost and that was unknown to me and I've been rejoicing ever since. Give me peace about this too...please. Amen."

When she opened her eyes and turned around, her eyes focused on Rice's phone numbers—cell and home. Somehow, knowing he could be reached was comforting. Several times, Simone had dialed his numbers, only to realize that she had been dreaming.

She refused to use Anthony as a substitute. He had called and sent flowers to the station. The attention was nice, but Rice denied being R. Anthony. So Simone promptly put an end to their communication, refusing any more of Anthony's calls and giving Annette his floral deliveries.

That was too bad, because Anthony was very attractive. Where was her boast that she was beyond looks? Shame on her.

A few hours later, Simone walked into the radio station like a zombie. Her goal was to make it through two shows. Prep for the next day's show and record some promos. She knew she was in trouble when a few guests commented she didn't sound her usual energetic self. During the break Simone had to re-focus, so she could 'perform'.

"Welcome back to 'Don't Get French with Me.' This hour I'm interested in your thoughts about the recent rash of police shootings of unarmed black youths. Talk to me—unless you're driving, then keep both hands on the wheel." Simone looked up to see Glen rolling his eyes. She grinned. The topic alone would jam the phone lines.

She lowered her voice to a pillow-talk tone. "If you're just waking up," she purred before clearing her throat and shouting into the microphone. "GET UP! You're already late for whatever." Simone giggled as Glen adjusted the audio level on the control board, rubbing his ears. That was fun. She had been too serious lately and that had drained her energy.

Fifty minutes later, Annette opened the door and stuck her head in the studio as Simone's theme music ended her show. "How police shootings translated to home schooling totally confused me, but as usual, the lines lit up."

"I know. A few callers tried to sneak that and other subjects in, but I wasn't having it. Police shootings are a serious issue. Since we had the sixth police shooting in south St. Louis in weeks, it's been front-page news. Everybody had an opinion."

"Keep the shows sizzlin', girlfriend."

Removing her headset, Simone stood and grabbed her notes as the next host stormed into the studio with his cup of java. Larry Wilson was a plump retired electrician who hosted a weekly Thursday show on home repairs.

Annette waited until they were alone in the hall before she whispered, "Tomorrow's the big date, huh?"

Later that night, Simone climbed in bed vaguely remembering the day's conversations or events. "I really need to talk to you, Rice," she whispered. She couldn't take her mind off him.

After clicking off the TV, Simone reached for her Bible on a nearby table. She wanted to do anything, but reread his letters, which would make her even more nervous. As she fingered through pages, she couldn't recall one scripture. That was bad. Getting up from her seat, she stirred around the house. After taking a deep breath and before she could talk herself out of it, Simone dialed Rice's home number, which her mind had already memorized.

As she gripped the phone, waiting for the connection, her heart pounded against her chest. Simone shivered from a sudden cold sweat. Simone bit a recently manicured nail as the first ring started. She hung up and collapsed back into her pillow, gnawing on her bottom lip. She was really freaked out.

What if he had picked up? What would he sound like? Would she be disappointed if his voice wasn't deep? Sitting up, she psyched herself with a renewed bravado. She touched redial, then disconnected again. Thanks or no thanks to Caller ID, Rice would know how fickle she was acting. Thank God, he didn't phone her back.

If she couldn't hold it together tonight, she would be a basket case tomorrow. Maybe she should call in sick. With that possibility, she turned off her bed lamp and feigned sleepiness.

***

Rice was simmering tomato sauce for his spaghetti dinner when his phone rang, but stopped by the third ring. He shrugged, thinking it was a wrong number. One thing he didn't do was call a person right back and ask if they called.

If a person didn't leave a message, then he assumed it was a wrong number. However, when his phone chimed three more times within ten minutes, he stormed into his bedroom and checked the Caller ID—S French.

The steam seeped as Rice smiled. "My lady." She was probably nervous. Rice momentarily forgot about his growling stomach as he relaxed in a chair next to the phone and waited. "Don't be scared," he whispered, coaxing the phone like a pet. "Call one more time, baby, and I'll pick it up faster than a DSL Internet connection." He laughed, willing for it to ring.

Seconds turned to minutes and finally an hour had passed. Rice concluded Simone wasn't calling back. When he sat to eat, but couldn't taste his dinner. He contemplated calling her back now that he had a number, then he resigned to the fact that he would just have to wait until the next day.

Later that night, after he stepped out of the shower, Rice checked his Caller ID—no more calls. He was too excited about the next day to be disappointed. He was relieved that their blind date frenzy would end in less than 24 hours.

He glanced across the room at the stack of letters from Simone—almost thirty to date. "That's a lot of love between us," he whispered. He climbed in bed, but couldn't sleep as he recalled his last letter to her.

Hi Babe,

I miss you like crazy, and I love you deeply. I had to write you again today. Are you willing to believe in our love and in me enough that you will say yes to marrying me—sight unseen? If you just fainted, then pick yourself up and sit down. Yes, I'm proposing. This is how strongly I feel about you, about us.

Her response had surprised him.

Rice,

If you are really everything that I've hoped for, and I pray you are, then I'd be a fool to say anything but yes. One condition, as long as it's not this Valentine's Day. I love you with all my being, but I'm still scared.

Simone

Folding his arms behind his head, Rice stared at the ceiling. His mind was made up. Regardless of how Simone looked or what she weighed, he would get on bended knee and ask her to be his wife. Rice didn't care about the outer beauty. He was in love. "Okay, I do care a little, but a sweet woman is a virtuous woman, finer than rubies and stones or something like that in the Bible."

As Rice prepared for bed, he wore a smile thinking about their love, relationship, and future. On his knees, he prayed for forgiveness of his sins and then asked Jesus for the desires of his heart... A few minutes later, he finished and got up.

Rice had just closed his eyes when his phone rang again.

***

"Hello?" Rice answered.

Simone didn't even hear the phone ring as she played a round of Russian roulette with his number. *Say something,* Simone's mind commanded. *Speak,* her mouth shouted. Simone couldn't utter a whispered word. She felt paralyzed.

Sleep had been impossible as Simone leaped out of bed after a catfight with her cover. Maybe because she never went to bed at nine-thirty at night, Simone was more of a nighthawk.

"Hello?" He repeated, chuckling. "Hey, babe. I'm glad you called back," he cooed.

"I'm sorry about hanging up. I was so scared. I'm a fake, a big chicken."

His soothing voice interrupted her babbling. "But you're my chicken and I love you."

His words, his voice, and his patience helped Simone relax. "I love you, too, but I don't know if I can do this tomorrow."

We're both scared," Rice replied in a reassuring tone. "God knows you've been a sweet torture to me. I'm praying I'm everything you want because you're what I desire."

"But—"

"Your looks can't change what my heart feels, Simi."

She smiled as the richness of his voice said her nickname. His rhythmic breathing hypnotized her, and his unwavering confidence in their love strengthened her. However, her doubts still remained. "What if my hair is shorter than what you like?"

"I'll buy you a weave," he teased.

"Funny, Mr. Non-Materialistic Man. What if I'm not the size of a model and overweight?" She compared herself with Hershey, the perfect height and small figure.

"I'll put you on a diet and promise to exercise with you."

Simone mimicked an offending gasp. "Rice!" She giggled as she sensed the love behind his words. They had promised to be truthful with each other. "What if my skin is a darker chocolate than what you want?"

"I'll find out what the late Michael Jackson used and get you a year's supply." They both laughed. "Look, honey. I want the woman who authored the words, the lady who controlled my heartbeat with the stroke of a pen, and the diva who slips into my mind when I'm lonely, driving, or trying to concentrate on something else. I'm all yours." He paused. "If you want me with a beer belly although I never touched the stuff."

Simone never thought about that. *If I want you,* she replayed his words. Rice had no idea as she closed her eyes to capture the sudden tears. "I love you," she whispered, thinking his voice was the best therapy.

"And I love you back."

The phone line went silent. "Rice?"

"Yeah, baby."

"I hear what I've been missing."

"I've longed for you, all of you—your enchanting smile, your revealing expressions, and only God knows what else."

Simone stared at the ceiling as tears escaped. "How can you be so sure when I'm petrified? I could have teeth missing."

"You aren't getting out of our date tomorrow, Miss French." He laughed, "Besides, braces and bridges work wonders."

"I think you are a wonderful man."

"If you believe that, then agree to be my wife."

The man wasn't backing down. He was bold enough to propose in a letter and over the phone. But, somehow, looking into his eyes and watching his lips move would still probably overwhelm her tomorrow. "You sound so sure of what you want, just like in your letters."

"Rice, are you sure when you haven't even met me?"

"I've met you in my mind, my dreams, and my heart. Don't think for one minute that I'm not in tune with your love, desires, and fears. I understand your confusion, but just remember this man loves you."

Simone questioned him about certain letters for hours, often asking him to repeat his thoughts. Time was forgotten until they competed in yawns.

"It's late, sweetheart. See you in the morning, okay?"

"Okay, Rice Anthony Taylor."

"Night, baby."

CHAPTER 11

Rice parked his Durango in front of the building housing KXNG-AM studios. He exited his vehicle with a swagger. Today was a good day to fall in love. He had dressed meticulously, experimented with new cologne, and began his day on his knees giving God thanks mixed with moments of pleading for a happy ending.

What could go wrong after all that? He wondered. Rice's confidence guided his footsteps into the elevator and then stepped off on the thirteenth floor. Flexing his muscles, Rice felt powerful, but very anxious to meet the woman who had seized control over his emotions.

His readied smile faded and the sparkle in his eyes dimmed as a heavy-set white woman stood in front of the receptionist's desk like a security guard, staring him down. Her eyes twinkled with mischief like she was sizing him up for battle. Rice knew Simone wasn't white, although they never had divulged any physical characteristics, but anything was possible.

Should he take the subtle hints and race down thirteen flights of stairs, leaving a trail of red roses?

Suddenly, he realized he was already on an unlucky floor.

Without a smile, in a nonchalant voice, the woman spoke. "Are you lost? May I help you?"

Add a gray wig and some glasses and the woman could easily pass as somebody's wicked step-godmother. With a bright smile, Rice pulled flowers from behind his back. "I'm here to see Miss Simone French, please." The chilling laugh emitting from her throat vibrated throughout the small lobby area.

Ya kiddin', right? Whom might you be young man?"

"Rice Taylor."

"So...you're the one keeping the United States Post Office in business," she said accusingly, shaking her head. "I told Frenchie she could do better. I hope she won't be disappointed."

It was perfect timing when Allan walked out of his office. He offered Rice a grin and a handshake. "Be nice, Annette. The big day, huh?"

"Yep."

"Good, so you're ready for the unexpected?" Allan asked cautiously. "Just remember Simone is a sweet and together sister. Hurt her, and I'll take it as a personal assault on my business. I'm not about to lose my best talent over any nonsense."

Allan glanced at Annette and gave her a sly wink before he faced Rice again. "She has been a nervous wreck for weeks, dressing without fashion coordination, and I could tell she even lost some weight, not that I would consider her overweight."

"Well at least her clothes are matching today," Annette injected.

"Ready for an escort to the studio?" Allan asked and began the trek down a short hall that seemed endless. Rice's uneasiness dissipated as Simone's sultry voice vibrated through the airwaves. This was it. The "on air" sign blinked above a closed door that separated him from Simone.

Allan ushered Rice into an adjacent room with a large window, overlooking historic mansions and Forest Park. "It's a little crowded in here, but you'll find a seat beside those mini disk racks." He pointed to a chair behind a grinning engineer.

"Besides, you'll be able to see Simone better."

Rice was tempted to peek. "Thanks, Allan, I can wait a few minutes longer." *We will do this together.* He closed his eyes, stroking his chin grinning as Simone's voice lulled, excited, and soothed him simultaneously.

"It's Valentine's Day on Friday's edition of 'Don't Get French with Me.' I hope today will be very special for you."

Rice smiled at the humor in Simone's voice as her words flowed with ease. Although he suspected she was on the edge of her seat. When the show ended, he prayed she wouldn't be afraid to begin a new chapter in her life.

Simone exaggerated a long exhale. "I must say, I'm impressed with the men out there, showing their ladies love through poems, songs, and other expressions." She sensed Rice was probably on the other side of the glass because she started experiencing major premature hot flashes. She fanned herself to slow her racing heart.

Minutes earlier, Simone saw Allan and a shadow of a man enter the control room. Glen had purposely turned off the lights—the snake. She couldn't make out any of the man's features except he wasn't short.

Glen's usual laid-back, bored-to-death expression had disappeared. Grinning, Glen hadn't shown his extremely large teeth since one of Simone's guests fell out of a chair while on air. She rolled her eyes.

Can someone let her in on the joke? Did Rice look that disgusting? If the sparkle in Glen's eyes didn't fade soon, Simone would probably throw up. She ignored his amusement and focused on another call. "Finally, I have a woman on the air, Gina, welcome."

"Frenchie, I'm really enjoying the men on your show this morning, girl. They make me miss what I had. But, I'm surprised your man hasn't phoned in. What about your honey?"

There was a pause before Simone responded, "Well, I've got thirty seconds before my next break. What about my man?" She hoped she was wearing extra-strength deodorant today because she was beginning to sweat like she was in the middle of a morning cardio-workout.

"I was kinda of interested in hearing about that special someone in your life. I've never heard you talk about your man. Give us some juicy details. Describe him and the romantic things he does."

Simone huffed. She straightened her shoulders. There went her show's high ratings. If she didn't say something soon, Allan would barge through the studio door for an explanation of dead space going over the airwaves.

She looked up at the studio clock. Five seconds had past. She was busted. She closed her eyes and began to describe the man she saw in her mind.

***

Gina? Had she been calling Simone's show all along or was this some type of a joke or setup? Rice's mellow mood immediately vanished as he sat erect in his chair and gritted his teeth, trying to keep his temper in check. *Please don't let Simone be in cahoots with Gina*, he pleaded.

That's it! Rice leaped to his feet, clenching the plastic-wrapped red roses. What was Gina up to? He hadn't determined if he was more annoyed or angry at Gina's call. Had she learned about Rice's interest in Simone and planned to humiliate her on air?

Well, it wasn't going to go down like that. A few long strides brought him face-to-face with the studio door. He forced it open, and froze. He blinked and commanded his lungs to inhale and exhale. God had indeed answered his prayers.

Simone French seemed to glow like a fuzzy vision. Rice captured the first sight of his angelic mirage and stored the image deep inside his mind for recall. Simone's shoulder-length hair was streaked with different hues of brown, which blended amazingly with her creamy caramel skin.

His eyes traveled downward to her off-white turtleneck sweater, then to her matching wool skirt. Rice guessed she stood about five-one or two without those stiletto leather boots. She was too shapely to be a model, but she could definitely be the mold for a Coca-Cola bottle.

Tears formed in her eyes. "Rice?" she asked in a soft whisper away from the microphone. Restrained by her headset, Simone remained seated, but opened her arms.

"Yes," Rice nodded as he slowly approached, staring into her brown eyes protected by thick black lashes. He knelt down as if he was worshipping her presence before gathering Simone's shaky body in his arms.

Her engineer played a Luther Vandross love song, momentarily taking her off the air. She sniffed and slowly smiled. Simone reached out and stroked his high cheekbones, whispering, "You really do exist," she said with such awe.

"For twenty-eight years."

She dropped her hands on his shoulders and hugged his neck.

The love song ended too soon for Rice as her engineer pounded on the glass, frantically giving Simone hand signals. She motioned for Rice to be seated next to her.

He reached for her right hand and mouthed, "You okay?" When she nodded, Rice caressed her fingers, and offered an encouraging wink.

Taking a deep breath, she spoke into the microphone, "Welcome back to Valentine's Day on 'Don't Get French with Me'. Sorry for the interruption, but my honey just surprised me with a guest appearance. Now back to Gina's question."

"I'd be more than happy to describe him, and then he can tell you what he has planned for us this weekend." She pointed to the extra headset. When she touched his cheek, he trapped her hand and kissed it. He smirked as she squirmed in her seat.

"Stop it," she mouthed. "I'm mesmerized by his six-plus-feet stature. He has the most expressive brown eyes. Silky thick dark eyebrows match a black goatee that frames his full lips." She scanned his chest. "He has an athletic build, but a gentle heart to match his tender touch."

"Humph! Sounds like you've found a winner, Frenchie," Gina sighed heavily. "I need me one of those."

"May I?" Rice mouthed, then adjusted the microphone in front of him. "Gina Larson, this is Rice Taylor. Remember me? You had a good man, and didn't appreciate what I had to offer, so stop your whining and lying."

Simone's mouth dropped. She frowned. He knew her questions were forming. "You dated her?" she mouthed.

Rice scooted his chair closer. "Although she's from my past, she's quickly becoming a present pest. You're my future."

Nodding, Simone disconnected the call. "Gina, Rice is an exceptional man, not only in looks, but also in his heart. The reason why I fell in love with him was his faith in our relationship. That's what held us together."

"Okay, enough of that, I need to regroup, and catch up on my sponsors. We'll take more of your calls on the other side of this break."

When the overhead on-air light blinked off, Simone snatched off her headset. Tears wet both their cheeks as they stood to hug each other.

"Hi again, baby," Rice whispered over and over as they rocked in a tight embrace. He sniffed the banana scent of her hair before he took her face in both his hands.

Silently, their eyes and smiles communicated a happiness that Glen suddenly interrupted, banging on the studio glass—again. With thirty seconds, Simone motioned for Rice to sit beside her. She handed him the headset again.

"Shame on me for doubting my feelings," she confessed. "I really do love you."

"I know." His lips stretched into a warm smile.

When the on air light flashed on, Glen surprisingly cued him instead of Simone. The expression on her face was priceless.

"I'm Rice Taylor and happy Valentine's Day on KXNG. I've stopped by to tell my special lady and sweetheart how much I love her," Rice spoke in a deep rich voice, ignoring Simone's startled expression as the phone lines lit up. Taking her hand he said, "...and to ask her to have enough faith in me to be my wife." His course finger touched her lips. "Baby, please."

Simone wanted to cry for happiness. She became intoxicated with his words and hypnotized by his pleading eyes. Simone realized she cheated herself from hearing his deep husky whisper, and cheated them both by delaying a face-to-face date.

Music and Glen's voice danced circles around her head. Vaguely, she heard herself faintly answer, yes.

"This is Glen Howard, Frenchie's engineer. As you can imagine a live daytime soap is unfolding before my eyes. Let's take a music break, and Frenchie will return in a moment."

Annette barged into the control room screaming, clearly flustered. "Glen, I'm glad you're on top of this show. The past hour has been emotionally perfect for Valentine's Day."

Stalling, Simone listened to every word of Annette and Glen's conversation right before she was about to answer Rice. Gina was the least of her concern at the moment.

Glen grinned. "Yeah...It's the goofiest show I've engineered in six years. I knew something was going down when I spoke to Simone earlier. Although she couldn't seem to focus, her clothes matched today. Now I know why. I don't know who's getting a bigger kick out of today's show, the listeners or management."

"By the looks of the blinking lights on the phone board, our listeners are eating this up."

"Get this...that Gina woman keeps calling back demanding to speak with Frenchie."

"Hmm, I hear firecrackers poppin.' Well, by all means, put her through."

"Certainly." Glen did a poor job on his Three Stooges imitation. "I can always nap with the next host. His topic is on foot care. I can only take so much excitement in one day."

Simone blinked as Rice's soothing words mellowed her during the break.

"We're back with only a few minutes left. I hope your Valentine's Day will be just as special as Rice is making mine." She gazed into his dark brown eyes and catalogued his long beautiful lashes, definitely too long for a man. Good-looking didn't begin to describe him.

She almost fainted when he barged into the studio. She hadn't been able to switch back to her professional mode since. She was ready to begin her dating adventure. Glen signaled for her to take line two.

Simone did as Glen instructed without looking at the name on her computer. "Let's wrap up today's show with your thoughts."

"Frenchie," Gina spoke in a monotone voice. "I can't believe you've hooked Rice Taylor; I guess you're as materialistic as the rest of us."

Rice frowned and reached for the microphone, but Simone held up her hand and smiled. "Gina, don't get French with me." Grinning in triumph, she disconnected.

CHAPTER 12

Finally, the show was over and Rice planned to have Simone to himself not only for the rest of the day, but his life. "Your eyelashes were driving me to distraction and to the point of insanity while you were on the air. You say my name so possessively like you named me …it's so loving and caressing." Rice released a throaty chuckle as his eyes slowly roamed across her face.

Blushing, Simone stood. Her shyness complemented her beauty. She stroked his hair-covered chin. "The way our relationship began and developed is still mind-boggling. You fascinate me."

"And you make me happy."

"Thank you for believing, even when my faith was beginning to waver."

"It was my pleasure." Rice winked, taking her hand. "C'mon, let's make our dreams come true. By the way, you didn't sound too confident when you answered a very important question. You know I'm going to keep asking you until you shout, yes."

"I know."

"As long as you know."

On the way out the station, Simone grabbed her coat and introduced Rice to her co-workers, then Annette, who was dangling the phone in the air. "Gina's holding for you, Frenchie."

"She's already been disconnected." They all roared with laughter, walking out the office.

Rice coaxed Simone into the elevator. When the doors closed, Simone pushed the lobby button and became quiet, not facing him.

"We're finally alone. Why won't you look at me?" He leaned against the wall and opened his arms. "Come here my paper doll."

Simone walked into Rice's arms and collapsed into tears. Rice held her tightly as her body shook with sobs, brushing soft kisses against her eyes. "Why are you crying? I love you," he asked puzzled as the elevator doors opened and an elderly couple eyed them suspiciously.

The gray-haired, pinned-curled woman tapped her cane. "George, maybe we should call the police." George nodded as granny pressed her fingers against her lips. "Get your hands off her!" she lifted her cane for battle. "Honey, are you okay?"

"Step back from that woman, young man." George threatened feebly.

Simone covered her face in embarrassment. "I'm fine, really." She grabbed Rice's hand. "I'm so happy. He just asked me to marry him."

The old woman sighed so heavy, Rice and Simone thought she was about to faint. "George, they're in love. You are going to say yes, aren't you, honey? Oh, I remember my wedding day almost sixty years ago."

Turning to her husband, the old woman smiled before lifting a wrinkled finger and wagging it. "See, George, you worry too much. I knew everything was okay." She patted the couple's hands and scuffled inside the elevator.

Rice threw his head back and released such a deep satisfying laugh that had his eyes watery. He stopped long enough to compose himself and pull Simone into his arms. Slowly he brought her knuckles to his lips for a kiss before he brushed her lips. "I guess we better go to lunch before we create another scene."

Outside, snow flurries drifted around them. Simone snuggled closer to Rice as he helped her into his Durango. They would come back later and get Simone's car. She reached out and held his chin while steady looking into his eyes. "If I wasn't already in love with you, then I would want to fall in love with you."

"Write that down and mail those words to me in a letter." Rice grinned. "My serenade ain't over. I plan for us to fall so deeply in love with each other this weekend, words won't be necessary. We'll celebrate today and then tomorrow post Valentine's Day. First, let's get lunch. I have worked up an appetite."

Less than fifteen minutes later, Rice memorized Simone's facial expressions as she sipped raspberry lemonade. The cozy atmosphere at the Central West End restaurant seemed to relax her. It didn't take long for them to place their orders. However, it seemed like it took forever for them to finish eating. Every few bites, they were feasting on hand caresses, winks, air kissed and smiles. Simone even asked him to recite lines from his past letters, which made her glow. "Remember this one? *'There is no other woman my heart craves. I believe you, Simone French, were made just for me. Although our relationship has been based on the written word, it has withstood four months. It's a relationship I faithfully honor. We've shared secrets of the heart, so close your eyes and count the days and baby, I'll be there.*

"You left out a few sentences, but I remember."

Rice smirked. "Oh, so you've memorized every line of my letters, huh?"

"As a matter of fact, I did," she teased and scrunched her nose at him. "'*Dear Simone, I'm flying to New York again, and of course, I was thinking about you. I know we've discussed so many things over the past weeks and comparing notes. Can I get personal? What makes a woman stay in love with her man? May your days be as lovely as you and your thoughts be filled with the passion of life.*"

Simone paused. "Okay, I want the truth and nothing but the truth." She reached out and touched his cheek with the back of her hand. "Were you trying to hit on me?"

"When I penned that letter, honestly, I don't think my mind knew what my heart was doing. On the surface, no, but my soul was connecting with yours, and didn't want to let go." Rice bit his bottom lip and nodded toward her. "Your turn, tell me you weren't trying to flirt with me with: *Rice, your letters are like a bowl of double-dip chocolate ice cream on a hot summer night. Believe it or not, you inspire me.*"

Simone groaned. "I can't believe I wrote something like that."

"I'm glad you did. Our love will make a believer out of anyone, including Gina." Rice shook his head. He should have never brought up her name. When Simone didn't comment, he gave his complete concentration to her. "Sorry, I'm very happy right now. If anything, Gina brought us together, in a sense; because of her, I stopped and listened to your show until the end to hear what lies she wanted to spin. That's over." Pulling money from his wallet, Rice paid their bill, left a tip and then assisted Simone with her coat when she stood.

After making sure she was bundled up against the cold elements, Rice drove them to *Generations Photography*, a small loft converted studio near downtown, known for its unique style. Photographer and long-time family friend, David Newsome had assured Rice he would be impressed.

"Rice, I don't want to start complaining, but it's getting colder and we're supposed to get more snow. Couldn't we wait for a warmer day to take pictures?"

It didn't take long for him to quickly develop a habit of stroking Simone's narrow nose when he talked to her. "You are my fantasy, woman. Indulge me." He placed a soft kiss on her thick lashes. "I love you so much." How many times had he said those words today?

Once they were inside the studio, Simone's eyes sparkled. David had frozen a video shot of a bright moon, illuminating a clear night sky against a large wall-size screen.

"It's beautiful." Simone turned in Rice's arms and offered him a tight hug.

"So are you."

When she stared lovingly into his eyes, he knew without a doubt they'd done it, blindly gained each other's heart, trust, and love. David flashed the camera capturing their embrace.

Rice exhaled. He had found her—a virtuous woman hidden behind her voice of seduction. As they continued memorizing each other's features, David's flashes continued around them.

"What would you've done if you thought I was disgustingly ugly?" she asked sincerely.

"Beauty is in the eye of the beholder and I was willing to accept my fate with you. You had already possessed my heart. Only God would have set us up like this."

Her fingers played in the waves in Rice's hair. "Do I still possess your heart?"

Rice blinked as David clicked. "Yes."

An hour later, their session was finished and the photographer allowed them to view proofs. Simone softly sighed as Rice alternated between scanning the portraits and her face, making sure his friend captured everything with the lens that he did with his own eyes. "I'm in love with you, Simi French."

David cleared his throat.

"Oh, sorry." Rice grinned. "Email me the proofs of all the shots, and we'll take the Valentine special *Love Story* deluxe package." Although he spoke to David, Rice didn't take his eyes off of Simone.

Shaking his head, David scribbled his order. "You two didn't need me to seize the moment." He examined one pose. "Anybody on the street could see you two glowing from miles away."

"We knew it would be like this when we first met. The sparks were burning up our love on paper," Rice said.

David frowned. "You lost me between 'first met' and 'love on paper'?"

Exchanging glances with Simone, Rice began their story of how love was blind between them. Simone concluded with what happened earlier in the day.

The photographer rubbed his chin. "A love letter, huh? No text or emails?"

"Every woman should get at least one love letter in her lifetime." Simone beamed.

Now Rice truly understood the saying and scripture, "He who finds a wife, finds a good thing." And the woman sitting next to him was not only a good thing, but a fine thang, too.

CHAPTER 13

Bright sunshine nudged Simone awake Saturday morning. It was post-Valentine's Day. She lay in bed with her arms folded behind her head. She glanced at the picture inside the crystal frame, which Rice had given her for Christmas, poised on the nightstand.

David had snapped a shot of Rice touching her cheek as he said something to her. He emailed her the proof while they spoke on the phone late into the previous night. Simone printed it and placed the picture inside the frame before going to bed.

What a difference a day made. The previous day at this time, Simone woke exhausted after tossing and turning most of the night. She had feared she had fallen for a man that she had to keep her eyes closed to love him. It would serve her right for the hypocritical feelings she was experiencing.

Now she reminisced about how their evening had ended. It was as if they had been dating for months as they enjoyed a stage play at the Black Rep, featuring local performer, Denise Thimes, who was hilarious in her role as a rejected lover. That fate could have fallen on them if it wasn't for the Lord playing a hand in their lives. Her phone rang as she was about to get up.

Simone sighed. "Now that's something your letters can't do."

"What?"

"Your voice makes a great alarm clock to wake up to."

"You're the radio personality." They spoke for a few more minutes before he said he'd see her later. An hour later, Simone received a letter via telegram. In it, Rice suggested attending an early morning church service the next morning in celebration of God bringing them together, then perhaps they could meet each other's family. "He's not fooling around." It was odd that he didn't tell her that over the phone.

She gave God a prayer of thanks for Rice making the suggestion. He could have been the type of man who a woman had to drag to church and then glue him to his seat. Simone had seen it happen, only for the man to gradually back out of his commitment to God. It was evidence that Rice had strengthened his walk, because he was taking the lead.

More letters arrived every hour. Rice's short love notes were creating havoc on her senses as she looked forward to their dinner date at six. At five, she expected another letter when she opened the door.

It was a good thing she was dressed, because Rice was on one knee. Simone had never met a man so sincere and yet intense with his feelings. They gazed into each other's eyes, and then exchanged 'I love you'.

Inviting him in, she rushed to comb her hair, and slip into her shoes. She could thank Annette for her fashion sense. Her friend had selected the red dress. Ready to go, they both acknowledged their increased temptation, so they hurried and left her apartment. Once outside, she gasped at the long red strip of fabric that started at her building's front door and ended at his vehicle.

Against the snow and moonlight, it created an elegant illusion as if she was among the elite, the rich and famous. "Rice, did you do this?"

"I know it's corny, but my intent was to make you feel special."

Simone shook her head in disbelief. "You're incredible."

Inside his SUV, Simone clicked her seatbelt, and then turned in her seat. Folding her arms, she watched Rice check his rearview mirror and pull into traffic. There was nothing simple about this man or his love. Simone's heart swelled with fulfillment.

His eyes sparkled when he stole glances in Simone's direction. Rice was well groomed, very attentive, and extremely handsome. How could Gina or any woman allow Rice to walk out of their lives? The thought caused a slow smile. *Thank you, lady.* "Rice?"

Grabbing Simone's hand, Rice guided her fingers to his mouth, softly brushing his lips against them. "Yeah, babe?"

"Are you going to tell me where you're taking me?" She squeezed his hand.

A deep laugh rumbled from Rice's throat. She enjoyed the rich sound.

"No. What happened to all that patience you had during the past months?"

"I lost it," Simone stated flatly, twisting her lips. "It was torture not seeing you, especially after I realized how much you really loved me."

"About us getting married..."

Panic hit her like a brick. Had Rice changed his mind? Simone's vision blurred. "You don't want to marry me now?"

"Where did that come from?" Rice checked his rearview mirror, turned on his signal and exited off the highway shoulder to a gas station. He shut off the engine and gave her a loving look before taking a deep breath.

"Listen to me, Simi." His finger guided her chin closer to his mouth. "I love you. I want to marry you now, right now, woman. But I'm leaving the date—whether it's next week or next year, up to you. I don't want you to feel rushed, pressured, or obligated. You told your listeners you would marry me—barely, but I heard a yes." Rice grunted in amusement, then he drove off the lot and got back on Highway 367. Soon, they were crossing the Missouri River into Alton, Illinois. Not long after that, they arrived at Pere Marquette Lodge in Grafton.

The earlier snow created a picturesque winter wonderland with scattered cabins and the lodge reminding Simone of a Christmas village. "Ooh, this is pretty."

As they trotted carefully through the wet snow to the main building, Simone peered through the large ceiling-to-floor window at roaring flames dancing in a massive stone-and-brick fireplace centered in a huge lounging area—a fireplace. "This is so beautiful."

Inside, Rice helped Simone take off her coat, then led her to an oversized black sofa and two matching love seats positioned in front of the fire. The room was enormous; it had four separate reclining areas, three with fireplaces, and massive overhead chandeliers glistening.

"When I heard about the multiple fireplaces, I thought about you, me, and a warm fire. I wanted to make sure we had time to relax before dinner." Rice glanced at his watch and they made themselves comfortable. "Unfortunately we've only got about fifteen minutes to unwind before our reservation."

The dancing flames were the perfect setting for snuggling. But the game area a few feet away with a room-size floor-model chessboard complete with life-size chessman fascinated her. She watched as children giggled as they played.

"Our first therapy session together."

Nodding, Rice dragged her closer and settled her on his chest. Within minutes, he pierced the quietness with the soft humming of gospel artist Darwin Hobbs' "So Amazing". Rice's smooth baritone voice was hypnotic. He stopped abruptly. "I hope you're extremely happy."

"I am."

Rice whispered as he inhaled Simone's hair. "I want a woman who loves me despite my faults and insecurities. If my woman has to re-mold me, I only want her loving hands to shape me." He gently stroked the soft-red knit jersey fabric on her arms. "I need a woman who's strong when I'm weak, one who's not afraid to love me from the depths of her soul."

She recognized the words from one of his letters. "I could spend a lifetime in your arms enjoying a cozy fire and listening to you."

After their dinner reservation was announced over a loud intercom, Rice slowly disentangled their arms and stood. He guided her down a wide glass-enclosed hallway that overlooked the outdoor wintry scenery. Once they were seated in the large, but cozy banquet room, soft jazz music began to romance them. Flickering candle light welcomed them as an assortment of aromas floated to their noses, enticing them to sample.

In the end, they chose the buffet rather than ordering from the menu. After dinner, they summoned the waiter for their dessert. He returned with a dozen white heart-shaped teacakes on a crystal platter.

Simone's eyes widened to see their names written expertly on each cake in pink icing. Touched, she glanced at Rice who sat quietly watching her.

"Happy post-Valentine's Day, sweetheart. Here, let me do that." He lifted a miniature cake and teasingly coaxed her to take a bite, then it was her turn until the treats were all gone.

"Ready to leave?"

"And realize that I've been dreaming? No," she said chuckling, applying fresh lipstick before standing and then accepted Rice's help with her coat.

During the ride back to St. Louis, they chatted about everything until he delivered her to her doorstep with a kiss that she would dream about all night.

Breathless, she stuttered, "You're not helping us live for Jesus."

"Then marry me fast!"

CHAPTER 14

Sunday marked the last day of their "discovery weekend" and they spent it at God's Blessings Temple. When Rice and Simone entered the sanctuary, people were in high praise. In the short time it took for an usher to find them a seat, the singing was coming to a close as Pastor Williams requested that everybody stand.

Rice grinned and whispered, "I guess we're late."

"We're here and that's what's important to me," Simone said as she knelt to pray and then stood.

The minster continued, "It's time for our one minute of praise, saints. We can't narrow down one thing that God has done for us. Just pick something special that happened to you this week."

All around them the congregation created a thunderous applause. High-pitched and deep baritone voices shouted together nonstop with praises like they were cheering at a baseball game.

Rice had a lot to be thankful for, including internal resolution to move on from the bitter breakup with Gina. Otherwise, his heart may not have been able to patiently hold out for the jewel standing beside him. God had done all right by him.

Simone's voice blended with the others in a shout, "Thank You Jesus for my salvation and bringing Rice and happiness into my life!"

He was humbled that Simone would consider him as a gift from God.

Gradually the praise died down. Re-linking fingers, Rice and Simone sat contently listening to Pastor Williams's sermon entitled, "God Makes No Mistakes in Our Lives."

As he preached from Psalm 37:23: *The steps of a good man are ordered by the Lord and He delights in His way*, Rice reflected on his prayer life that changed for better when Simone entered his life.

"Don't you know that God delights in doing great things? Then why are we depriving Him of blessing us? Sometimes we hinder ourselves…" the man of God continued.

Almost an hour later, the pastor wound down his sermon and appealed for sinners to repent and be baptized. "Acts 2:38 says, '*Repent, and be baptized every one of you in the name of Jesus Christ for the remission of sins, and ye shall receive the gift of the Holy Ghost'*. Salvation is a process that includes repentance, the cleansing of your sins through simple water baptism, and then the anointing of the Holy Ghost. God will speak through you with tongues. Come today." He stretched out his arms.

"Have you been baptized?" Simone asked.

Rice shook his head. He never thought it was necessary. "Have you?"

Leaning closer, she lowered her voice, "Yes, but I never thought the Holy Ghost was necessary."

The pastor pressed the crowd, "You don't have to leave church today the same way you came in. This is a weekend of love. Besides showing your sweetheart you love her, show God. Surrender to Jesus this moment. Obey His Word and God will make a promise to you and your generations after you."

Frowning, Rice considered the invitation. He had attended this church off and on for years and never stayed for altar call.

Abide in Me, and I in you, God spoke in the wind.

And Rice caught His whisper at the same time Simone squeezed his hand. He looked into her soulful eyes.

"Let's do this together. If we believe God brought us together, then let's surrender, and believe that Jesus will keep us together."

Standing, Rice entwined his fingers with hers. Together, they walked down the aisle to complete God's plan of salvation.

At the altar, a minister prayed for them and explained the power of the Water and Holy Ghost baptism. Minutes later, Rice had exchanged his suit and tie for a white T-shirt, pants, and socks. As he descended into the pool, a minster was waiting for him while Simone stood nearby to witness his surrender.

He mouthed 'I love you' to her, and then repeated the declaration to God. Seconds later with his arms folded, the minister said, "My dear brother, upon the confession of your faith and the confidence we have in the blessed Word of God, concerning His death, burial and Grand Resurrection, I now indeed baptize you in the name of Jesus for the remission of your sins. Amen." The minister buried him under water, then Rice came up rejoicing for every blessing in his life.

Once he changed back into his street clothes, he and Simone were ushered into a small chapel where women were praying for individuals. One instructed them to have a seat anywhere. An elderly woman came and sat next to them and instructed them to pray in a manner like never before.

"I'm Mother Hines. Now, I want you to open your mouth and let your heart speak to Jesus. Remember, we can't pray to the Lord without worshipping him first…"

Closing his eyes, Rice fell to his knees and began to cry out to Jesus. Soon he heard an explosion of tongues come from Simone's mouth. Before he could open his eyes to see the manifestation of what people called the Holy Ghost, the anointing hit him and he was speaking uncontrollably in a language he hadn't learned in school until tears streamed down his cheeks.

A while later, after Rice composed himself, Mother Hines congratulated them on their new lives and hugged them. The church was almost empty when they, along with others who were in the room, left.

"Thank you," Simone was the first to speak inside his vehicle.

Rice rubbed his thumb over her hand. "For what, sweetheart?"

"For including church in our weekend dating plans. I might not have ever experienced this on my own and I'm so glad I did with you."

"Me too." He squeezed her hand. "I think I can be a good boy around you now until our wedding day."

"Me too." She smiled. "Ready to meet my siblings, the twins?"

"Yep. After that sermon, I'm ready for anything."

But thirty minutes later, Hershel and Hershey French proved to be a challenge to Rice's newfound happiness.

"You're getting married?" They yelled in unison.

"Not to *the* paper man?" Hershey queried with a worried expression.

Hershel frowned. "He delivers paper? Simone I'll not allow you to support a man who won't get a decent job," he threatened.

"What?" Rice asked Simone.

Holding up her hands, Simone tried to calm them down and began to explain how they met.

"I can't say I'm getting good vibes about this," Hershey paused. "What do you really know about him? Are you sure he has never served time?"

"What!" Hershel jumped to his feet, standing erect with fists thrust in his waist. "You sure know how to pick them, baby sister. Of all the men I could have fixed you up with, you chose a parolee." Hershel paced the floor like he was prosecuting a criminal in the courtroom.

"Rice, you're saying you had no idea what my sister looked like, huh? Why do I find that hard to believe, considering her picture's in the paper every now and then?" Hershel folded his arms. "Your game is weak, if you expect me to believe something like that, man."

For the next hour, Rice was cross-examined about his education, financial portfolio, and family background. The twins took notes, compared notes, and held conference breaks before mellowing down.

Mimicking her twin, Hershey folded her arms and tilted her head. "My brother does make an excellent point. Well, Rice I guess you won't mind if we run a police check on you."

This time Simone jumped up. "What!"

Rice held up his hand. "Hershel and Hershey, you two don't know me, but Simone holds all my secrets. I will not let you tear us down," he stood eye-to-eye with Hershel, well almost. "Although what you're asking me is an intrusion into my privacy, I will gladly submit to a police, credit, and physical exam if that will make you feel better."

"Done. That way we'll know what we're dealing with," Hershey and Hershel responded together without hesitation.

Rice enfolded Simone in his arms to soothe her downcast look. "It's all right, honey. I have nothing to hide."

Less than an hour later, the couple left in a sober mood. Rice expected some resistance, but the prison thing was a stretch. "Well, babe, God prepared us for this, because prior to church, I wouldn't let another man insult me like that and still have his front teeth.

"I guess it's our first test…I think you passed."

Twenty minutes later on the other side of town, Rice parked in front of his parents' home.

Simone was twirling hair behind her ears.

"Nervous?"

"Should I brace for a repeat performance?" She asked.

"Not even close. Let's pray," he suggested, reaching for her hands. "Jesus, Lord we know we are walking in Your will. Please fight our battles. Amen."

Rice got out of his SUV and walked around to the passenger side and helped Simone out. Strolling up the walkway, he squeezed her hand. His mother opened the door before he could insert his key.

He encircled her in a warm hug, and then made the introductions. "Simone, this is my mother, Sharon Taylor."

His mother embraced Simone with genuine warmth and that's when Simone physically relaxed.

"She's much prettier than the last one," Sharon commented proudly, "and not as snooty and uptight. I like her."

"Mom." Rice said a second prayer, hoping his mother would be on her best behavior.

Sharon stepped back, held her hands to her chest, and released a hearty laugh. "Sorry, I'm not usually rude and forgetful, just forgetful." They all laughed.

A booming voice approached from around the corner. Winston Taylor strolled out of the kitchen clenching a thick, double-decker sandwich in one hand. He was known for raiding his parents' house for a snack before heading to his own apartment minutes away to eat again. As Winston approached the foyer, he stopped dead in his tracks.

"Whoa, bro, who is this?" shock, surprise, and amazement played across his face. Winston easily forgot about his food as he leaned against the wall. "Please tell me she has some sisters?" he asked. "I'm harmless, really. So, this is the woman behind the voice?" He took a bite from his forgotten sandwich and started chewing, thinking out loud. "How…when…where did you two…so this is the one…hmmm. Really, do you have any sisters as gorgeous as you?"

"I have a sister who *is* gorgeous, but she's more than a challenge."

Winston's laugh was deep and rich like Rice's. "I'll remember that when I'm mentally ready for a battle. It's still nice to meet you, Simone."

Rice's sisters walked into the foyer and barely hugged him staring at Simone as he grabbed her hand. "Simone French, these are my two sisters, Brenda and Tina. Ladies, the woman I plan to marry, so don't scare her away," Rice said as he pulled Simone through the hall, ignoring their gasps and Winston gagging on his food.

"You're engaged?" Tina asked in a whisper.

"To the most sought-after female media personality?" Tina added, trailing behind them.

A few hours later, after re-hashing the details of their meeting, the Taylors congratulated the happy couple and then left them alone in front of a warm fire in the family room.

Rice exhaled and stretched his arm along the back of the couch around Simone. "Since we have God's blessings, my family's blessings, why wait on your folks to get married? Two out of three ain't bad."

CHAPTER 15

On Monday morning, Simone was back at work, behind the mike, and a different woman than she was when she left on Friday. She fingered her bracelet from Rice as she was about to broadcast the last hour of her show, Rice was probably boarding the plane.

"Hey, St. Louis, it's Monday, and I'm Frenchie comin' at ya in three, two, one... Before I open the phone lines for your calls, I want to say to my female listeners, I hope your sweetheart made you feel real special this weekend."

"You're my first caller. Talk to me," she said with a smile.

"Good morning, Frenchie, my name is Jason. This past weekend marked my mother's tenth year cancer free, so we had a big Valentine's party for her and other breast cancer survivors attended."

She wasn't expecting such a serious topic, but Simone welcomed the topic that addressed serious issues, especially those affecting the Black community disproportionately.

"What a wonderful expression of love. Praise God she's a survivor. Blacks are usually diagnosed in the latter stage of the disease when it's too late. The lack of adequate medical insurance, proper education and the lack of trust in doctors are factors that cause us to die at a higher rate," Simone snuck in that shout out to God and hid her giggle.

"I agree, Frenchie. Although my mom's doctor didn't waste any time on her treatment once she was diagnosed."

"Thanks, Jason, for setting us up this hour. Women who have survived breast cancer—their treatment and the illness, call in and share your personal experience right after this short break."

During the commercial, Simone's phone lines lit up. As the music faded, Simone punched line two. "Welcome to the show."

"Hi Frenchie, this is Gina…"

Not again. Simone rolled her eyes and held in a sigh. Before her show on blind dating, she couldn't recall the woman ever calling in.

Gina continued, "I know how sweet Rice can be. How sweet was he to you this weekend?'

How dare this chick call and jeopardize the serious nature of her show with a personal vendetta. "Gina, that's not the topic for discussion this morning."

"Let's make it the topic. After all, it's open line," the woman snapped.

"Let's not. As a matter of fact, don't get French with me." She disconnected and signaled Glen to block out her number. The show continued without another hitch.

Afterward, Simone walked out of the studio heavyhearted about the large number of young women battling cancer. She would have to pray for them, then she was irked that Gina had the nerve to harass her over the air.

Annette stood waiting for Simone at the receptionist's desk. "Good show, crazy woman, and sad topic, but you held it together. Rice would be proud," she said, grinning like a proud mother. "Okay, details girlfriend about the weekend, details." She smacked her lips like a dog waiting for mealtime.

"And if I don't," Simone teased, trying her best not to smile.

"Oh well." Annette shrugged and began to walk away before glancing over her shoulder. "I guess this letter from fine Mr. Rice-a-Roni remains in my hands."

She tried to yank the envelope, but Annette moved back. "Don't play, or you will get hurt." She grinned, but was really serious.

"Okay, I'm sold on Mr. San Francisco Treat." Handing over the goods, Annette laughed and headed back to her office.

Simone caressed the pink envelope tied with a rose-colored wired ribbon. "When did he have time to do this?" she wondered.

To my baby,

I know words brought us together, but now there are no words to express my feelings for you and every sweet moment we shared this weekend. I fell in love with you over and over, woman. Thank you for letting me love you. The unexpected plus was sealing our relationship with a commitment to God.

I'll call you as soon as I return Thursday night. Have a good show today, and smile often when you think of me. Hugs, kisses, smiles, and more kisses,

Rice

Simone refolded the letter with misty eyes. She gathered her purse and left. As she was about to step into the elevator, an extremely beautiful woman walked off.

"Frenchie?" the stranger asked, but her tone indicated she already knew.

"Yes."

"I thought so. I recognize your voice."

Simone recognized the attitude. "Gina." *God, You just saved me, please send this devil back.*

CHAPTER 16

"She did what!" Rice was heated after Simone retold Gina's stunt. His ex had crossed the line. He didn't care if Simone did put her in her place—in the sweetest Holy Ghost spirit she could muster—while Annette was ready to lash out. In the end, security escorted Gina out of the building.

Somewhat placated, Rice switched subjects and started talking about his favorite topic—Simone. They regaled about their past weekend and whispered words of love until she begged off the phone, so he could get back to work.

Now, glancing out his hotel window, Rice was itching to call Gina and threaten her to stay away, but God intervened and told him to pray for her instead. Once he did, Rice returned to his work.

Before Simone called, Rice was in the process of reviewing marketing concepts to expand new pharmaceutical drugs in larger markets. He shared his findings in morning seminars and at a luncheon.

His eyes blurred from reading sales figures and performances. *Enough,* Rice's brain screamed from fatigue as he stood and stretched his weary body and massaged his stiff neck. Since it was late evening, he showered and ordered room service.

Rice was about to turn in when he realized he hadn't checked his voice messages at home. One was from a solicitor; the other was a husky voice he recognized immediately.

Rice,

You are so sweet and thoughtful. You overwhelmed me before last week, your love saturated me Valentine's weekend, and even now while you're away, you are still incredible. Thank you for the letter that was waiting for me this morning. Now, when I close my eyes, I'll see you.

I keep asking myself if I'm dreaming. Did you have any idea it would be this wonderful between us? I called because a piece of paper and pen can't hold my words of love anymore.

Bye.

Smiling, Rice saved the message and disconnected. He wondered how long Simone would have him wait to marry. He wanted to make love to her so badly—before and after he met her. Thank God that Jesus saved both of them in time before their innocent love would have shamed them both. Despite talking twice earlier, he had to place one more call before he read his Bible and went to bed.

"Hello? Rice?" Simone's drowsy voice whispered into the phone.

"Hi, babe. Sorry, it's so late."

"Your calls are always welcome."

She always made him feel privileged. "I loved your message as much as your letters." They chatted for about an hour until Simone yawned. "Say you miss me," Rice demanded softly, listening for the response he knew would lull him to sleep.

"Of course, I miss you." Simone paused. "And, I love you, too."

"But I love you more."

CHAPTER 17

If the rain, sleet, hail, and snow didn't stop the postal service from delivering mail, then the weather wasn't going to keep Simone away from surprising Rice later at the airport. Forecasters had predicted two or more inches of snow, gusty winds, and bone-chilling temperatures.

Dressing warm, but fashionable against the elements, she boarded the city's light rail to the airport, so she could ride back with Rice. Simone had almost gone insane with loneliness while he was away.

Once inside Lambert airport, she purchased two long-stemmed roses at a kiosk. Waiting outside the security checkpoint, Simone occasionally sniffed the flowers as she eyed the terminal for arriving flights.

She fingered the Mahogany pocket-greeting card in her hand. Simone couldn't resist the tiny pages filled with one-liners that described so eloquently how she felt about Rice.

Her sister, who somewhat accepted her relationship with Rice, and a couple friends had always warned her against "surprising *your* man because *you'll* be the one left with a surprise." Rice was not that kind of man.

Checking the monitor confirmed that his flight was on time. Simone's heart raced as she leaned against the wall, waiting. She didn't encourage a few men's appreciative stares and flirtatious hellos. Usually she shied away from attention, but that night she felt like taunting every man with an *eat-your-heart-out-I-belong-to-Rice* attitude.

Simone inspected her makeup again. It was flawless. She shifted in her heels, growing impatient. Finally, through the throngs of travelers, she spotted Rice. She admired his Shemar Moore handsome looks and confident gait with a physique that drew the attention of several ladies in the terminal, which he ignored.

Although it was her surprise, Rice searched the faces, as if he sensed her presence. Once they locked stares, his features softened as his smile widened. Swiftly he approached Simone as a predator and without saying a word, lifted her off the ground and presented her with the sweetest kiss.

"Did I tell you I love surprises?"

"You just did," Simone said.

EPILOGUE

On the first night in June, about fifty family members and friends gathered in a small, white renovated historic chapel.

Simone was in her dressing room when a pink envelope slid under her door. There wasn't a knock, just the heavy footsteps of someone walking away.

Scooping it up as if it were a precious gem, she smiled and sniffed the envelope—the scent of roses. As she opened it, white rose petals spilled to the floor. In gold ink, he had penned his last love letter as a single man.

There were only a few words, but their value was worth a fortune to her.

Simone,

Words of Love are meant to linger long after they're written. I can't wait to show you that I'm indeed the man worthy of your love, trust, and desire. Watch me, baby. I plan to back up my words until I take my final breath.

Rice, your soon-to-be husband

LOVE AT WORK

CHAPTER 1

Desiree King looked forward to each New Year. She couldn't help but be excited about the new possibilities, blessings, and yes, even challenges she was sure to experience.

Normally, she didn't get caught up in the yearly craze of making resolutions. Besides, it was a matter of time before each declaration began to fizzle.

But this year, on a whim, Desiree decided why not toss a few of her own resolutions into the ring. She had her priorities set.

First, Desiree vowed to God to increase her prayer life, then maintain a healthy lifestyle, and last, get back into the dating scene to attract a good Christian man. To help in that department, her best friend, Malinda Thompson, suggested the two of them should try some gradual makeovers to snag a brother's attention.

Although Desiree agreed, it really wouldn't matter. Who would notice her? Desiree's job had been the real culprit that hindered her from attending many of the Friday night services at church that catered to singles.

Then one week into January, something unusual occurred. Never in her three years as an assignment editor for KDPX-TV had Desiree received an anonymous letter. The sealed envelope was hidden among other items in her designated mail slot.

Tucking it under her arm, she headed to her work station. Jokingly, Desiree called the assignment desk the circus area. On some days, it was like a zoo when everything exploded, overwhelming the newsroom.

The assignment desk was more like a service counter rather than an actual desk or cubicle. It was the newsroom's central command center. The person manning the post had to monitor several radio and television stations' news stories.

If that wasn't enough, emergency, fire, and police scanners occupied most of the back wall. When breaking news happened, it was Desiree's job to dispatch a photographer with or without a reporter to any location to cover the story.

Her goal, along with the entire news team, was to beat the competition to the scene and report it first on the air.

At her work station, curiosity about the envelope got the best of her. She broke the seal.

Desiree, I'm not shy, but I'm respectful of your time while at work as well as my own.

Oh boy. She took a deep breath. What rumor was stirring in the newsroom now? Bracing herself for some kind of complaint or gossip, Desiree continued reading.

I'm very interested in getting to know you. Besides being gainfully employed, I'm single, never been married, and have no children. I do have three adorable little nieces. You would like them. They're heartbreakers in training, thanks to my sister.

Huh? Frowning, Desiree was dumbfounded. Was this supposed to be akin to a love letter?

If so, she had not received one of those since…first grade when cute Peter Jones was practicing his cursive letters and sent her a sloppy I love you note. Desiree exhaled and finished.

I'm a Christian who believes in practicing what the pastor preaches. I give God more than lip service. If my approach is too forward or too juvenile for you, and you don't wish to receive another letter from me, you can unsubscribe from any more of my intentions by marking on the outside of this envelope, "return to sender."

Okay. This had to be a prank. Although Desiree didn't preach the Word per se at work, she did wear her allegiance to God on her sleeve in her treatment of others. Dismissing the note, Desiree shoved it to the bottom of her purse and forgot about it.

A week later, another sealed envelope was tucked in her mail slot.

Yesterday, as I sat in the newsroom, your beauty constantly distracted me. If you're thinking this is a prank, it's not.

I'm just a man who appreciates God's amazing handiwork. I hope your interest is at least piqued. Texting, phone calls, and dates are more my style, but I'm biding the right time.

Her so-called secret admirer had lost his mind. It was a well-known fact among her colleagues that she did not date on the job. There were no exceptions!

Cheez, did she have to send out a mass email to reiterate her position? If she received one more letter, Desiree would take it to personnel and let them deal with the harasser.

At twenty-seven years old, Desiree had, so far, evaded potential coworker-wannabe-suitors at the St. Louis NBC affiliate. When someone tried to cross the line into her personal affairs, she steered them back toward topics she deemed work-related.

She had good reasons to be so adamant. Then there were the cheating spouses right under her nose. One, in particular, came to mind. The sheriff had delivered divorce papers from John's wife who worked upstairs in the business office. Stupid. How he thought she wouldn't find out was mindboggling.

It had been a big mess. Newsroom staffers didn't need to post anything on Facebook or Twitter. The blabbermouth mill was faster than the Associated Press news wire service. If she had been the judge and the jury, Desiree would have fired the offender on the spot, but she had no say in other people's affairs.

Desiree had been up-close-and-personal with a few female coworkers when they got trashed through office gossip about their sexual escapades. As her heart bled for them, she did her best to offer them kind and encouraging words. However, the damage had been done. Two of them never regained their respect from their peers.

At the start of another week, Desiree walked through the newsroom door with a smile. She hibernated all weekend except for church. Shifting her coat in one arm, Desiree nodded at a few coworkers.

She stopped at the bulletin board to read the latest company news and then strolled to the mail slots. It was amazing how much mail was delivered on Saturday in a mad rush to get press releases there by Monday. Without looking through it, she headed to her work station.

Shifting in her chair, Desiree laid her mail aside as she logged into the computer to scan the notes from the overnight crew. Multitasking, she absentmindedly fingered through the stack. She froze when she spotted another letter that bore the same handwriting.

This had to stop. Angling her head, Desiree performed a slow sweep of her surroundings. She took in every nuance of everybody and -thing in her peripheral vision.

Most of the day-shift reporters and writers hadn't arrived yet, so the newsroom was fairly empty. "This is getting old—quick," she griped, ripping the thing open.

The third note went for the kill: *I can continue to write you letters, but I don't want that. I need to know would the affections be mutual if you learn who I am. Will you meet me for dinner this Friday at 7 P.M., at the Melting Pot in Chesterfield? I'll do everything in my power for you not to regret it.*

"Hey, Desiree," someone called out, approaching her.

Startled, Desiree looked up, almost falling out of her seat. Bunching up the paper, she shoved it under a stack of folders. "Good morning, Greg." Desiree felt like a robber caught with stolen money glued to her hands.

She groaned, hoping she didn't look guilty. But to any seasoned news hound, she probably did.

"I need…" He paused, blinked, and then stared at her. "Wow. Whatever you did to your hair, it's working for you. You look hot." He peered over her shoulder to a classroom-size white chalkboard that listed the schedule of who was working that day.

"Thank you." She got her first compliment on the subtle highlights in her normally dark hair. Plus, Desiree let Malinda talk her into getting soft bangs. Even her stylist agreed that it gave her a sassy look.

"Can you spare a photog so I can get a couple of random shots of downtown St. Louis businesses for my story?"

Turning around, Desiree checked the chalkboard, too, against what was scheduled for the day. From that moment on, it was one request after another. People asked, and Desiree was expected to make it happen.

Surprisingly the day was filled with more compliments. All of them didn't come from her male coworkers. Desiree's female counterparts also raved about the outfit she was wearing. She blushed from the accolades. Desiree had simply added bold shades of red to her dark clothing.

Throughout her busy day, her mind drifted back to the third letter. She questioned if it was an ambush to humiliate her or genuine adoration. Any other time, there wouldn't be any hesitation. Her answer to going on a blind date would be an automatic no.

That was before her New Year's resolutions and her pastor's request that all members adhere to 3 John 1:2: *Beloved, I wish above all things that thou may prosper and be in health, even as thy soul prospers.*

Elder Harrison instructed, "Don't get sidetracked. I don't want you to focus only on the financial prosperity. Seek a healthy walk with God and a healthy lifestyle, which includes taking care of your body." He added, "Do this for a year, and see what God does in return."

So it was her pastor who caused her to reflect on other aspects of her life in conjunction with that scripture. Health wise, she was in fairly good shape. She exercised at home. Plus, Desiree naturally preferred fruits and vegetables over junk food. She was already increasing her prayer life daily.

In regards to her social calendar, Desiree needed divine intervention to prosper in that area, too. Working sporadic excessive overtime put a damper on attending church sponsored singles events.

If Desiree did make a function, she was literally part of the Johnny-come-lately news team. With women outnumbering men in the churches, Desiree didn't stand a chance.

Suddenly, the last note came to mind.

Will you meet me for dinner at the Melting Pot in Chesterfield this Friday at 7 P.M.?

Was this a serious date proposal or a practical joke disaster? Maybe she should go just to put a stop to the distracting notes. Evidently, someone thought he could bend her rules. Maybe it was time for her to set him straight. Yeah, that's exactly what she was going to do. Set him straight.

***

Friday morning, Desiree and Malinda coordinated Desiree's dinner date. While Malinda was excited, Desiree was skeptical if this was God's setup.

"I'll follow you to the place," Malinda confirmed.

Desiree nodded even though they were on the phone. "Yeah, it's time to put an end to this secret admirer finale." She gnawed on her bottom lip, which was already sore from the previous night's jitters.

"I still can't believe I'm stupid enough to fall for this. My integrity is on the line."

"Who knows? Your future happiness could be at stake, too. If this is the real deal—which you won't know until you go—then I wouldn't chance missing out." Malinda had recapped the admirer's messages. "He said he was single, a Christian and attracted to you. That alone makes him three strikes ahead. What else do you want from the man, his DNA?"

"Honestly? For him to get another job. We work in a busy newsroom where rumors are breaking news. How do two coworkers basically work undercover to find romance?"

"Ooh, I would love to be a fly on the wall to find out. Desiree, you can't let other people's bad choices keep you from experiencing God's blessings."

"If this blows up in my face, my reputation will be ruined and I'm ex-communicating you."

Malinda laughed. "Girl, please. We serve a great big God. We're committed all year to petitioning Jesus for our spiritual growths, natural needs and desires of our hearts. Put this under the wish list."

Desiree was having second thoughts. This was not how she envisioned God blessing her social calendar.

"Wasn't that why we bought that book with advice on doing different fashion tips every day of the year? Girl, your makeovers are probably what did it, and just think, the month isn't over."

Sometimes, Desiree thought, her friend was too whimsical in her thinking. Their makeover goal was to attract single brothers in the church, not single coworkers.

"We already went through this last night. I'll wait in the parking lot. If it seems like a setup, text me, then I'm coming in to be your date for the night. Girl, if I have to do that, then you'll owe me big time for splitting an eighty-dollar dinner tab."

"Right." Money was the least of Desiree's concerns.

"Shouldn't we give each other code names like the first presidential family?"

Desiree chuckled. "No. This is not a covert operation."

"This could be so much fun if you'd use your imagination. Speaking of which, you don't have any idea who's behind the notes?"

With fifteen reporters, nine of them were male, which included six new hires in the past months. It could be one of the three Black men, but one was supposedly happily married. There were the two Latinos and a White guy. She had to give KDPX their kudos. They enforced diversity in the workplace. It was a plus that all of the male reporters were good-looking.

"I'm clueless."

CHAPTER 2

Will she show tonight? Brooke Mitchell wondered as Desiree sashayed into the newsroom that morning. Leaning back in his chair, he grunted as men around him drooled. Women near him whispered about Desiree's attire. She was a showstopper with little effort.

Oozing with confidence, her mannerisms were professional at all times. Black women would be proud that she led the pack at KDPX when it came to breaking news.

Unfortunately, there was no hint in her mood that she was eager about anything special happening after work. Brooke hoped, he prayed, and he even wished she would take a chance and accept his blind date request.

As an award-winning investigative reporter who hailed from Little Rock, Brooke did his research on her and assessed his findings. She wasn't married, didn't have any children, and as far as word from the newsroom rumor mill was concerned, Desiree King didn't bring drama into the workplace.

She guarded her personal life like a bank vault. If Desiree entertained a male friend, no one had ever met him. Some even joked that if she was an axe murderer, it would be news to them.

He smirked to think this station recently won an Emmy for the number one investigative team in St. Louis. Yet, that was the best information they could learn about one of their own.

Brooke worked among the elite. He dug deeper for any blemishes in Desiree's character. So far, they were as clear as her flawless honey tone skin. Her eyes were a rich dark brown. She was a knockout. How could any man not fall for her?

What was Desiree's story?

Even after his last dating disaster on a job a few years ago with reporter Andrea Turner, that fiasco didn't scar him for life. At the time, Andrea wasn't a Christian and neither was he, so the score was even. Her objective was to snag the new kid on the block at the station: him.

After the messy fallout, the woman moved on emotionally. After Brooke's contract ended, he moved on physically. He was still willing to take another plunge at finding love. At thirty-one years old, he was ready to settle down.

From what Brooke could surmise, Desiree was a genuine Christian woman. She always had kind words and compassion when circumstances arose out of her control.

As she slipped off her wrap, he assessed her again. Did he say she was gorgeous? His mind answered, *You did.* How could she be stunning in a black knee-length sweater dress, black tights that showcased shapely legs, which were his weakness, and black ankle boots? It wasn't the first time he had seen her in black, but she glowed tonight.

Brooke was sure he wasn't the only one to notice Desiree had tried different styles with her vibrant tresses all week. What was up with her? Was another man outside work wooing her, or was it because of her secret admirer—him? Brooke exhaled.

Wouldn't that be wishful thinking? Clearing his thoughts, Brooke returned to work mode. With leads to chase down on a story, he picked up his phone and got busy making calls until the morning staff meeting.

Afterward, Desiree assigned Brooke a photographer and dispatched them to a breaking news story. Students were trapped inside a school building whose roof had collapsed because of a recent snowfall. Grabbing his stuff, Brooke and Sylvester "Sly" Westin didn't waste any time heading out the door. By the time they arrived on the scene, all of the children were out and a few adults were injured while trying to rescue them, but the building sustained some major damage.

Brooke returned to the newsroom hours later with unanswered questions. Yes, St. Louis had some recent heavy snow accumulation, but that building looked fairly new and should have held up. He went to work researching back stories that talked about any problems with maintenance of city schools.

He had lost track of time when Desiree approached his desk. "Brooke, I need you and Sly to give me a live shot at five in front of Styx School. If you need anything, let me know. I'm sure you'll do a good job."

Not waiting for his response, she walked away, but her sweet fragrance stayed behind.

"Blink, man." Sly chuckled. The veteran photographer was the first one to befriend him when he arrived. Brooke soon learned why. Sly told things as he saw it, and he didn't care who it was. Sly was also a prankster when the mood hit him. "Stop watching me and pack up your gear," Brooke joked then turned back to his computer to log off. A few minutes later, his eyes strayed back to the assignment desk.

Desiree's curls were piled on top of her head with a few riotous strands framing her face. Her earrings were larger than usual, but not gaudy. To him, she always dressed nice, but not over the top. Not like someone who might as well work in a nightclub. *Would she show?* Brooke wondered one more time. He glanced at the time on his cell phone, knowing he needed to hurry and get back to the location of the roof collapse. The good news was the principal was able to get all two hundred and fifty-three students out safely. The bad news was classes would have to be held elsewhere.

Clearing his throat, he trekked across the room. This was his last chance to feel her out. She was on the phone when he approached the assignment desk area. Desiree held up her finger. Her nails were polished, but nothing extravagant.

Brooke stuffed his hands in both pants pockets and waited. Lowering his lashes, he continued his assessment. *Lord, let her show.*

When her conversation seemed like there was no end, he pivoted to leave. He didn't want anything anyhow.

"Ready?" Sly asked as he finished packing up his tripod and camera.

"Yep."

Brooke was almost out the door when Desiree called his name. She was on his heels. "I'm sorry about that. I was on hold to get an update on a patient's condition for Brad's fire story. Did you need anything for your live shot?"

With Sly and Desiree staring at him, Brooke wracked his brain for an excuse. "I'm set. The school superintendent is meeting us there for an interview. Have a good weekend." *And meet me for dinner.*

"You too." Nodding, she hurried back to the assignment desk as the phones started ringing.

Inside the news van, Sly grunted as they buckled their seat belts. "That is one fine woman. Too bad she plays hard to get with her sweet self." He twisted his lips as if he was enjoying the last bite of a homemade dessert.

Brooke fingered his mustache and glanced out his window. He shrugged. "Maybe she's just waiting for the right man to come along."

"Well, here I am, brother." Sly laughed. Checking his rearview mirror, he pulled off all while Brooke wondered if she would show.

CHAPTER 3

After the five o'clock broadcast, Brooke raced home to freshen up. He took a record-breaking shower and dressed in black slacks and a turtleneck. He wanted to be early. If he wasn't, she was sure to think a number of things, including it was all a joke.

He chose the Chesterfield suburb location because of its distance from the station. Unfortunately, it was a half-hour drive from his apartment. He planned to make it in twenty minutes—twenty-five tops. Unless there was something major happening in West County, he didn't expect to run into anyone from KDPX-TV.

Twenty-three minutes later, Brooke sat in the restaurant's parking lot and took a deep breath. He didn't see her car. Either he had beaten her or Brooke Mitchell was dining alone. *Lord, let her show up.*

He got out of his car and donned his hat and coat. Grabbing the envelope and a long-stemmed rose, he strode with a purpose through the restaurant's door. Glancing around, Brooke noticed no one was waiting in the lobby. A pretty petite Latina woman standing behind a podium got his attention.

"Your name, sir?" Squinting, she gave him an expression like she knew him from somewhere, but couldn't place him.

He smiled as he walked closer. "Brooke Mitchell."

"I thought so!" She cut him off and blushed. Her name tag read Lana. Flustered, she couldn't hold her pen steady.

"My party isn't here yet." He pointed to the leather cushioned bench. "I'll wait."

The young woman beamed and nodded.

Sitting, Brooke stretched his legs. So far, the ambience was what his older sister described. It was Debra's suggestion when he told her of his plan to woo a coworker.

At first, Debra sounded concerned that he was about to get caught up with another "crazy", as she had described Andrea. Brooke assured Debra that Andrea and Desiree were as different as Satan and an archangel.

Brooke reached for his cell phone to check the time. Desiree had fifteen minutes. If she was anything like when she came to work, she was punctual. He prayed she would walk through the door any minute.

With five minutes to go, Brooke started counting: three...two...okay two again...one hundred seconds, ninety-nine...

The door opened and Desiree made her appearance. Instead of her confident strut, she walked in hesitantly.

Yes! She came. His heart beat wildly. Brooke wanted to pump a fist in the air in victory. His throat was suddenly dry. *Not so fast for the celebration,* he thought. *Her being here is only the first battle. Whether she would be glad it was him would be the second.*

Brooke regulated his breathing as he observed her through bushy decorative plants that gave him a temporary hiding place. Desiree had released the curls she had trapped earlier at work. Now, they cascaded to her shoulders.

He allowed Desiree's eyes to adjust to the dimmed surroundings as she strolled farther into the lobby. When Desiree saw him, she smiled.

"Brooke, what are you doing here? It seems we're both craving the same food, huh?" She seemed nervous as her gaze darted around the restaurant. Desiree was searching for someone other than him.

Uh-oh. This wasn't the reaction he was expecting. For a smart woman, she had not connected the dots.

Before he could say anything, she sat down, whipped out her iPhone, and started texting. Frowning, he retook his seat next to her.

When Desiree finished, she looked up and smiled again. She had sparkling eyes. Before he could say anything, another text grabbed her attention. Immediately, she replied with a heavy sigh.

The same hostess walked up to Desiree. "Is your party—"

"Uh." She cringed and whispered, "My party hasn't arrived yet." She appeared embarrassed.

Her expressions were a mixture of trepidation and irritation. Clearing his throat, Brooke's spirit plummeted. He was practically invisible to her. "Your party's been here waiting on you."

When he handed her his signature envelope, the light bulb seemed to come on. Desiree's gloved hand flew to her mouth. "You?" Her eyes widened as her hand shook when she accepted it.

"Disappointed?" Brooke then presented the long-stemmed rose.

She blinked at the same time she received another text. Her lips formed an "o", then she whispered, "No." Breaking the trance, she replied to her texter. This time, Desiree sent a short message, and then gave him her attention again. "No, I'm relieved."

Another hostess gave them the strangest look, then cleared her throat.

"We're ready." Brooke stood again and waited for Desiree to confirm.

Nodding, she got to her feet. Brooke helped her out of her coat and scarf. There was no hint of nervousness as she followed their hostess.

Her light scented perfume drifted to his nose. His nostrils flared. It wasn't the same fragrance she wore at work earlier. The belt around her small waist was replaced with a colorful scarf that rested on one side of her hips. Brooke blinked at the ankle boots that were now transformed into knee-highs.

Jesus, You brought her here. Now, please don't let me run her away.

CHAPTER 4

"When you sashayed through that door, my heart dropped. Although I was hoping and praying you wouldn't stand me up, I didn't think you would come," Brooke confessed once they were seated. Relief filled his face.

Desiree imagined that unbelief was still etched across hers. Brooke Mitchell was attracted to her? There were at least three other coworkers who were trying to get their claws into him. She was not tossing her hat into the ring for that kind of drama.

Brooke was her secret admirer. She was flattered, but now what? Nip it in the bud before something started blooming or... Nope, there were no other options.

She had never been in a restaurant where she couldn't make eye contact with another patron. The booths were designed to be cozy, intimate and private. Unless a guest stood in front of the booth, no one would know they were there. Brooke's eyes danced with amusement as his fingers softly drummed the table like a keyboard.

"There are no monitors or scanners here, Desiree, so what's got your attention?"

Shaking her head, she couldn't face him. The environment had changed. She was no longer in control.

Although they were still coworkers, the atmosphere suggested otherwise. Brooke didn't know how many times she thought about backing out while working. "I didn't think I would come."

"Why did you?" He leaned closer, invading her personal space. He waited patiently as she struggled to be honest with herself first and then him. He said he was a Christian, and she took the bait. Could she trust him with her truth or did she need to keep walls erected?

"At first, I thought it was a prank, and then your notes kept coming. That was creepy."

"I know. I took a chance," Brooke admitted sheepishly. The confidence he portrayed on camera had vanished. There was a hint of vulnerability with which she could connect.

"My stance on mixing my personal matters with the workplace is well-known. The outcome is never good. "

"Not always," he challenged.

Anchoring elbows on the table, Desiree rested her chin on top of her linked fingers. "Excuse me? I was one note away from going to human resources and filing a sexual harassment complaint."

"I thought about that." He paused and toyed with the hairs on his trimmed mustache. "I took a chance writing those notes and you took a chance coming. I know why I did what I did, but why did you come?"

"If you knew that, why did you think you could go where no man has gone before?" She evaded his question because she didn't really know the answer herself.

"I'm noting that you have not answered me." He winked and reclined in his seat.

Desiree almost slid down her seat. She needed a fan. Brooke's closeness and his command of their conversation fluttered her because she was attracted to him. She was no different than any other woman. She appreciated beauty and he was the epitome of handsomeness.

"Since you're evading my question, I have no problem putting everything out on the table. I'm confident I have something to offer you. I've learned to pray for what I want."

Hmm. What could be more appealing than a self-assured man who lived to please God? She liked the sound of that. Without mentioning the prayer, Brooke would have come off as cocky.

She swallowed. Now it was her turn to pray she wouldn't regret this night and have it backfire on her. She was not about to play all her cards.

"My girlfriend, whom I was texting in the lobby, encouraged me to meet this Christian man."

"What did she say when she found out it was me?" His expression was hopeful.

"Malinda texted that I was in good hands and that she was leaving." Picking with her napkin, Desiree wasn't totally convinced that Brooke was a good guy. To top it off, she felt vulnerable. So much for her tough exterior reputation. Word would get out she was a desperate woman.

Brooke relaxed. "Whew. I have an ally. By the way, I liked your hair on top of your head this morning and the way it's teasing your sweater." His eyes twinkled. "I like what you're wearing."

Remember to breathe, Desiree coaxed herself. Otherwise, she would faint from his compliments.

"You're so much more than your looks. I've seen you in action. You're demanding, but considerate. You're easygoing, but not a pushover. What really attracted me to you is the Jesus in me connecting with the Jesus in you."

That sucked her in just as their server approached.

"Welcome to the Melting Pot. I'm Jason." He was tall, white, and almost too good-looking not to be in front of a television camera. She guessed he might be a college student, working to pay his tuition.

He clasped his hands together. "I'm here to ensure your fondue experience is memorable. Have you ever dined with us before?"

Both shook their heads. Jason reached over and turned on their small fondue pot. "Don't let the size fool you. This thing gets hot."

Jason placed menus before them and began to explain the process of the four-course meal. "We'll start off with me creating a cheese fondue of your choice. The wine we recommend—"

"We don't drink," Brooke spoke up.

"Okay. Well, the salad will follow. After that..." He paused and winked. "Hopefully you'll cook your first meal together."

Brooke grinned and nodded. His expression must have jarred Jason's memory because he asked if he was the reporter at KDPX. After the fan adoration wore off, Jason continued.

"I'll let you two look over the menu, and I'll be back."

When Jason disappeared, Desiree turned to Brooke who was already watching her. Neither seemed interested in their menus. *What is he thinking?* she wondered. Yes, she noticed his good looks when he first arrived at the station and every day after that.

The cameras couldn't do him justice. Desiree witnessed Brooke's charisma when he interacted with people, whether he was on or off camera. He was well respected.

Despite his major and her minor attraction to each other, the fact remained she didn't engage in office romances. Even though Brooke Mitchell was the latest craze in the city, Desiree couldn't let her thoughts linger on carnal desires. As a Christian, wasn't that what God commanded her to do—flee temptation? Knowing his interest, which flattered her, how could she see him every day at work and turn away this Christian man? She could feel his eyes on her as she fumbled with her menu. Then she had to force herself to read the selections. "See anything you like in here?"

"What I like is sitting next to me in this booth. Now that you've asked, there really isn't anything Jason can bring me from that kitchen."

"Brooke Mitchell, I walked into this place with pure thoughts. I want to leave here the same way, please."

"I can compliment you, admire you, and even kiss you without crossing the line. I'm still a man, but a Christian. That separates me from the rest."

Whew, a sexy Christian male. You created him, Lord, with the right amount of seasoning. He made Desiree want to salute him with "yes sir!"

"I am curious about your reaction when you first walked in here. When you saw me, it seemed as if you didn't connect the clues that I was the one who invited you. That's an automatic F in Investigative Journalism 101, Desiree King."

"I flunked." She laughed, then looked away, thoughtful. "I feared some disgusting coworker with bad breath, beer belly...you know, using me for an office joke."

"But you came..." Brooke left her to fill in the blanks. She nodded. "And you saw me..." Desiree nodded again. "And..."

She blushed as he coaxed her. "I relaxed." She stuck out her tongue. "You weren't the Big Bad Wolf."

"But it didn't click it was me?"

"No. I never thought you were or would be interested in me. You do have options at the station—and plenty of them."

Twisting him lips, he stroked his goatee. He frowned and smirked. I've got options, huh? Well, I choose you."

Reaching for her glass of water, Desiree almost choked as she tried to gulp down as much as she could in one swallow. She underestimated how much temptation there was being in close proximity to a Christian man.

She wouldn't contemplate this setting with an unsaved man. Not realizing Jason had returned, Desiree blinked to concentrate.

"Which cheese fondue would you like to try?" Jason grinned, eager to get started.

"We don't know," Brooke admitted guiltily. "What's popular?"

"The spinach artichoke."

Brooke looked to Desiree for her approval, and then Jason left.

"I thought he'd never leave," Brooke teased.

Her thoughts were too jumbled to respond. The air became thick between them, or maybe it was the steam from the fondue pot. Surely, the man had to know he had her discombobulated. Regaining control, Desiree tapped on the table. "So why did you pick this place to shame me?"

"Never to shame you. My sister—the one I mentioned in my first note with the little angel-face daughters—raved about it. My brother-in-law took her out for their tenth anniversary. Debra's only complaint was the experience seemed to take forever as she constantly checked her watch, mindful of their babysitter. She confessed she and Devin were probably the worst customers that night.

"Her husband has high cholesterol, so he asked for the sodium intake of each dish. She says, at thirty-five, they acted like senior citizens with their ailments."

He paused and laughed with Desiree. "I figured if I only had one shot, I wanted to mingle the Mitchell experience with a night-long fondue experience. I might need as much time as possible."

Jason reappeared with bread, apples, and veggies for dipping, then he dropped the cheese cubes in the pot. Once it melted he added other ingredients. He demonstrated the dipping. A few minutes later, he left again.

"I don't know if this is going to be enough food." Brooke tried dipping an apple slice.

She munched on the bread cubes she had dipped into the pot. "At least it's a four-course meal. We better look at this menu."

Their server's timing was uncanny. Since they were almost finished with the cheese fondue, they ordered the Melting Pot house salad. Desiree tried shrimp as her main course, while Brooke asked for the herb-crusted chicken breast.

The night turned comical when Jason brought raw shrimp and chicken to the table.

"Hey, man, that's not done." Brooke seriously pointed out.

"Right." Jason snickered. "You're going to cook this yourself." He recited the instructions as if turning in their food orders to the cook. "Remember to add your vegetables after three minutes…"

Shrugging, Desiree teased him. "It's all about the experience, remember?"

"Right." He grinned, concentrating on cooking their meat thoroughly.

As the evening progressed, their conversation stayed on safe territory as they discussed their hobbies, families and commitment to God. Surprisingly to Desiree, they talked very little about work. Initially, that was the only thing she thought they had in common. By the time Jason brought out their dessert, they were stuffed.

"So did our four-course meal create a memorable experience? Don't ever say I didn't cook for you."

Brooke took a bite of his chocolate-covered strawberry while she swirled hers in white chocolate.

Desiree laughed. "This was different and nice. This has been an enjoyable fondue and Mitchell experience."

A few minutes later, Brooke paid the bill, but made no attempt to leave. "This is who I am outside work. When I'm in the newsroom, I get paid for working. I'm not the Big Bad Wolf, but I'm hoping I've convinced you I'm Prince Charming." He took a deep breath. "So, are you willing to date me undercover?"

Her heart skipped. Yes, they had a good time. She had finally relaxed. Still, Desiree was hesitant as she stared into his eyes. When she frowned, Brooke seemed to brace himself behind his enticing smile.

"I don't know. My name and reputation are important to me. I just don't think romance and work go hand-in-hand. Once people lose respect for a peer, their name is tarnished. How does one get it back?"

"See, that's an *if* question, and we have control over *if*s." He reached for her hand. "I'm in a good place right now. I'm content. I'm happy if you're happy. Not only will I protect your heart, but also your name."

"What about your name? Aren't you concerned other reporters will blame you for getting assignments they wanted or…"

"Believe me, I've been down that road once before with a coworker. I was sincere while she was the gamester," he said dryly.

"It's because of that road I sought Jesus. My sister ministered to me like never before when it seemed like my lifestyle crossed wires with my workplace—"

"See what I mean—"

"Actually I don't, Desiree, because after that experience, I re-evaluated my life. I attended church, but for all the wrong reasons. My best judgment was flawed. I was powerless, so I gave up and handed my life over to Christ. My mind was like a rolodex, recalling every sin I committed and I repented."

Closing his eyes, Brooke shook his head as if he was reliving the memory. His testimony was her deal breaker. Desiree respected him as a professional, but this intimate look at the spiritual side of the award-winning reporter was making it hard to turn down his request.

"I went to the altar for the works—the baptism in the name of Jesus and the fire baptism. Afterward, ministers prayed for me, and an overwhelming power exploded within me. I heard myself speak in unknown tongues that I couldn't control. I didn't want to. What I witnessed and experienced made a Bible believer out of me."

"Amen." She sniffed.

"Does that mean you're willing to give *us* a try, Amen?"

She nodded.

Pumping his fist in the air, Brooke lifted his voice. "Hallelujah."

Jason appeared as if he were on roller skates. Concern was etched on his face, "Is everything all right, sir?

"It's breaking news. The Mitchell experience was a success!"

CHAPTER 5

It had been worth the wait. Despite Desiree's protests, Brooke insisted he trail her home to make sure she made it all right. *Lord, did I say thank you? If I didn't, thank you.* The night ended outside her front door—not with a kiss like he wanted, but a short sweet prayer like she requested. At least they had exchanged phone numbers before leaving the restaurant.

"Thank you," Brooke whispered once they said Amen. He stared into her eyes. They were beautiful but tired. It had been a long, hectic day at work for both of them.

"I'm glad I came," Desiree confessed, then warned, "but come Monday, I'm back to being your assignment editor and bossing you around."

Brooke lifted a brow. He didn't dare challenge her because he would be the one to come up with the short end of the stick.

"I don't know if I can look you in the face and not remember the things you shared with me from your heart." She patted her chest.

"I'll help you. I won't force your hand. I'll protect your honor at all costs."

When she teared-up, Brooke took that as a sign he had gained her trust. God help him to keep it in an atmosphere where the practice of invading privacy was big business.

"Good night. See you next week." She turned to insert her key.

"You didn't invite me—"

She stomped her boot-covered foot. "And I'm not going to invite you in. It's late and—"

Brooke chuckled. "Ah, the suspicious nature is back. I'm talking about inviting me to your church tomorrow. I'm off Sunday, as you know. I don't want our dates to be limited to dinners in hideaway places. Surely, we can worship openly together."

Desiree sighed. "You amaze me." She blushed and stared so long into his eyes, Brooke was sure a good night kiss was coming. "I attend Bethesda Church near the airport. Worship starts at ten A.M., service at eleven. I'll look for you. Good night."

Without another word, she proceeded to insert the key in the lock and go inside. Stuffing his hands into his pockets, Brooke smirked. The woman was definitely in control at work and outside. He liked that in her, he realized, as he spun around and walked back to his car.

***

Sunday morning, Brooke woke eager to get to worship service. This morning, he would experience the Desiree King experience at her church. He showered, ate, and dressed within an hour. After double-checking his appearance in the mirror, Brooke grabbed his Bible and car keys.

Once he was behind the wheel of his sedan, he headed toward the highway. Following the directions on his GPS, twenty minutes later, Brooke drove into the parking lot without any missed turns.

After he got out of his car, almost everyone he encountered on his stroll to the entrance greeted him with an enthusiastic "Praise the Lord." Some seemed to recognize him from the newscasts, but none detained him for an autograph as if he was more than a man who needed Jesus just like them. That was refreshing, considering some members at the church he had been visiting since he moved to St. Louis, always made a point of pointing him out to visitors as the local celebrity who picked their church to worship.

Brooke had barely cleared the door when he felt the overwhelming power of the Holy Ghost filling the building. True to her word during their conversation, which lasted almost three hours the night before, Desiree was standing near one of the doors to the sanctuary. She waved and her eyes lit up.

If he thought she was pretty at work, he was floored now. She wore a classy strange-shaped hat that was angled on her head. Her cascading curls remained in place. The two-piece gold suit appeared to be a custom fit for her curves—stunning. In a black tailored suit, Brooke felt underdressed next to her.

"You came."

"You act surprised. Did you doubt me?" Brooke quizzed her.

"Well, talk is cheap." Before he could respond, she added, "Hey, I'm from Missouri—the Show-Me state, so you've shown me, but I'm glad you're here."

Brooke had to remind himself to be patient. One dinner date and a long phone call couldn't constitute trust. He nodded. "Me too. Come on, as the song says, I'm here to worship."

Grabbing his hand, Desiree smiled and tugged him along. "Then let's do it."

Brooke saw where she received her inspiration. The worship in the place was contagious and fulfilling. The sanctuary was huge, but not a mega-church. Brooke estimated a couple thousand members and that was pushing it.

With or without another personal invitation from her, he would be back. For months, he felt like he was church hopping as he visited different congregations until he settled on the present one he had been attending for a while. Brooke felt like church hopping again.

This time, he might finally be at home. As the saying goes, home is where the heart is and Desiree was definitely the desire of his heart.

CHAPTER 6

On Monday, it was back to reality for Brooke. He held his breath as Desiree breezed through the newsroom door. She was wearing her beautiful game face over her light makeup. Brooke angled his head so as not to ogle her. If he did, his attraction would be obvious to anyone who glanced his way.

He couldn't wipe the smirk off his face, recalling the time they'd spent together since Friday. As a man who uncovered secrets for a living, Brooke was prepared to guard his business with all he had in him. It wasn't going to be a problem to detach his personal life from his work responsibilities. One thing was for certain, she was making it challenging.

Sometime later as he pecked away on his computer keyboard, her smile seemed to flash in his mind. Taking his eyes off his screen, Brooke had to steal a glance at the woman who was basically off limits from nine-to-five.

Desiree was leaning against the desk with her back to him. She had the phone jammed between her ear and shoulder. She seemed focused on the overhead TV monitors nearby. Slowly, she turned around and stared out into the newsroom. Their eyes met. If Brooke had blinked, he would have missed their brief connection.

Exhaling, he ached to wink, smile, or blow her a kiss—considering he had yet to kiss her. He could wait. Brooke wanted to do everything right this time. Whenever she granted permission, Brooke was ready to pucker up.

Stretching, he cleared his mind. He had a job to do. And this was the time of year where every news story had to count.

During February, May, and November, the competition among television stations was brutal. Whoever aired the best reporter stories to sway or sweep viewers away from one station and to another scored the winning touchdown. The high ratings translated into charging top dollar to advertisers for the months ahead.

Plus, to earn the status as an Emmy award–winning journalist for the best news coverage did come with its perks—besides a coveted spot on the reporter's résumé, ego, and an extended contract with an increase in pay.

The winter sweeps was days away. Brooke had double checked his sources' information for his investigative story. He had worked undercover for a month to expose the mastermind behind trafficking children as drug dealers.

A few hours later, Brooke and his photographer strolled out of the editing booth down the hall. Together, they had collaborated on choosing compelling video to visually expose the criminal activity.

Sly was sharp. He had an eye for detail, even though he had been on the clock since before dawn. As they headed toward the newsroom, the medical, fire, and police scanners were blaring. Not a good sign.

"Brooke and Sly to the newsroom a sap," Desiree's animated voice came over the intercom.

Entering the newsroom, supervisors were huddled around what Desiree often joked about as the circus area. The day had been relatively quiet across the city. There wasn't even a shooting or knife fight. Suddenly, a storm was brewing.

"What's going on?" Brooke asked as he and Sly joined the group.

"I have a three-alarm house fire. It's bad. There might be children trapped inside. Witnesses say a few people jumped from windows." She seemed to struggle with her expression to maintain composure despite the severity of the situation. "Dispatchers are calling firefighters to evacuate the building. Move now!" She added, "Please."

He and Sly seemed already forgotten as she picked up the phone and started making calls. Multitasking, she asked writers to look up the names of any residents living on the same street, using the Haynes Directory, a resource book that systematically listed every street, house number, and resident's name that lived in St. Louis city and the surrounding counties. It never failed; someone in the newsroom would reach a neighbor.

People liked to talk. If a reporter shoved a microphone and a camera in front of them, some would ramble on for days.

Bystanders were always a good resource for information at the scene. They had no problem telling other people's business. Unlike a company spokesman and public figures, they hated the media and would run the other way if the camera wasn't rolling on them.

Back at his desk, Brooke didn't waste time as he grabbed his belongings. He whirled around, expecting Sly to be behind him. Instead, his photographer was still at the assignment desk, trying to get Desiree's undivided attention. Brooke backtracked.

"C'mon, Desiree," Sly argued. "I've worked a ten-hour shift already. I've missed lunch, and now there's no telling how long we'll be at this fire. I'm ready to get home."

"Sly," she tried to reason with him. "I agree with you, but we're in the news business. You know it's not nine-to-five. I'll make it up to you later.

"We're pulling a crew off another story as backup. They'll head to the fire as soon as they break down the equipment. But Thomas and Jerry are at least thirty minutes away. Once, they're there, you can leave and Brooke can ride back to the station with them."

The assistant news director intervened on her behalf as if she couldn't hold her own. "We can disagree later," Todd advised Sly, ending the dispute.

That was the catchphrase managers had borrowed from Desiree. She used it at the end of conversations when she knew somebody wasn't going to be happy in the situation. *Disagree.* Desiree never used the word *argue.* Diplomacy.

Begrudgingly, Sly stalked away and swiped his camera equipment off the floor. He mumbled a few choice words and yelled, "Let's go, Mitchell."

Sly spit out his order as if Brooke wasn't standing a few feet away, waiting on him. If his photographer called him by his last name, then he was hot. Brooke couldn't blame him. Unfortunately, he was going to be the only person who had to endure Sly's tantrum.

Brooke exhaled. Desiree was right. Long hours were part of their job. Viewers were clueless about what it took to get a story on the air. The public had the perception that a television personality's job was glamorous.

It was just the opposite in most cases. In severe weather, meteorologists urged residents to stay indoors, while assignment editors dispatched crews in dangerous conditions to report to viewers first-hand accounts of what was going on.

News reporting could be stressful. In Brooke's nine years in the business right after college, he had covered deadly crashes, child drownings, and house fires as well as happy occasions like celebrations, dedications, and commemorations.

His photographer wasn't a newbie in the industry either. He had been at KDPX for twelve years. Sly had won numerous awards for his coverage of abduction cases, the St. Louis Cardinals World Series champs, and countless other headline news makers. Together, they made a good team, but probably not today.

The overnight assignment editor had called Sly in early to cover a police car chase, which ended when an SUV crashed through the bedroom of a house. It was God's grace that nobody was killed while they slept. But the damage to their home was extensive.

Roger's only concern was to get video of the scene. After that, it would be the assignment editor's headache to deal with the details of adjusting schedules. Basically, the overnight assignment editor was passing the buck to Desiree to deal with the fallout.

As expected, once inside the news truck, Sly's griping didn't cease. "That woman is evil. That's why Desiree ain't got nobody. She just dogs a brotha out. I'm hungry, I'm tire—"

"Exhale, pop a mint, and when you get home, take a bath," Brooke told him, and he wasn't kidding. The evidence of Sly's long shift was evident in his physical appearance and odor that he had to endure a few hours longer. Brooke needed him to calm down before they arrived on a traumatic scene.

After checking his rearview mirror, Sly cut his eyes. "You've got jokes about me, huh? My water heater went off. Trust me, your day is coming when that woman will force you to go to Chicago and back in one day. She doesn't care what you've planned outside of work—whether you're tired, got a hot date, or overdosed on caffeine to stay awake. That woman's evil."

It wasn't unusual for a photographer or a reporter to bad mouth an assignment editor for an undesirable job assignment. Even if he wasn't a Christian, Brooke wasn't going to dog Desiree to play his undercover role. Protecting her name meant standing up in her defense at all times.

"I'm sure she'll make it up to you. Now, let's get going, man, so you can go home."

Sly sneered. "Yeah, Miss King can make it up to me with a hot date and hot sex."

"Watch it," Brooke said. He did his Holy Ghost best to keep his composure as his muscles tensed.

"Recycle your mind. If you need help doing that, God has the tools to clean it up.

"Protecting the honor of another one of your lady coworkers, huh?" Sly grunted. "It won't win Desiree over. Nothing will."

Tuning him out, Brooke glanced out the window. He hid a smile. *You'd be surprised what a God-fearing man can get from his daddy, Jesus.* If only Sly knew his secret weapon: the scriptures. John 14:14: *If ye shall ask any thing in my name, I will do it.*

They were about ten minutes from the location, and Brooke heard sirens in the distance. Black smoke billowed into the sky.

"Jesus, save the children," Brooke murmured as Sly sped toward the scene.

CHAPTER 7

"Spill it," Malinda demanded over the phone. As promised, Desiree called her the minute she got into her car after leaving work. "How did the first day of secret love go?"

"Love? I don't know about that." She laughed. Although she didn't text while driving, she tried to limit her talking for safety reasons, so she sat in the garage. She didn't care whether she used a Bluetooth or the car speakers. Distraction was distraction.

With Malinda on the other end, a brief conversation wasn't going to happen. It's not like her friend wasn't up to speed anyway. Desiree had already given her the details about the dinner date.

Actually, Malinda didn't give her a choice, waking her Saturday morning before daybreak. She called until Desiree answered. Her friend didn't have an ounce of patience.

At times, their personalities were at odds because Desiree could hold out until she was ready to make a move. Maybe that's why they were good friends. They balanced each other.

That morning, she had refused Malinda one morsel of information until she got a few more hours of sleep. Two hours later, with the sun barely as a backdrop, Malinda banged on her door with doughnuts as a bribe gift. Minutes later in her kitchen, Malinda practically salivated as she recanted everything Brooke had said.

"He's the one," Malinda had said steadfastly as she sipped on black coffee.

She couldn't get rid of her friend until late on Saturday when Brooke called. Then on Sunday, Malinda was disappointed when she missed meeting Brooke at their church. Malinda couldn't believe of all days for her company to plan a mandatory event, it would be that one.

"So, how did it go?" Malinda repeated, firing off more questions. "How did Brooke act around your coworkers? Did you two use hand signals? What do you think? Can it work?"

Desiree replayed every moment of the day, even the times she wanted to go near him just to say hi. "Brooke acted normal. I think he purposely stayed clear of me. I've got to respect him for that." Blushing, she giggled. "I do wonder how long we can keep up the charade. We're in the news business." The thought saddened her. *What if it is impossible?* she questioned herself. "The big test will be impartiality on my part. There's not one reporter or photographer there I haven't bumped heads with—some more than once."

"Girl, don't think negative thoughts. Think of it as a game to win," Malinda suggested at the same time Desiree's other line beeped.

Checking the ID, she smiled. "Hey, your time is up. Brooke is calling me."

"I'm getting dumped."

"Yes, you are," she teased, ignoring Malinda's wounded tone. She swapped calls. "Hi, Brooke."

"Hello, boss." His baritone voice made her ears tingle. "How did I do my first day on the job?"

"You're good."

He laughed. "Well, if I want to keep my assignment, then I've got to impress the boss."

They chatted a few more minutes before Brooke learned she hadn't left the parking garage. He scolded her for still being anywhere close to their job, then possessively told her to be careful on the road because there were a few slick spots from the brief shower.

"I will." Desiree disconnected and grinned all the way home. Later that evening, they spoke again. Their conversations added excitement to a life she didn't consider dull.

While they talked about his family and her lack of one, Desiree had a Lifetime movie on mute. She wouldn't mind if he was there to watch a movie with her, but she didn't want to go too fast.

Brooke jokingly complained about being the little brother. "But I thank Jesus for a praying sister."

"I wished I had siblings, but I'm an only child."

He confessed he had many acquaintances, but only a handful he would call friends, like those from his childhood in Little Rock.

Besides sharing their favorite scriptures, Brooke revealed he enjoyed bike riding in the summers. It had been a while since she had climbed on one. "I would

probably need a helmet, knee pads, and neck brace—"
Brooke barked out a laugh.

Desiree did the same. When she regained her
composure, she finished. "Seriously, I prefer winters. I
know that sounds crazy. When you're hot and the air
conditioner breaks, you'll fry. I always tell people I
can't stand the heat here, so I'm going to make sure I
miss hell."

"That's a subtle witnessing tool. I'll have to borrow
that."

Desiree nodded. She always got a response with
that one. "I like fireplaces, snowmen, and winter plays
and dance troupe performances. I enjoy bundling up in
winter coats, hats, and boots, but I do have my limit. I
don't want to move to Alaska."

"If you relocated, I would follow because I feel
that's where God would want me."

***

By Wednesday, Desiree questioned whether dating
incognito at work was worth denying herself of
laughing, smiling, and getting lost in Brooke's clear
brown eyes, even for sixty seconds. She masked the
longing in her heart with an eager willingness to assist
all reporters who came to the assignment desk.

The undercover was Desiree's idea and mandate,
so she had to live by her own rules. The week ended
without any slipups from her or Brooke.

The next Sunday, Brooke attended her church
again and met Malinda who gushed over him as if
Brooke was a Hollywood star. Behind Brooke's back,
she gave her the thumbs up.

Smiling, Desiree admitted she was in a content
state. She had a Christian man she so desired; she just

never expected to work with him. Still, there was no reason for her to complain. The next week, Brooke continued to play his uncommitted-to-her role convincingly.

Unfortunately, the following Sunday, on Brooke's day off, he had to work. "Pray for me and jot down the scriptures for me," he had said. His request only made him more endearing to her.

Because of his upcoming series on child drug dealers, Brooke had to meet with some of his informants to double check his facts. Desiree wanted to interrupt him, take him a plate of food to eat or just pop in. Her presence would surely pique the weekend assignment editor's suspicions.

When the first week of February sweeps kicked in, Desiree stepped up her game. She was not about to let another station out scoop her on any breaking news. Management was depending on six of its top reporters to take the station to ratings king.

Brooke's five-part series began airing during the ten o'clock newscast. After the second night, viewers called, tweeted, or emailed, applauding his work.

By the end of the week, their station was in the lead. Biased, Desiree believed Brooke's hard work gave them the edge. She was proud of him. She craved one moment of celebratory praise with him.

Giddy with excitement, she could barely contain herself at work. Hoping her timing was right, Desiree strutted down the corridor where Brooke had disappeared minutes earlier.

As she rounded the corner, Brooke swaggered out of the edit booth. Desiree admired the slight bow in his legs, which was noticeable with his swagger. He was tall with broad shoulders. His rich dark skin made her wish she was a coffee drinker. She was impressed with how neatly he kept his mustache and goatee trimmed.

Desiree sucked in her breath when their paths crossed. She blushed watching him check her out. Maybe it was her attempt at a new style technique with her colors: bold mustard yellow and red accents, which included a scarf, tights, and jewelry. It actually turned out nice. Once again, her fashion book was right on the money. But the way he made her feel beautiful didn't have anything to do with her experimental fashion statements.

When their eyes connected, Brooke's danced with merriment.

As they passed each other, Brooke whispered, "You're gorgeous. You are the peace God sent me in the middle of this crazy sweeps storm." He didn't miss a step as he kept going.

No sooner had she entered the bathroom, she received a text: *But my beauty queen looks tired. Call me when you're on your way home and I'll bring dinner.*

Desiree's heart warmed. Yes, she had made the best decision of the New Year when she asked God to bless her social life. Not only did she increase her prayer time with Jesus in the mornings, she and Brooke exchanged scriptures and Biblical phrases throughout the day.

She had given love a chance.

Hold up. Wait a minute. Would what they began turn into love? *Lord, could I love a man on the job and not give him preferential treatment?*

***

It was Friday night, and instead of Desiree being with or talking to Brooke, she was in her living room with Malinda, rearranging her furniture. They had a mime performance the next day at an event, and Desiree was the cause of their slack in practicing for it.

After moving her coffee table to the side, she inserted William McDowell's CD. Getting into position, they waited for "I Give Myself Away" to begin. In sync, they swayed their bodies to the rhythm.

The art of miming was a perfect fit for Desiree because she couldn't hold a musical note to be on the praise team or in any of the church choirs. Taking pity on her, Malinda looked for another avenue for her to serve the Lord in music.

Her friend suggested mime as a form of spiritual expression. It only took one time for Desiree to witness a performance, and she was hooked.

Tuning everything and everyone out of her mind, including Brooke's smile, she focused on God, then on their facial expressions. She and Malinda allowed the Holy Ghost to descend upon their spirits.

It never failed, soon after, their practice turned into praise as they worshipped in the spirit. As tears stained their cheeks and they moved their arms in the air, they spoke in unknown tongues.

An hour or so later, they sat in Desiree's kitchen. Burning up hundreds of calories was cause for a celebration, so they rewarded themselves by pigging out on Crab Rangoon and two orders of special fried rice.

Desiree's pledge of maintaining her healthy eating lifestyle had been put on hold for two days. Since her affirmation was part of her New Year's requests, she was certain to get back on track.

During the weekend, Brooke would be sure to guide her back to the straight-and-narrow road with baked dishes and plenty of vegetables.

"So, it's been more than four weeks since the letter, the date and the dancing around your feelings for Mr. Mitchell. Now what?" Malinda asked.

"I don't know." Desiree sighed, shrugging. "Truthfully, I didn't think it would work."

"Brooke is serious about you. Maybe it's time to break your silly rules and go out on a real date. This hide-and-seek or hide so no one can see you is no way to really date. What's more important than a special someone in your life?"

Desiree scrunched up her nose. "I had a career before Brooke and plan to have one after he's gone. Sweeps is hard on a dating schedule."

Standing, Desiree cleared off the table. Malinda followed and began to rinse off the dishes.

"I didn't know what I was getting myself into when I agreed to date a man on the job. I didn't think it would be this hard to resist telling my coworkers how wonderful and kind Brooke is," she said as they walked into her den to put the table back in place.

"Should I remind you that you requested this covert dating operation?"

"No, you shouldn't." Desiree stuck out her tongue. "I guess I should've been careful what I asked for because I sure got it. I honestly don't know what to do next."

"Start with coming out of hiding."

CHAPTER 8

It was risky, but Brooke decided to go for it. Desiree King would get flowers delivered on the job Valentine's Day. Brooke ran the idea by his sister.

"I think it's romantic that you're going through all this trouble for a woman who doesn't want outward affection. It's almost as if she's ashamed of you."

"I respect her, sis."

"You have no complaints, bro?" Debra quizzed him.

"Oh, I have a couple. One is watching her have a bad day and not being able to comfort her. That's torture. Another is she works too hard and doesn't know when to go home."

Brooke ignored the fleeting thought of how he felt when Desiree had to make tough calls and ask reporters and photographers to stay on the scene and sacrifice whatever they had planned.

Although she was doing her job, he didn't like her putting herself in the position to be the bad person. He had seen firsthand some disappointed men call their wives or girlfriends and tell them they would be late. In her defense, she did scramble to get crews replaced and off the clock as soon as she could.

"Somewhere down the line, Desiree's going to have to make your relationship a priority, which means she doesn't care who knows how she feels about you."

"You're being too hard on her," he defended. "It's only been a month."

"All I'm saying is you should have passed her test by now."

After she reminded him of the fiasco with that woman at the other station, Brooke said it was time to go. "This is so different. I've captured her heart, and she's filled mine."

"Okay, well, be prayerful. I hope to meet her soon."

After they disconnected, Brooke prayed, "Lord Jesus, I know Desiree and I aren't married, but I became a man when I left home for college. I grew up more when my parents died in a car crash. It's time for me to go after a woman who may be a perfect wife for me if it is Your will."

Taking a deep breath, he waited and listened for God to speak. When no words came, Brooke logged onto his computer and Googled a florist in the area. It didn't take long to make up his mind.

He chose A Girl's Best Friend Florist. The owner didn't have a problem sending flowers to KDPX-TV, especially when she learned she had the ear of the award-winning reporter Brooke Mitchell.

When it came to booking a dinner reservation, even his name couldn't get him a table. Every place was packed, so he had to think quickly. As a member of the media, he ran the risk of violating his payola contract, which was basically a conflict-of-interest clause, if he called in a favor. If he ever had to investigate that person or business in the future, it wouldn't look good. His judgment could be tainted.

Brooke needed to come up with something memorable for her, in lieu of eating at a posh restaurant. Any man with respect wouldn't miss cherishing his woman on Valentine's Day. He would have to make it up to her another way.

As he wracked his brain, God placed into his mind that he was a storyteller. A silly notion came to Brooke. He thought about penning a poem. "Nah." He was far from poetic.

What about a romantic story with them as the characters for Valentine's Day? He questioned himself. Although his storytelling abilities were limited to a minute and thirty seconds on camera, he would give himself a try. It should be a piece of cake, right?

It took him three hours to handwrite five half sheets of paper. Brooke smiled as he uploaded a picture of her and then himself from the station's employee profile. He searched for an online editing website where he played around with photos, drawing crowns on both their heads, and then he picked a cover.

He would take his masterpiece to the printer the next day where they could guarantee a fast turnaround. Leaning back in his chair, he hoped she valued his simplistic juvenile approach to wooing her. Personally, he was getting a kick out of it as if he had just completed his art project in third grade.

Brooke's jubilant mood turned frustrating. He was no longer a kid in primary school. He was a grown man ready to take the next step and he needed Desiree to be on that same page. How long could his woman hold out with this madness?

CHAPTER 9

On Valentine's Day, Desiree hadn't been at work ten minutes when the security guard from the lobby called the assignment desk and said she had a package. Walking out of the newsroom, she wasn't expecting a bouquet of red roses to be waiting for her. She had never received flowers on her job.

Brooke. After she smiled, she thought about strangling him for his public show of affection. She wasn't to that point in their relationship yet. Removing the card, she stuffed it in her skirt pocket.

Bracing herself, she could only imagine the whispers and the rumors that would begin to circulate around the office. It was her coworkers' closer scrutiny she didn't want or welcome. Still, accepting the vase of flowers, she sniffed and walked back through the newsroom doors. Her package suddenly became a magnet. She could feel the eyes on her.

"So Cupid's arrow found you, huh?" Dianne, a producer, teased before she could make it back to her area.

"Wow, Desiree, flowers? I definitely could have done better than that," Brian, an overhyped reporter cooed. Coming to investigate, he perused her more than the flowers. To say he was a company flirt was an understatement.

Once she was behind the assignment desk, more coworkers made a beeline to her. A few female staffers were greedy for the identification of the sender. They were disappointed when they didn't see a card. "You have no idea?" one said with an accusatory tone.

Keeping a straight face, she refused to lie. When they realized she wasn't about to be forthcoming, they lost interest. As the excitement died down and Desiree could safely steal sixty seconds alone, she dug into her pocket for the envelope. Slipping out the note, her heart melted: *You mesmerize me. Me.*

Wow, I see someone beat me to it," another reporter teased as he approached the assignment desk, snapping his fingers. "Who are they from?" A nosey producer who came alongside him asked, peeping over Desiree's shoulder.

"So you really do have a boyfriend," Sly said, approaching from across the newsroom.

Desiree wanted to scream, "My life is not news, people." Unfortunately, that outburst would have been out of her character. She continued to neither confirm nor deny. Although Brooke's gesture touched her heart, she wondered if her reputation as serious and detached from office politics was compromised.

Wait until she saw Brooke Mitchell. If she didn't like the flowers so much, Desiree would throw the vase at him. As she fussed at him in her mind, the object of her desire swaggered into the newsroom, carrying another vase of roses. She inwardly groaned. Brooke was testing her.

Brooke didn't even look her way. "Elaine, the guard asked me to bring this in for you." He grinned to a beaming coworker as he placed it on her desk.

Leaping from her chair, she screamed and clapped before ripping off the wrapping in search of the card. After plucking a small envelope off a plastic stem, she read the card aloud.

"It's signed a secret admirer," she squealed, blushing and grinning.

The scene was repeated twice more to other single women in less than thirty minutes. In total, four of them received the same flowers with different messages. Desiree was perplexed about what was going on.

With the scent of roses permeating in the air, her coworkers settled down. A few hours later, she walked down the hall. As she approached the bathroom door, her cell phone beeped, indicating a text. She recognized Brooke's number. *I hope you enjoy the flowers from your sweetheart on Valentine's Day. Unfortunately, I didn't know how to get my mission accomplished without throwing everyone off.*

Shaking her head, Desiree felt ashamed for being ungrateful for his thoughtfulness and ingenuity and doubting his commitment to her request. *Lord, please forgive me for my negative musings.* Brooke had gone through great lengths to pull that off for her. She didn't even want to think about the money he dished out, blessing others because of her. *That was so sweet of you,* she texted back.

The bad news is I didn't plan ahead early enough to make dinner reservations, so I cooked. Disappointed?

Another sweet gesture. She replied: *Not at all. See you around six-thirty or seven.*

For the remainder of the day, Desiree, along with her other three coworkers were teased unmercifully. Even Brooke joined in.

"Looks like you've got a secret admirer." Brooke's eyes sparkled as he walked up to her assignment desk under the guise of asking for a contact's phone number.

"Don't be jealous," Desiree flirted.

"I'm not." He winked and headed back to his desk.

After Elaine made pit stops to the women who were the recipients of the anonymous admirer, she stopped by the assignment desk. "That is one fine man." She sighed. "For a moment, I thought he was bringing me those flowers.

I thought he was bringing you those flowers, too, Desiree didn't dare to voice.

"Well, a girl can dream. As long as I've been here, a man has never sent me flowers. I used to envy other women whose boyfriends and husbands were so romantic. Evidently, I've got someone's attention."

Elaine grinned and almost glided away. Closing her eyes, she took another whiff of her flowers on her desk. After Elaine took her seat, she rearranged the vase.

Desiree swallowed. *Lord, I got what I asked for on my social calendar, but at work? What if the word gets out and it doesn't work between us? How will that affect others' respect of me?* It seemed as if she could hear God laugh at her and say, "You worry too much."

CHAPTER 10

The day had been full of firsts: flowers delivered on her job and now, Desiree's first time going to Brooke's house. Although she agreed, she was leery. The greatest temptation known to woman was being alone in a romantic setting with a sexy man.

She thought about a sermon Elder Reed had preached recently on 1 Corinthians 10:13: *There hath no temptation taken you but such as is common to man: but God is faithful, who will not suffer you to be tempted above that ye are able; but will with the temptation also make a way to escape, that ye may be able to bear it.*

The bottom line had been that God wouldn't send her into battle without the armor to win or a way to survive the combat wounds. He had recited an example about not giving a College Board test to a kindergartener because that would be a sure way to fail.

Walking with Christ for at least sixteen years, Desiree had gone through many trials. It didn't matter that she was thirty-one years old, grown, and had been gone from her parents' home for at least ten years. She was also someone who denied herself Brooke's affections throughout the work day. *God help me.*

As a woman striving to live holy unto God, the devil marked her as a constant target for temptation. And right now, she was no different than any other woman caught up in the Valentine's Day hoopla.

A half hour later, Desiree drove into a revitalized neighborhood in South St. Louis city. After verifying the address, she parked but didn't get out. Instead, she sat in her car and closed her eyes while her emotions clashed. Or rather, her spirit battled against the devil.

"God, keep me. Your Word says You can keep me from falling. Keep Brooke and me from falling."

A tap on the window startled her, she opened her eyes. Brooke stood outside, wearing a concerned expression.

"Are you okay, babe?"

Babe. She liked the sound of his endearment as her heart pounded with excitement. "Yeah," she said with a sigh. Desiree unlocked her door, and Brooke helped her out. Tenderly, he paused to make sure she was bundled against the sudden chill.

After she activated her car alarm, Brooke took her hand and escorted her up a short walkway to his place.

As Desiree cleared the threshold into his townhouse, she blinked. A magnificent table set with stemware, china, and candlelight took her breath away. "Wow."

"Wow is right. Look at you." He whistled, helping her remove her coat. "How can you look pretty at work and a few hours later, be just as gorgeous?"

He didn't wait for an answer. Turning Desiree around, Brooke engulfed her in a hug that she couldn't deny she indulged in his cologne and the strength of his arms. *Traitor,* her body scolded. How soon was she giving up the temptation battle?

Slowly, they separated. As she stared into his eyes, pleading he was asking her for permission to kiss her. Swallowing as her heart continued to pound, she nodded. Brooke must have felt her nervousness as he brushed a soft kiss against her lips. Her lids fluttered, but didn't close. Their first kiss and she wanted to give in to more of his sweetness, but it appeared they both held back.

"I couldn't help myself." He paused as he rested his forehead on hers. "That's not true. I could have, but I think every woman deserves a kiss on Valentine's Day. Desiree, you're torturing me."

"I'm torturing myself, too," she mumbled. Taking a deep breath, she spun around to create some distance between them. Desiree focused on the table and walked closer to his masterpiece. "This is beautiful."

"My sister says it's all in the presentation. I copied a display I saw on a website. You might want to reserve your accolades until after you've eaten."

"Fair enough." She admired his decorating flair or lack of overdoing it. There were a few print arts, and the necessary reclining chair near a large-screen TV. Instead of a sofa against the wall, Brooke had an overstuffed cushioned love seat between two end tables with stylish lamps. The unblemished hardwood floors were evidence that Brooke rarely had visitors.

As cozy as his living room was, Brooke's dining room begged for attention. It was basically a thick oak square table and four chairs. A large palm tree occupied the corner.

The neatness ended there. Peeping through an open half wall to the kitchen, she found the telltale sign he did indeed live there. The remains of his eye-stopping preparations littered the countertops.

Brooke pulled out a chair for her. Desiree thanked him and made herself comfortable as she watched him lazily walk into the kitchen and return to the table with a small basket of rolls and butter.

He always complimented her dress, but she liked men that dressed with attention to their attire. It was something about turtlenecks that covered a man's chest at the same time showcasing his biceps, and Brooke wore his turtleneck well with his broad shoulders and muscular build. She admired his walk and then stopped herself. This was what she was afraid of—lusting and then losing control.

I am attracted to him, and that has to be enough. To catalog all of his assets and features would defeat her will power, so she blinked and cleared her throat. "Thank you for the flowers."

Brooke stopped in his tracks with a bottle of sparkling juice. "You're welcome. I'm new at this undercover romance thing, bab—I mean Desiree."

"I like your term of endearment."

"I wanted to say it sooner, but I have tried my best to play by your rules." He smirked. "Okay, baby. I hope you didn't mind the other ladies getting flowers to throw off the staff."

"That was sweet of you to send flowers to Elaine, Becky, and Sharon. I know that wasn't cheap. You're a wonderful man, and you amaze me." Desiree paused.

"You're worth making happy. I want to impress you, so I'm hanging in there."

"Brooke, we can spend a lot of time complimenting each other, but I'm just as adamant about my salvation—actually more—than you respecting me on my job. I can get lost in you and caught up in the moment. Our emotions are high and the setting is tempting. Would I be even more demanding if I asked that we steer our conversation away from our hormones?"

"My heart is in this too, Desiree. I want to do this right, guided by God's rules and your requests. He placed their plates on the table. The food looked delicious. Taking his seat, Brooke reached for her hand.

"I rethought my plan to cook a fancy dinner at the last minute. I didn't think you could stomach my half-done hen."

"I have no complaints."

He snickered. "Okay." He winked and squeezed her fingers, then bowed his head. Desiree copied him.

"Jesus, we thank You for Your presence in our lives and the food we are about to eat for the enjoyment and the nourishment for our bodies. Please sanctify it and remove all impurities...and God, I thank You for this incredible woman You brought into my life. Amen."

"Amen," she repeated.

They were silent as they indulged in the chicken Alfredo and ham. She would have to give him a lesson later about the four food groups. Desiree sipped on her sparkling white grape juice. "This is good."

He nodded his thanks, and cleared his throat. "Let's revisit the under the radar dating thing we have going on. Have you thought that if the women at work knew I was taken by the gorgeous eagle eye assignment editor, they would stop flirting with me?"

"Or they would step up their game when they realize the competition isn't a threat."

"Oh, you're a threat to those she-demons. We're both saints of God and can show people how Christians date, our honesty, and the way we adore each other without compromising our duties at work or each other," Brooke said, trying to reassure her.

Desiree wasn't one hundred percent convinced. She hadn't reached the confidence level that it appeared Brooke had. As they finished their meal, they steered clear of any more mention of work.

When she rested her fork on her empty plate and declined seconds, Brooke wiped his mouth and stood. He disappeared down the hall and returned moments later with a small gift-wrapped box.

Her eyes danced with excitement. She loved receiving gifts as much as she enjoyed giving them. She whispered her thanks as she fumbled with the amateur bow. She smiled at his attempt. Removing the lid, she recognized a book.

Brooke retook his seat and watched her. She lifted it out the box and turned to the first page, then she realized Brooke had written the story.

Once upon a time, a prince came from a faraway land in search of his princess. In the night sky he saw a television tower reaching into the stars. God's finger came down from heaven and touched it, causing it to shine bright, so it would act as a beacon to the prince.

Page two: *The damsels flirted with the prince to get his attention, but the prince knew he had not found his princess. Until he looked into the eyes of a woman so beautiful no man could win her affections.*

Page three: *The prince knew she was the one, so he went to his father. "Daddy, I see this pretty girl I want. The Lord said: 'What is her name, son?' He told Him, "Desiree."*

Page four: God said He would work on it according to His Word Psalm 37:4: Delight yourself in Me and I shall give you the desires of your heart.

Page five: *Desiree, God works in mysterious ways, but the most important thing is He is working on us. THE END or it could be OUR BEGINNING.*As she fingered the last page, she sniffed.

Facing him, Desiree smiled. "Do you really believe I'm the one?"

"I do. I can prove my worth to you."

"You already have," she whispered and leaned closer to Brooke's waiting lips. They struggled to control themselves. Brooke moved away first and allowed Desiree to recover.

"Expect more kisses, babe. I can't stop giving them now, but God can help me control how far they should go."

Clearing her throat, Desiree changed the subject. "Uh, I checked the schedule at work. I see Wanda has you down to work next Saturday. Malinda and I are performing our first miming to William McDowell's song during a Black History celebration event. If you're not too tired after that, I hope you can come and support me."

Brooke smirked. "I want to be part of every aspect of your life. Whether we are at work or outside, even in your dreams. I'll be there."

CHAPTER 11

Brooke wasn't going to make it to Desiree's first performance. Not only did the weekend assignment editor send him to cover a story an hour away, but his sister, Debra, decided to visit. How inconvenient for him that she had booked a flight with a three-hour layover in St. Louis, so now he had two women who he cared about vying for his attention.

Once he returned to the station, he jumped into his vehicle and headed to Lambert Airport. Brooke made it there in record time only to learn that Debra's flight was ten minutes late. He huffed, groaned, and mumbled under his breath.

His attention alternated between watching the arrival monitor and counting down the minutes before Desiree's event began. Finally, Debra's plane landed and then it seemed like forever before she cleared the terminal. Brooke walked swiftly to meet her and gave the briefest greeting.

Debra blinked. "Did you kiss me? Because if you did, I missed it."

"I did. Now come on. Desiree is performing today, and I don't want to miss it. Any luggage?" he asked and rushed her along, not waiting for her answer.

"Whoa. Slow down. It's just me and my purse." She patted her oversized bag.

"Good. We don't have time anyway. Let's go." As Brooke left the airport garage and exited onto the highway, he considered the time and traffic. Brooke didn't believe in speeding unless it was the impending death of a loved one or close friend. Neither scenario was at hand, so Brooke questioned more than once why he was inching ten miles over the speed limit.

"Slow down, B. She'll still be there," his sister advised.

"You're right." He eased up on the pedal. He—they—were already late. The event started twenty minutes ago. If anyone would understand why he missed her debut, it would be Desiree.

Out of the corner of his eyes, Brooke could see Debra staring at him before she said, "I can't wait to meet this woman who is making my brother lose control."

"Funny." Brooke turned into the parking lot at the University of Missouri at St. Louis, called UMSL by the locals. He didn't want to chance texting her in case she was performing.

Now as he ushered his sister out the car, he prayed for two things. He didn't miss too much of her performance, and that somehow he could send a vibe, letting Desiree know he was in the audience.

They hurried across the lot to the Blanche Touhill performing arts building. By the time he opened the door into the lobby, Debra was winded. Evidently, she needed to hit the gym again. His haste was no different from his early morning brisk walks.

As they neared the auditorium door, Brooke froze. "I Give Myself Away" by William McDowell was playing. Desiree and Malinda had to be on stage.

The usher quietly opened the door. Brooke squinted to the front where a spotlight was shining on the stage. The place was crowded, but Brooke asked the usher for two seats as close as possible. What he and Debra got was ten rows from the stage. Despite Debra's objections to interrupting the guests who were already enjoying the entertainment, Brooke convinced her to climb over several people to settle into their seats.

Focusing on the stage, it didn't take long for Brooke to become enthralled with Desiree and her friend as they moved in sync. Resting an ankle on top of his knee, Brooke intertwined his fingers and watched. He was drawn into Desiree's facial expressions. Just like the note he had written Desiree on Valentine's Day, she mesmerized him.

Debra whispered, "Which one is she?"

Without taking his eyes off her, Brooke replied, "The beautiful one." She elbowed him, and he frowned at her distraction. "What?"

"They look about the same to me. In case you haven't noticed, both have white paste on their faces and their hair is pulled back."

Brooke was agitated at her nagging. He huffed. "She's on the right. *Shh.*" He turned back and gave Desiree his full attention.

His woman did mesmerize him. In the thirty days they had been dating, Brooke's feelings were growing stronger. But how could he treat her the way she deserved when she was concerned with what others said? How long would it take for her to say yes to tell others that they were an item?

Their movements slowed as the music began to fade. As Desiree searched through the audience—he hoped for him—it seemed so natural as if it was part of the routine. Willing for her to glance in his direction, their eyes connected, but it was only a split second.

The audience, including him and Debra, stood with an enthusiastic applause. Not to be outdone, Brooke jammed two fingers in his mouth and whistled.

Debra shoved him. "You're an award-winning television reporter, and people are seeing you act a nut."

Brooke laughed, then whistled again just to irritate her. When she gave him a warning look that would scare his nieces, he wrapped his arms around her and kissed her cheek. "That doesn't work anymore," he whispered.

After the crowd settled down, Brooke sat impatiently through the remainder of the program that honored the pioneers in Black History. Although, he had to get Debra back to the airport soon, Brooke hoped she could see Desiree before flying back home.

Finally, the program concluded with the singing of the Negro National Anthem, "Lift Every Voice." With forty minutes to spare, Brooke grabbed his sister's hand and concentrated on getting to the back of the stage. He ignored the whispers as some wondered if he was the reporter from KDPX.

Desiree was standing near the back entrance, speaking with the other two ladies when Brooke snuck up behind her. He covered her eyes and whispered into her ear, "You mesmerize me." He brushed a kiss against her cheek and stepped back.

She twirled around, furious.

"Brooke," she hissed, clearly upset, "we're in public." Desiree was visibly shaken.

"I forgot."

"Yeah," she said disappointedly, "but I didn't."

Brooke glanced at Debra. She wore the oddest look as if she was contemplating to whose side she would pledge allegiance.

Keeping his agitation in check, he introduced his sister who shook hands, but didn't say a word. He nodded at Malinda and left with a weak good-bye.

He and Debra got into his car, and he silently headed toward the airport in record time. As he parked to walk her in, he asked, "How come you didn't say anything back there?"

"Besides the Holy Ghost wouldn't let me? I wanted to give Desiree a piece of my mind and let her know a lot of women would love to be in her shoes."

Debra was right. The only problem was he liked the legs that were in Desiree's shoes.

CHAPTER 12

"You've got some serious issues," Malinda scolded Desiree as she trailed her to the car.

"I know." Her voice quivered as tears blurred her vision. "Did you see the hurt on his face and the scowl on his sister's? It's not going to work, Mal."

"Why, because you don't want it to?"

"I've got two things going for me." Desiree held up her fingers. "My job and Jesus. This isn't about hearsay. I've seen with my own eyes the fallouts from office romances that go wrong. It's not the brokenhearted who suffer. It's the coworkers who have to pick sides and tiptoe around the opponents."

"The next time you pray for something, make sure you're ready for it," Malinda said softly, still wiping at the white mime makeup residue in her fine black eyebrows.

Desiree nodded. Her friend was right.

"Listen," Malinda said, giving her a hug, "I'm your girl and prayer partner, but when it comes to matters of your heart, it has to be a personal conversation between you and God. If you didn't like Brooke, you would have walked out that restaurant last month and never looked back, but you didn't. Brooke may have agreed to your terms, but for your sake, I hope he doesn't call it quits. Then don't go back to God asking for a mate.

***

Brooke never had to second guess his affections toward a woman in the past. Even before God had saved him, he never, ever disrespected a woman in public. That wasn't his makeup.

His day was going downhill fast. From the politician's story he had to cover to the incident after the event, and now, Debra's plane was canceled due to an impending storm back in Indianapolis.

Although he missed home and never passed up an opportunity to be with family, this was a day he wanted to be alone to nurse the hurt Desiree inflicted on him from her actions. His gesture was harmless, and they weren't even at work. Granted, people recognized him…

"I know you're really into her," Debra said hesitantly.

"Personally….hmmm, never mind." She paused. "You and Desiree need to sit down and talk about if this is what you really want. You two can go your separate ways. It's not like you're in love with her."

"I'm not so sure, Debra. She may be the one."

"Without a test, you two won't have a testimony, but the affections can't be one-sided. Desiree has to give, too. I don't see what the big deal is about dating on the job. I know a lot of people who have gotten married—"

"And divorced—" Brooke answered absentmindedly as they got back into his car, left the airport a second time, and headed to his home. Office romances happened. He respected Desiree's wishes, but if she was going to keep him at arm's length all the time, then maybe...

"What you need to do is confront her and see if she's committed to making this work because you may be crazy about her, but what I just saw was crazy on her part—"

"Sis?"

"Yeah, bro?"

"Please be quiet." He could fight a man, but he couldn't withstand Desiree's rejection. She didn't cause a scene, but her body language spoke volumes.

Back at his townhouse, Brooke helped his sister out and escorted her inside. "Make yourself at home. I'll be back." Stepping outside, a blast of air slapped Brooke's cheeks. He zipped up his jacket, stuffed his hands in his pockets, and began walking toward the end of his block where the neighborhood transitioned from townhouses to ranch and two-story homes.

"Jesus, I don't even know what to pray." And Brooke didn't. He continued walking until the wind picked up and forced him to turn around. That's when he realized how far he had strayed from his home.

As he increased his strides, his cell chimed. It was either his sister or Desiree. He didn't want to speak with either. At that moment, only a Godly intervention could determine his next move.

The caller left a message. Did he dare see if it was from Desiree? Was this their first official argument? He wanted to hold out for as long as he could, but curiosity got the best of him. Brooke wanted to know who called. He yanked his phone off his belt.

Desiree. His heart pounded with uncertainty. Brooke debated whether Desiree calling first should be viewed as a victory. He retrieved the voice message.

"Brooke, I'm sorry about how I responded to you." Her sweet voice warmed him. "I know this is no way for a woman to treat the man who adores her. You deserve so much more. My mouth is saying, 'we tried and it didn't work,' but my heart is drowning it out saying, 'make it work.' I can only imagine what your sister thought of me."

She sighed. "If I have really messed up, I accept my mistake. If you don't call me back, then I'll see you Monday and be nothing more than the assignment editor."

They both were hurting, but something had to give. Debra was right about one thing. Desiree was going to have to find a way to give more to their relationship to make them work.

He picked up his step and hustled back to his townhouse. The aroma of chili welcomed him at the door. He shook off his jacket and headed to the bathroom to wash his hands.

"It's about time you came back. If I wanted to cook, I could have stayed at home with your nieces and brother-in-law," Debra said as she scooped up healthy portions into two bowls. "You didn't have any crackers, so bread will have to do."

They said grace then ate in silence. Brooke knew his sister was itching to say more. He hated she had witnessed Desiree's reaction, but this was something he was going to have to work out.

"Do you know what I think?" she asked.

"Nope." Shaking his head, Brooke swallowed his last spoonful. "And I didn't ask to know."

"Don't worry. My advice is free. Desiree is going to have to decide if she wants a good man or any man. And then she's going to have to prove it."

For free advice, his sister was right.

CHAPTER 13

Desiree hoped Brooke had listened to her voice message and accepted her apology, but he hadn't returned her call, so she was in limbo. That night, for the first time since she had went out to dinner with him, Desiree cried herself to sleep.

On Sunday morning, she dressed, giving extra care to her hair, makeup, and perfume. Desiree chose a red suit because her fashion chart said the color complemented her honey skin tone. Since she and Malinda were trying to adhere to their weekly style book tips, Desiree experimented with a scarf-tying technique.

"Not bad." She admired her handiwork. Instead of curls, Desiree opted to brush it straight.

Now what? She asked her reflection in the full-length bathroom mirror. She and Brooke were at a stalemate. She couldn't back down. If he was not the one for her, then she would have risked her heart for nothing and compromised on something that she had steadfastly said wasn't negotiable—dating a coworker.

By the time Desiree walked into the sanctuary at

church, the Spirit of praise overwhelmed her as she surrendered her worries to Christ. Yet, her heart still longed for Brooke's presence. The choir sung two selections and Brooke was a no show; the preaching started. Still, there was no sign of him.

There was no hope to keep alive. Brooke wasn't coming to her church any more. He had only missed one Sunday since they started dating and that was because he had to go in to work.

Even Malinda had skipped church this morning because she was tired after clocking more than sixty hours of overtime for the week, and they had performed the previous day. Of course, Brooke could have been called into work for a major news development she reasoned, but Desiree wasn't buying that.

Whenever something big went down, reporters and staffers were automatically expected to report to duty, but no one called her, so that wasn't it. There was a possibility that Brooke had simply returned to his own church.

Sitting in church, Desiree was tormented as she chided herself for getting into this sad state. Somehow Desiree was trying to avoid heartache, and a cluster of them had snuck up on her anyway. She didn't know if her heart would recover.

"Open your Bibles to Colossians," Elder Reed instructed his flock. "I want to concentrate on verses nine and ten in chapter one: '... *that ye might be filled with the knowledge of His will in all wisdom and spiritual understanding; That ye might walk worthy of the Lord unto all pleasing, being fruitful in every good work, and increasing in the knowledge of God.*'

"The key words in these scriptures are *spiritual*

understanding and *knowledge.* There is a purpose to everything that is happening in your life. Your heartaches and triumphs are all under the watchful eye of the Lord Jesus. Therefore, if you've got a problem with what's going on, it's prayer time…"

Desiree began to silently pray, *Jesus, please give me the strength to go on.*

***

On Monday morning, Desiree was on a mission when she got in to work. This was the part in a movie where the heroine went ballistic and asked her lover why he didn't call that weekend, but her life wasn't a movie.

Jesus was her only lover, and He had already written her script. From this moment on, Desiree would treat Brooke cordially as a coworker and brother in Christ.

After clearing the door to the newsroom, Desiree was surprised to see Brooke in an hour early and at his desk. She swallowed. Not yet. *Bide your time,* she coaxed herself. Desiree wasn't ready to face him, so she headed to her mailbox. Her heart thumped in her chest, just knowing he was near, but they were mentally so far apart.

As she flipped through her letters and packages on the way to her circus area, Desiree spotted a familiar piece of mail. Could it be? She held her breath as she examined it closely. It was Brooke's handwriting on the envelope. Settled behind her desk, Desiree glanced across the room. Brooke had disappeared down the hall.

Shrugging, Desiree did a quick head check to see if anyone was watching her as she broke the seal and slid out the card.

You know how I feel. I think maybe I know how you feel, but the ball is in your court, beautiful. So what's it going to be: a) walk away, b) stay and fight for what we have, or c) get married?

Desiree barked out a laugh. She didn't know marriage was on the table. His sense of humor chased her emotional fear away. She shuffled through stacks on her desk until she found a piece of paper. She tore off a piece and scribbled her answer: *B. How?*

After stuffing the envelope and card into her purse, she got up; Desiree was about to go in search of him. Then the phone rang and distracted her. By the time she finished with the call, others were arriving in the newsroom, but she refused to be deterred.

"Good morning," she greeted several folks on her way to Brooke's desk. One minute he was alone, and then the next Sly cut her off and beat her to Brooke.

Desiree wracked her brain for an excuse. She was saved when someone called Sly away.

"Good morning, boss." Brooke grinned. That was the first time he used the nickname some of the other reporters called her.

"Morning. How was your weekend?"

"It was good. My sister was in town, so we enjoyed a performance Saturday evening, and then she left late yesterday morning."

His sister—*great.* She had seen the worst side of her. At least she knew why Brooke wasn't at church. Nodding, she handed him the scrap of paper. Instead of heading straight back to her desk, she made a few more pit stops.

Of all the days to be a slow news day, Monday was it. She needed crime and mayhem to keep her mind off

Brooke.

It was almost time for the evening news. Brooke and Sly left to go back to the scene of an earlier group arrest over the petty theft of items from a thrift store. That was the best hard news Desiree could scrounge up.

After Brooke's live broadcast, Desiree was sure he would head home. Not surprising, ten minutes from getting off, calamity reigned when a ten-car pileup on an icy road caused injuries.

The downside was the scene was an hour away. She assisted the evening assignment editor with re-directing crews. Again, Desiree was about to grab her purse and the scanners went crazy.

Firefighters were racing to a three-alarm warehouse fire. Roger had her call the crew back. She knew they were chewing her out royally, but it was not her call. She was only the backup. She suggested activating the news chopper to fly to the scene of the crash. Roger agreed.

At least Brooke was safe from being dispatched to the warehouse fire. The evening reporter and photographer were itching for somewhere to go. They were out the door without being told.

An hour and a half later, Desiree was exhausted when she gathered her purse and coat to leave. The roads weren't icy downtown, but she took her time driving home. When she unlocked the door to her condo, she still hadn't heard from Brooke. She hoped he hadn't changed his mind about making it work between them.

As she warmed her Sunday leftovers, he called. "I missed you."

Closing her eyes, a tear escaped at the sound of his

deep baritone voice.

"I missed you too," she whispered. "I'm sorry again."

"I know, and I'm sorry, but if we're going to give us a serious try, then we have to spend time together outside the office. In the newsroom, I can't even wink at my lady. Our relationship should not be on the clock all the time. I want a date where I have the liberty to flirt, hold hands, and even steal a kiss with my woman, and you better believe I intend to take full advantage."

"I agree." *Lord, give me strength to hold on.*

CHAPTER 14

A few weeks later, Brooke had no complaints about his social life: dinners, movies, and even attending some church functions. He and Desiree were still discreet at work, but she had let down her defenses enough so he could spoil her like he wanted. Brooke was falling hard for her.

"What's got you so happy?" Sly asked as they lounged around the newsroom, waiting for something to go awry. It was a slow day. Sly believed in knocking on wood. Brooke preferred to thank Jesus for the downtime.

"I've got plans." Brooke crossed arms behind his head.

This was their first big date since they met at the Melting Pot. He had learned Desiree enjoyed ballet and a major performance was coming to St. Louis. Tonight was the night.

Stunned, Sly leaned closer. "I wouldn't say that too loudly. You know this job is a life-crasher. Plus, Desiree is on the desk and she has no problem assigning you to a story, I think, just because she can."

She already knows, dude, and she can't wait. Brooke shrugged.

"That woman has ruined many of my few dates. Whatever you do, don't let her know about it."

There were only so many times Brooke could hold his peace. "You need to find someone else to pick on. Desiree is not the source of your lackluster love life."

"Desiree is hot. I'm just going to keep wearing her down."

"That will never happen." Sly was testing him without knowing it.

Sly propped his booted foot on a nearby desk in a vacant cubicle as the scanners went berserk. The managers gathered around Desiree, Brooke didn't move. He wasn't looking to volunteer his services to cover any breaking news. Besides, Desiree knew they had somewhere to go. Still, he didn't want to give the other supervisors any ideas.

As the only day side reporter left in the building, Brooke heard his name called along with two night side reporters who had minutes earlier clocked in.

Brooke went to meet the other two at the desk. "What's going on?"

"We've got two officers down at two different locations. We don't know if it's connected. It's a mess in Jefferson County. Brooke and Sly, forget about your story you had for five. I'm going to need both of you outside the hospital. Fred and Greg take your photogs and head to those scenes," Desiree said.

Brooke sucked in his breath. Desiree couldn't be serious about sending him forty-five minutes away. They would definitely be late for the ballet. Sly seemed to read his thoughts.

"This man has a date," Sly informed Desiree, pointing to Brooke.

"I'll make it up to you," she said hesitantly. She schooled her expression, but he recognized the hint of disappointment in her eyes. Even if he did get off on time or a few minutes late, that didn't mean she would be right behind him.

Tickets for the Alvin Ailey dance performance weren't cheap. If there was any time to make him and her a priority, it was that moment. With one of two night side assignment editors on deck, Brooke wanted to tell Desiree to let Dennis handle his shift.

Taking a deep breath, Brooke spun around. He headed to his desk and grabbed his things. "Come on, Sly," he said over his shoulder.

Sly roared. "Told ya so."

Unless God intervened, Brooke knew how this was going to play out. It was going to be the lead story again at six o'clock and then at the ten o'clock newscast. To beat KDPX's competitors, their news team would cover the story at every angle. Network affiliates would get wind of it and want footage and on and on.

Brooke didn't say another word as he climbed into the news truck with Sly behind the wheel. He wanted to lash out at someone. It wasn't about the money he spent on the tickets that was important, but the special time he craved to be with Desiree.

This was the night he planned to discuss how they saw themselves a year from now. He definitely wasn't feeling that now. Brooke didn't want to think about ten minutes from now.

"There goes your hot date. I told ya, man. It never seems to fail. I bet your girlfriend is going to be hot."

Brooke worried his mustache as he looked out the window. "I think my lady will understand. It's me that's hot."

"Desiree didn't need us to go. The night crew could handle this. Why make us stay? Jefferson County is at least an hour drive. I could make it in forty-five," Sly griped as he exited on I-55 going south.

"Nah. You don't need another ticket. At this point, take your time." Was Desiree trying to sabotage their relationship to prove her point that a workplace romance couldn't stand against pressure.

CHAPTER 15

Desiree wasn't happy, but the needs of the business always had precedence. Brooke had to be steaming about their plans, but they were alive and well and not experiencing a crisis. Two police officers were clinging to their lives and their families were in turmoil.

She said a silent prayer for the victims as she began to make phone calls to gather more information while the reporters were en route to the scenes.

It was still a possibility that she and Brooke could make it to the performance, but that would be a stretch. Desiree refocused as the chaos at both crime scenes was mounting. As she tried to get a hold of the public information officer for the Jefferson County Sheriff's office to get a statement, the night side assignment editor tried to contact the hospital to verify the victims were coming to that location and not being airlifted to another hospital.

As the reporters arrived at the scene and the news truck had established a satellite signal, KDPX went on air first with the breaking news. She watched as Brooke led the newscast. The man was a professional. Despite being thrown in at the last minute, he was able to interview a couple of distraught family members with sensitivity. The man had such a compassionate approach. She loved that quality in him.

Brooke definitely had the qualities that would cause any woman to fall for him, and Desiree wanted to be that woman, but work interfered, especially with their plans for a night out. She was determined to get to the Alvin Ailey performance, even if she was only able to see the last thirty minutes.

Once the news director cleared Brooke from the scene, Desiree grabbed her purse. "Okay, Dennis. We did it." They high-fived each other. "I'm heading out. I'm passing the torch to you."

"Okay, dawg," the older white man said, as usual, using lingo that was always outdated. They both chuckled.

Desiree hurried to her car in the garage. Once she got on the highway, she called Brooke, hoping Sly wasn't nearby.

"Hello." Brooke didn't sound happy.

"We can still make it. I'm fifteen minutes from home. I'll be ready, or I can meet you at the Fox Theatre."

"Neither. Dennis hasn't cleared us. As a matter of fact, my photographer and I are forced to give another report," Brooke said in a professional manner.

"What?" Desiree stuttered, "Okay. Well, maybe I can meet you there."

"Sorry, babe. The needs of the business. Plus, I don't half-step on my dates. I go all the way. Maybe next time. I've got to go." He hung up.

Desiree couldn't plug her sinking feeling. Brooke sounded as if he had given up trying to make them work. He couldn't be, not when Desiree's determination had just kicked in. She blinked as her eyes misted. Her coveted job, which was her livelihood, had interfered big time with her personal life and she had paid the price for it.

CHAPTER 16

I'm through.

Desiree was right, Brooke hated to admit it. Office romances didn't work. He had tried it twice. His first experience had been a disaster. Now the one woman who could make a difference in his life was giving zero effort.

Clearing his head, Brooke gave a live update and fifteen minutes later, Sly was breaking down his camera equipment. Brooke refused to check the time as they got in the truck and headed back to the station so he could get his car. His night on the town was ruined.

Brooke wanted all the blame to lie with Desiree, but then when he spoke with the families of critically wounded officers—one a rookie—he prayed to Jesus for peace in the middle of their storm. He had no reason to complain, but he had every reason to be disappointed.

"No sense in sulking, man. Desiree is the culprit." Sly's taunting didn't help his mood either. "She earned her rep with you today. I don't care how understanding your woman is, she won't like being stood up."

Glancing at his watch, Brooke didn't bother to respond. They were twenty minutes out from the station. Even if he rushed home, they were going to be an hour late. They had missed out, maybe for the last time. *I am so through!*

***

When Brooke got back to work, he made a beeline for his car. There was no way he was setting foot in the newsroom until Monday. It would be just his luck another news story would break and he would be the scapegoat. Once he was behind the wheel, he called his sister.

"You were right. I'm through with this undercover romance assignment. I'm moving on," Brooke said, barely letting her get a hello out.

"What happened now?" Debra asked.

She was silent as he roared his complaints about everything.

"Start from the beginning and tell me what happened," she encouraged.

By the time Brooke finished his recap, he was turning the corner into his neighborhood. He frowned when he saw Desiree's car in front of his townhouse. "What is she doing here?"

"Who?"

Brooke didn't answer as he hurried her off the phone. "Talk to you later." He parked behind her. Desiree stepped out and waited by her car. She had changed. She looked gorgeous. He couldn't believe that one look at her could deflate his anger.

They stared as he approached slowly. "What are you doing here?"

Jutting her chin, Desiree lifted a brow. "We have a date. Did you forget?"

He grunted. "I thought you did when you dispatched me to that story. It's too late now. The performance already started." He stepped closer. "We missed out, Desiree."

"Wrong. I don't plan to miss out on anything with you, so go and get dressed. Since you don't have to put on makeup—" she paused and checked her watch— "you should only need thirty minutes to shower and change. Go." She nudged him toward his front door.

"Des—"

"Brooke, don't give up on us. This is the career path we chose. We have to deal with a certain amount of interruptions. Now hurry, please."

"Bossy," he taunted her as he did as he was told. Exactly thirty-two minutes later, he was ready and escorted her out the door. Once at the theater, Brooke used the valet to park his car to save time.

They were an hour and forty-five minutes late. When they strolled into the lobby, neither expected to see that an intermission was underway.

Brooke guided Desiree through the maze of guests. He even relaxed long enough to mingle with a few adoring television fans. With his arm securely around Desiree's waist, he lazily strolled up the winding staircase to the mezzanine.

Their seats were near the balcony. Once they were settled, a hostess appeared with a menu. She greeted them warmly after recognizing Brooke. She gave them a few minutes and returned for their order.

Stretching his arm across the back of Desiree's chair, he brushed a kiss against her waiting lips. "You

are one determined woman. I was ready to call it quits."
And he meant it until he looked into her soulful eyes.
Brooke quickly changed his mind. "That was before
you showed up on my doorstep."

Desiree nodded and glanced away as if she was
digesting what he had said. She looked back with a
hopeful expression. "So what do you have planned this
weekend?"

He grinned and wiggled his brow. "Kidnap you
beginning tomorrow morning for breakfast and sharing
lunch and then top it off with dinner. Sunday, I'll
prepare breakfast, then church—"

Stroking his chin, Desiree stopped him. "Sunday
night, I'll cook dinner—"

"Then we'll go grocery shopping together," he
countered.

"If I survive this marathon dating, then maybe we
can watch a movie."

"You got it, babe," Brooke said as his cell phone
vibrated. He answered without checking the ID.

"Are you okay?" Debra asked.

"I'm in a perfect place right now." He hurried off
the phone and winked at Desiree as the lights dimmed
for the second part of the performance was about to get
underway.

"I hoped that wasn't any breaking news calls from
Dennis," Desiree whispered.

"News flash: Brooke Mitchell is already working
undercover on another important assignment." He
placed a soft kiss in her fragranced hair.

CHAPTER 17

By early spring, Brooke and Desiree had survived sweeps, breaking news, and office gossip. For months, they had been on the same page. Debra had finally met Desiree. The two hit it off once Debra understood Desiree's position on work-related affairs.

On Easter Sunday, they professed their love over a romantic dinner. Desiree cried tears of joy as Brooke comforted her, then they realized that their temptation would consume them if they ignored their prayer time with Jesus.

Desiree agreed it was time to come clean with their coworkers. "I'm in love with you," she told him one night.

"And my heart knows it." Brooke had a plan, and he prayed God would hold the world still for three minutes from any mayhem or disaster.

The next day at work, it seemed like business as usual and some things never change. Sly continued to harp on his conspiracy against the assignment editors, namely Desiree. The man was going to have to find someone else to pick on soon.

Brooke couldn't wait to put a lock on Sly's mouth once he learned that he and Desiree had been dating since the first of the year. He snickered. "You've been grinning all day." Sly spied him suspiciously.

"I'm about to pop the question." Brooke smirked.

Sly's jaw dropped open as he set up his tripod and camera for broadcast live in the newsroom. He wormed his cordless microphone through his suit jacket and clipped it on his shirt. With his earpiece in place, he listened to the news intro music.

The anchors, Maurice and Cindy, welcomed the viewers. They broadcasted the first and second segments and finally sports. When it was time for the show closer—some called it fluff news, Brooke was cued.

"Thanks, Cindy. Employees at KDPX have been in the dark about a story that is about to come to light. Since the beginning of the year, I've been working undercover in this very newsroom." Brooke began to walk toward the assignment desk. The expression on Desiree's face was priceless. "This is Desiree King, one of the station's most talented assignment editors. She is responsible for dispatching us to stories viewers see every day, including breaking news stories." He reached for Desiree's shaky hand. Brooke squeezed it. "This woman won my heart and respect. Today, I am reporting that she has captured all my love."

Getting on one knee, Brooke looked up. He was sure Sly had zoomed in for a close-up, but Brooke didn't care as his eyes glazed. "I love you, Desiree. You are part of me. When I moved to St. Louis, I was chasing the big stories, and then months ago, I realized that the story of my life was right in front of me. So now, as millions of viewers are watching, I'm asking you to be my wife."

Desiree nodded, but their coworkers wouldn't be placated. They hooted, cheered, and some chanted what they wanted her to say.

"Yes, Brooke. I would be honored."

As he slipped on the ring, the closing music played and employees released a thunderous applause. Brooke was certain the angels began to sing.

EPILOGUE

Three months later...

Desiree and Brooke exchanged their wedding vows in a small ceremony. The station producer suggested that the couple allow their nuptials to be streamed live over the internet.

"Not only would viewers feel a part of your happiness, but it'll be good for ratings," the producer had said with a wry grin.

They consented and so now they stood at the altar reciting their vows.

"I, Desiree, take you Brooke for better, for worse, for richer, for poorer, in sickness and in health, to love and to cherish..." her voice shook as her vision blurred. She was really committing herself to this man who had against all odds wooed her on the job. Brooke's worried expression prompted her to continue. "I will honor our love and submit to you in Christ until death us do part."

Cupping her chin under the veil, Brooke brushed away Desiree's tear and smiled. "I will love and protect you, your body, mind and soul. I will honor you as my wife and as the weaker vessel in Christ, I will yield to the Lord as the Head of our household...and this day, I am committed to making our love work at home and on the job; I will always love you."

When the minister cleared his throat, he interrupted their trance. Brooke mouthed his declaration again, "I will always love you." Desiree inhaled his words.

Together, they faced the minister who warned them about not allowing any man or woman by any means necessary to separate them and then pronounced them husband and wife. "You may now salute your lovely bride."

As Brooke lifted her veil and was about to lower his lips, Desiree whispered, "Remember, the cameras."

"Let them roll, baby. Let them roll," Brooke teased and kissed her deeply.

OTHER WORKS

Thanks for reading! Please try my other eBook novellas:
HER Dress
Love at Work
Words of Love
Cameron Jamieson (A Back Story)
A Mother's Love
A Christian Christmas
A Woman After David's Heart
Coming soon: Stopping

Books in Print:
The Acquittal (coming March 2013)
Guilty by Association
The Guilt Trip
Free from Guilt
Crowning Glory
Guilty of Love
Not Guilty of Love
Still Guilty

ABOUT THE AUTHOR

Pat Simmons is a self-proclaimed genealogy sleuth. She is passionate about researching her ancestors, then casting them in starring roles in her novels. She hopes her off-beat method will track down distant relatives who happen to pick up her books. She has been a genealogy enthusiast since her great-grandmother died at the young age of ninety-seven years old in 1988.

She describes the evidence of the gift of the Holy Ghost as an amazing, unforgettable, life-altering experience. She believes God is the author who advances the stories she writes.

Pat has a B.S. in mass communications from Emerson College in Boston, Massachusetts. She has worked in various media positions in radio, television, and print for more than twenty years. Currently, she oversees the media publicity for the annual RT Booklovers Conventions.

She is the author of nine single titles and several eBook novellas. Her awards include *Talk to Me,* ranked #14 of Top Books in 2008 that Changed Lives by *Black Pearls Magazine.* She is a two-time recipient of the Romance Slam Jam Emma Rodgers Award for Best Inspirational Romance for *Still Guilty* (2010) and *Crowning Glory* (2011). Her bestselling novels include *Guilty of Love* and the Jamieson Legacy series: *Guilty by Association, The Guilt Trip,* and *Free from Guilt. The Acquittal* (A Guilty Parties novel) is her first of two 2013 releases.

Pat has converted her sofa-strapped, sports-fanatical husband into an amateur travel agent, untrained bodyguard, and GPS-guided chauffeur. They have a son and daughter.

Pat's interviews include numerous appearances on radio, television, blogtalk radio, blogs, and feature articles.

Please visit Pat at www.patsimmons.net

Or contact her at authorpatsimmons@gmail.com or

P.O. Box 1077

Florissant, MO 63031